At sixteen, Zeno Anderson is on the cusp of graduation. He's anxious to leave for college in Illinois come fall, but his cautious parents have their doubts about letting him out of the nest before he's eighteen. Zeno worries he's doing more to hurt than help himself on that front.

The thing is, Zeno has a tendency to run from problems, and he's a bit confused in his social life. After a terrible misunderstanding, he's been avoiding best friend, Marvus, for months now, only to find himself semi-crushing on Jemma, who seems to be catching feelings of her own. When something serious happens to Zeno at Jemma's unsupervised party, threatening their friendship, Zeno doesn't do himself any favors by not letting his parents in on it.

Then, there's tall, handsome Dalvin Drake, wide receiver on the football team. Zeno is surprised to discover, as his crush on Jemma wanes, his feelings for dreamy Dalvin fast-track from buddy zone to full-on flirt. With two friendships already on the rocks, Zeno doesn't want to risk losing Dalvin. Yeah, but the thing is, Dalvin's suddenly dropping hints that he's into Zeno too.

Life is so complicated. What exactly is a fella supposed to do with all this?

ZENO

GENE GANT

A NineStar Press Publication
www.ninestarpress.com

Zeno

First Edition, May 2025

ISBN: 978-1-64890-849-1
Also available in eBook, ISBN: 978-1-64890-850-7

CONTENT WARNING:
This book contains sexual language, teen underage sex (off page, non-explicit), underage drinking and the use and effects of GHB at an unsupervised party, police harassment (on page).

For Patrick Ross

Chapter One

"ARE WE READY, Zeno?"

I looked up, the smile automatically spreading across my face. Mrs. Herron stood in the middle bay of my dad's auto shop, smiling back at me. For a thirty-something sister, she was really pretty. And hella hot in her tight jeans and blue turtleneck.

"Sure thing, ready to rock," I replied in my most upbeat, customer-friendly tone. For the record, the "we" she was referring to didn't include me. She meant herself and her baby, the cherry-red Lexus NX 300 whose hood was currently undergoing a power-buffing at my determined hands.

This was my quasi-new hustle. Almost a year ago, in April, I started working part-time at Dad's shop doing janitorial work—dumping trash cans, cleaning bathrooms, sweeping and mopping, that sorta stuff. Four months later, a dude brought in his muddy pickup for a new transmission and offered to pay extra for a wash and shine. When Dad turned him down on the cleaning, I volunteered my service, accidentally starting my own car detailing business. After scrubbing abused toilets and emptying absolutely unholy garbage cans, this was definitely a less disturbing and more lucrative livelihood.

Mrs. Herron, one of my best customers, was a corporate attorney who could've easily passed for a Memphis Grizzlies cheerleader.

"Well, let's see about that." She stepped from the shaded opening of the bay into the afternoon sunshine. Her short black Afro sparkled in the bright yellow rays. So did her eyes as she angled her way between me and the right front fender of her car. With blue microfiber towels clutched in both hands, I moved back to give her room.

I smiled, aglow with pride as she inspected my handiwork. The car interior had been thoroughly vacuumed and dusted, the leather seats and trim wiped down with honey-inspired leather conditioner. The windows had been polished inside and out, totally free of streaks. And the exterior, tires and rims included, bore a super shine worthy of a new car fresh out of the dealership.

"Well," Mrs. Herron sighed when she completed the circuit of her car and stood next to me. The citrusy smell of her perfume tingled in my nose. Man! Mr. Herron was one lucky dude. "Baby looks like she just rolled off the showroom floor."

See? I wasn't exaggerating.

Mrs. Herron lowered her chin, looking directly into my eyes. The smile she gave me now was quite pleased. For some reason, my whole face suddenly flared hot, and I had to look away for a moment. She opened the little black purse she carried, pulled out a neat green roll, and handed it to me. "Great job as usual, Zenie. And you got Baby ready in time for me to make my meeting downtown as promised. Thanks. See you in two weeks."

"Sure thing, Mrs. Herron." I opened the driver's door for her. She slid behind the wheel, fired up the engine, and backed carefully into the street. With a casual wave, she took off.

I'd put away the hose and bucket after finishing the wash and rinse. Humming, I tossed my buffing towels into the old toolbox with the rest of my detailing supplies, grabbed the box, and walked into the service bay.

Bobbo, one of my dad's mechanics, got in my face right off. He was, like, in his forties with a thin body, a bald head, and a wiry black whisk broom of a goatee. His dark red coveralls were so smudged with grime they looked black. After my last growth spurt, he was now maybe five inches shorter than me, which meant we stood with his nose about level to my chin. He still managed eye contact. His smirk was the kind you'd probably see on an anthropomorphic cat who'd just left a fresh hairball in one of your shoes.

"You don't count your money, kid?" he said. "That ain't good policy."

"I trust Mrs. Herron." I tried to step around him.

He got in my way again. "Don't let the pretty faces make you stupid. This is business. Even if they ain't cheats, people make mistakes. How do you know your customer didn't accidentally shortchange ya?"

"Uhm?" Okay, he had a point. I unfolded the roll of bills Mrs. Herron had given me and counted them. My mouth dropped open. "Dang. She paid in full and threw in a fifty-buck tip!"

That smirk on Bobbo's face turned evil. "Hell, I got it all wrong. Lady Law wasn't the one who played on pretty, huh, 'Zenie'?" He tweaked my nipple.

"Ow." I jerked away from his pinching fingers. "What're you talking about?"

"Yeah, right. Like that tight-ass T-shirt of yours got wet by itself." Bobbo shook his head, chuckling, and turned away.

"You got it wrong, Bobbo," I protested, but he waved me off as he went back to work on the car he had hoisted in the air. I felt stung. Let it be known that I'm not a tease, especially when it comes to grown-ass married women who happen to be customers of mine. My T-shirt was tight because I'd been working out a lot over the past few months, bulking up, and neither Mom nor I had gotten around to buying bigger shirts for me. My T-shirt was wet because I'd just finished washing two cars, and I was kinda sloppy when it came to water hoses. Any tips I earned were for doing a thorough, most excellent job and not because I showed off my muscles.

I worked hard and gave my best, principles Dad had drilled into me all my life. There was no reason for me to feel ashamed. Still, I couldn't shake the guilt that pulsed in my face. I hated for people to think badly of me, especially when I hadn't done anything wrong.

There was no time for me to freak out over my besmirched reputation. In the employee dressing room, I stashed my toolbox in my locker and stripped off the embarrassing T-shirt, which I left hanging on a hook to dry. I pulled on my blue University of Memphis sweatshirt, grabbed my backpack, and shut the locker. I was heading out in a rush when the door swung in suddenly, and I almost barreled straight into Dad.

"Watch out now!" he said, laughing, and faked a couple of jabs, making me flinch. Forty years old, and the man behaved like a happy kid most of the time. When I was a little guy, his six-foot frame seemed giant-sized to me. At six-three now, I'd overtaken him.

"Yeah, okay. *Sir*." Stepping around him, I dismissively gave my dad the same calm-down-little-dude pat on the head he used to give me when I was in my tantrum-throwing phase.

"Boy! Who're you short-shankin'?" In a flash, he caught me by the ear.

We were both laughing as I doubled over and stumbled back, my head crashing into his chest.

"Okay, okay!" I said. "I'm kinda fond of that ear. Let go, please."

"I made this ear, and I can take it back. Better recognize."

"I recognize, Dad! Okay? Now leggo, or I'm gonna be late getting back to school."

He released me with a tender flick to the side of my face. "Back to school? I thought you were done for the day."

"Not really." I finger-combed my curly hair, trying to make sure my 'do was fresh after suffering Dad's abuse. "I've got a Film Club meeting in thirty minutes. And no, I can't skip it. We're making a movie that's also gonna be our senior project."

Dad's smile vanished completely. "Zeno, aren't you spreading yourself a little thin these days?"

I hesitated a moment, watching him carefully. My dad and I had the same warm, medium-brown complexion, the same friendly hazel eyes, and the same radar for picking up on each other's moods. It had been a long day, and honestly, my ass was dragging. More than anything, I wanted to go home and sleep for an hour or two. But I didn't have that kind of time to spare.

I puffed up my chest and widened my smile. "Just doing what I gotta do, Dad."

He looked so worried I wanted to hug him. "Zeno—"

"Gotta bounce." I gave his shoulder a squeeze and then backed away quickly.

Dad backed up, too, tacitly letting me go. Never one to go home dirty from work, he unzipped his gray coveralls as he moved toward the showers. "I'm cooking a good dinner. Chicken burritos and corn on the cob. It's going on the table at seven. Be there, Zeno."

"I will." Backpack slung over my shoulder, I retrieved my bike—shiny black frame with yellow seat and handlebars—from the service bay and rode off.

It was a gorgeous day, thank God. Or thank climate change. Blue skies, scattered white puffs of cloud, and an unseasonably hot mid-March were much appreciated but alarming. There'd been no dreaming of a white Christmas this past time around. The winter solstice had announced itself in Memphis with a summerlike eighty-nine degrees. Last-minute Christmas shoppers descended on stores in cutoff jeans and flip-flops. On New Year's Eve night, Dad and I had stretched out barefoot on the roof in sleeveless tees and basketball shorts to watch the fireworks.

At the opposite end of the current weather extreme in my hometown, the upper Midwest was being treated to the most powerful blizzard in two decades. Parts of Kentucky were drowning in waist-high flood waters brought on by three days—and counting—of hellacious downpour. Scientists declared last year one of the three hottest years in recorded history. This year was already angling for membership in that notorious club. Or maybe it would take the crown. Keep pumping that soot in the air, world! We can do it! Yay!

Senior year, so far, had been a monster for me. I skipped a grade in elementary school, which made me sixteen, and I carried one of the graduating class's higher GPAs. Still, I gave extra to the academics these days, hoping the additional effort would be taken as a sign of maturity. My parents were skittish that I'd be well under eighteen when I started college, so worried they might make me live at home freshman year. I was crazy about my mom and dad, but I didn't want to stay under their roof forever. I wanted to watch *OnlyFans* and bring home dates late at night and cuss whenever I chose. You know. Like a man.

Keeping up a solid academic performance was important for any student at Memphis Technical Fine Arts High School, aka MemTech.

A particular focus of MemTech was to provide a diverse and inclusive learning environment, one that encouraged open-mindedness, mutual respect, and a willingness to compromise. Of course, that very attitude was one of the reasons the Tennessee state legislature had been trying—so far unsuccessfully—to strangle MemTech out of existence.

To achieve its goal of sending well-rounded, open minds into the world, MemTech required every student to participate in at least one group extracurricular activity for a minimum of one academic year. After a failed attempt as a freshman, I tried to satisfy that requirement sophomore year as a football player. I was good at the sport, having played in a peewee league when I was a little guy, and I'd bulked up some by working out and maxing on protein over the summer. I made the team easily. Once the season started, I played first string, racking up some pretty impressive stats.

That all came to a screeching halt in game six when I faked out the center and sacked the opposing quarterback. Doing what I was supposed to do, right? Yeah, but I wasn't supposed to leave dude screaming on the ground with his right leg bent at a grotesquely unnatural angle.

To this day, I shiver when I remember that. The injured quarterback was really gracious about his broken limb when I visited him in the hospital, brushing it off as just one of those things. Didn't seem that way to me. I quit the team, unwilling to risk hurting anyone so horribly again. It took a long while for me to stop kicking my own ass over that.

The notion of fulfilling the extracurriculars requirement had sorta leaked from my brain until I hit senior year, whereupon the guidance counselor sent an email reminding me I was running out of time. I chose Film Club for no other reason than I had to choose something. (Well, it helped that one of my best friends was already a member.)

So, after a 5:00 a.m. wake-up, a quick workout and shower and even quicker breakfast (an apple), I biked to MemTech for an hour-long session with my study group. Seven grueling hours of classes later—five of them AP—I biked to the auto shop for two carwash appointments, after which I, once again, wheeled back to MemTech. The fun never stopped.

With my bike secured, I scurried down the empty, echoing main corridor toward the Arts wing and a muted tangle of sound coming from that direction. Once I pushed through the insulated doors, the tangle swelled into a cacophony of voices, ticks, taps, claps, and at least three competing streams of music. Band practice was in full swing, the Glee Club warbling. Mr. Collinde's theater students ran lines for their spring production, and the contemporary dance troupe stomped away to recorded jazz music. As I rushed to meet with my fellow movie clubbers in the classroom at the end of the hall, the door to my left abruptly swung outward, releasing an also rushing Jemma Haynes.

"Oop!" I pulled up short, avoiding a collision. Jemma jerked herself backward and lost grip on her backpack, which hit the floor with a thud.

Jemma immediately flashed an impish smile that lit up her blue eyes. "Sorry, Zeno. Thank God for my catlike reflexes, huh?" She started to reach down.

"Allow me," I said in an awfully fake British accent. I scooped up her backpack and presented it to her with a bow.

"Thank you, kind sir." Jemma's voice had a snarky edge to it. I liked her snark. She wore some kind of dance getup—a black leotard and white ballet shoes. Appropriate for a ballet dancer just leaving practice. Her blonde hair was tied atop her head in a haphazard bun, and she was a little sweaty. Oh. My bad. Southern females "glow," thank you very much.

I'd seldom seen this side of Jemma before, a little flushed, a little grubby. She usually kept herself polished and primed during regular school hours and when I visited her house for movie nights or to work on school projects. In addition to an athletic, curvy figure and a gorgeous face, this up-and-coming ballet artiste captained the girls' swim team, carried a 4.2 GPA, and had already been accepted to her dream school, Juilliard.

Me, I still wasn't quite sure what I wanted to be when I grew up.

Jemma's eyes shifted to the top of my head. "I'm so happy. You finally started wearing a helmet on your bike rides."

"What're you talking about?"

She reached up, plucking at my hair. "You have a bad case of helmet head."

Jeez! I *didn't* wear a helmet when riding my bike for precisely this reason. I should've checked myself out in a mirror after my head got pressed against Dad's chest. Given my family's budgetary limitations, I accepted that I'd live out my teen years in a Walmart wardrobe. But *dang* if I'd ever accept jacked hair. I made a move for the restroom. "'Scuse me, Jem. I gotta fix—"

"Hang on." Jemma kept finger-combing my hair. The fluffing felt really good, tingling over my scalp. Then she leaned back and assessed what she'd done. "Okay, you're good."

"You sure?"

"Zeno," she said, one hand going to her hip, her tone reproachful. "Have I ever not done right by you?"

I smiled. "Thanks. Gotta go. Film Club."

"I should go too. I have to pick up my sister. See you tomorrow." She grabbed me by the bicep, gave it a lingering squeeze, and then slipped past me.

As we moved in opposite directions along the hall, I looked back at Jemma, just as she looked over her shoulder at me. She smiled. I gave her a wink. That seemed to put an extra pep in her step as she disappeared around the corner.

Chapter Two

"YOU'RE LATE."

I'd barely stepped across the threshold of classroom A-14 when Oliver Gates, president of Film Club, brought out his talons. I glanced at the big square digital clock mounted on the wall over the teacher's desk: 5:32 p.m.

"Two minutes," I protested. "That's not even... Heck, that's almost early."

Oliver, a thin, angular dude of medium height and Irish descent, leaned back against the teacher's desk with his ankles crossed and skinny arms folded over his chest. Permanent outrage and a spray of fine red freckles clouded his square face. He had his brownish-red hair slicked back so severely a miniature human could belly slide off it.

"Anderson, I was here at five. *That* was early. Five fifteen would have been all right. Five thirty would have been tolerable, barely." He glanced back at the clock. "*Three* minutes past is absolutely unforgivable."

Yes, Oliver Gates was so anal if you x-rayed his head, all you'd find was one big pucker.

"Hey, can a brother put his butt in a seat before you rake him across the coals?" I tried a tired smile as I crossed the floor.

Oliver literally turned his nose up at me. "Will somebody please explain to Anderson what he missed by not being here when the meeting was officially called to order?"

In AP American History, Oliver once told the class he would be president of these United States one day. That scared the piss out of me.

I reached the narrow area where five chairs had been arrayed in a semicircle facing the teacher's desk. Slumping heavily in the unoccupied fifth chair, I accidentally bumped shoulders with Dalvin Drake. Cool name, cool dude. He had light brown skin, dark brown eyes, and wore his hair in a thick black, curly frohawk. A mustache and the shadow of a beard enhanced his face, which made me all kinds of jealous; when it came to facial hair, I barely had eyebrows. His chiseled cheekbones probably cut his pillow into confetti every night, and girls said his smile was killer. He turned that magic smile on me now, and hell, even I shivered. Here was the aforementioned friend whose Film Club membership had enticed me to join.

"Okay, Z, here's what you missed," Dalvin said. "Oliver called the meeting to order at exactly five thirty and reminded everybody that we all agreed our club project has to be at least thirty minutes long. He said he did a Zoom read-through of the screenplay with our actors last night and timed it, and the whole thing came out to nineteen minutes—"

"Oh, okay. We need a thirty-minute script. Got it." I nodded, eyeing our two actors seated beyond Dalvin, Tish Cooper and

Hyun-woo "Kipper" Yang.

Looking back at me, Tish and Kipper both raised eyebrows.

"I have to come up with eleven more pages for you guys to flesh out the time," I told them. "There's this scene I had in mind but never added, so I'll throw that in. I can start on it tonight and have it done in a day or two. Problem solved, and you all are welcome!"

The other members of Film Club stared like a group of kids whose friend had been caught shoplifting. Only then did it hit me; those raised eyebrows were a warning.

"Uh...okay, problem not solved?"

Oliver sniffed, firing a frustrated glare down his nose at me. "Anderson, if you'll stop babbling for two minutes, Drake will finish bringing you up to speed. Is that agreeable?"

What could I say, really? "Okay, sure."

Eyes on Oliver, Dalvin sucked his teeth. It was common knowledge that Oliver loathed the sucking of teeth, and he predictably clicked his tongue in disgust. I could never figure why dude found one mouth noise rude and the other perfectly okay.

"Well," Dalvin said, turning to me. "We talked about it, Z, and decided not to expand the screenplay. We're going to add, like, this documentary at the end. The movie's about two high school kids facing their biggest fear, right? So, the documentary will tie into that. We'll get a couple of MemTech kids on film talking about their fears and what they're doing to deal with them. Or how they overcame them. You know, inspirational while also helping us get to know some of our fellow students."

I found myself nodding. It was actually a pretty good idea. I wanted to say as much, but...I blinked at Oliver.

He sighed in this loud, irritated way. "Don't be a dick, Anderson. Go ahead and speak."

"Thanks, Ollie. That doc actually sounds great. I say go for it."

Oliver pushed away from the desk and started pacing back and forth. "Glad you agree, Anderson. Your vote makes it unanimous. I'm sure you'll come up with some interesting questions for the subjects since I'm making you our documentary's interviewer."

Huh? Back when I attended my very first Film Club meeting, we arrived at a fair and balanced labor agreement. Thespians Tish and Kipper would handle the acting in our film; Dalvin would take care of camera duties; Oliver would serve as director (of course); and I'd write the screenplay. What was up with this interview stuff?

"Wait. What now?"

Oliver kept pacing, something he did when his mind was churning through ideas. "I think the documentary will work better with an interview format, instead of letting the kids ramble. That way, we can be sure to keep things focused. And you, Anderson, will handle the interviews."

"But I'm the screenwriter."

Oliver stopped pacing, focusing on me. "Why are you reminding me of that?"

"Wouldn't it be better to have someone else do the interviews? Someone who's...more into the public speaking stuff?"

"No, it wouldn't. Cooper and Yang are responsible for set designs and makeup in addition to playing their roles. Along with camera work, Drake's handling the making of props, special effects, lighting, and location scouting. I'm directing *and* editing *and* doing the credits. The rest of us are multitasking, Anderson, so why not you?"

"I can do more, okay, but let me say—"

"It's settled. You're on interviews." Oliver clicked his tongue again, totally dismissing me and my concerns. He looked at his phone, which, no surprise, displayed an actual agenda for the meeting. "Now, next item..."

I sat there, staring at dude, like, *Seriously?*

*

THANK GOD THE meeting finished about thirty minutes later. I grabbed my backpack, muttered some see-ya-laters, and bolted.

I checked the time on my phone: 6:20. If I hurried, I could get home and grab a quick shower before dinner. As I rushed through the Arts wing, music and clapping and grandiose oratory still streamed from certain rooms. The sounds must've masked the footsteps closing in my wake. Something flicked my ear. I jerked away, swatting at the intrusion, and looked over my shoulder.

Dalvin smiled close behind me. "Hey man, where's the fire?"

I chuckled at myself, a little embarrassed. "Was I movin' like that?"

"I just about had to run to catch up." He fell in step with me as we rounded the corner into the main hall. "So, these interviews, is that really gonna be a problem for ya, Z?"

"I don't know...maybe? My dad tells me I'm stretched too thin with my classes and my job and everything. I think I'm starting to actually feel that way."

"I get it, man. Senior year, trying to stay on top of it all. That shit can weigh you down. If it'll help you out, I can do the interviews."

"What? No, Dal. I didn't mean for you—"

"It's cool. I'll tell ole Ollie the interviews are on me. I can even come up with the questions myself...probably not as good as the ones you'd write but, hey. Main thing is, you get some breathing room."

Oh damn. Like, somebody change my diaper and burp me

already. "Dalvin, listen man, I appreciate the offer. You don't even know how much I appreciate it. But dude, you've got the football team on top of Film Club and classes and all that. You're probably more swamped than I am. Ignore my whining. I'll do my part for the movie project."

"Cool. But if you change your mind, let me know."

Dalvin and I met on the first day of our freshman year at MemTech. We were in the same homeroom and algebra class but didn't notice each other until we literally collided. That happened at soccer tryouts the next afternoon. Two tall, skinny dudes crashed their bodies on a bright grassy field while executing the same scissor move in a bid to impress. Neither of us made the team, sadly, but we walked off the field together laughing at ourselves, and we've been friends ever since.

Dude was my best friend, along with Jemma. Really.

Dalvin's football tryout, a few days after the soccer fiasco, had a much better outcome. He was now MemTech's star wide receiver and ranked fifth on the state's top ten list of high school football players. After setting up an online recruiting profile and jumping through other requisite hoops (in addition to his stellar moves on the field), he got the attention of football coaches at several prominent universities, including the head coach at his dream school, Howard.

"So tell me," I said as we pushed through the main entrance into the warm winter twilight. The street in front of the school was deserted and quiet. "Have ya heard from Howard?"

Dalvin laughed, a cozy, comforting sound. "Man, if I get into Howard, you'll definitely know. I'll be screaming in your ears."

We stopped on the steps, facing each other. He rubbed his nose with the back of his hand. Dude would turn eighteen in June, but that move made him look like a little boy, and my mouth twitched. I fought back a smile.

"I got an acceptance letter from Stanford yesterday." His voice was quiet.

"What? That's awesome, man." But he looked down at his big feet, and I could tell it wasn't awesome for him. "Oh. No scholarship offer, huh?"

He shook his head. "Nah."

Dalvin's folks didn't want him saddling himself with a ton of student loan debt. They were all set to fund his higher education even if that meant taking out a second mortgage. Dalvin was as determined to avoid burdening his parents with his tuition. To fund college himself, he'd have to land a scholarship or get a job and pay as he went. Unless the job came with a six-figure salary, a place like Stanford was definitely out of the running.

"Howard's gonna come through, dude," I said, "with a full ride. No doubt."

"You're right, Z. Thanks." His eyes bugged suddenly. "Dang, man, you're really getting cut!" He reached out, his hand tracing the shape of the toned-up muscles in my arms without touching me. "You must have a monster workout routine."

"Not really. It's a few exercises my dad showed me. Brother gotta look good."

He grinned. "You're a vain mothersomethin'."

I shoved him on the shoulder, mock offended. "You're *way* more cut than I am, but I'm the vain one?"

"I got cut for football, ya narcissist."

"So did I."

"But you quit the team over a year ago."

"And that means I can't work out anymore?" I cocked my eyebrows at him. "'Narcissist.' Listen to you, tossing out those SAT vocabs."

"Hey, my parents paid good money for all that SAT prep. They deserve some kinda return on their investment."

We stopped talking for a minute after that. Nothing awkward about it; we just stood there, taking each other in while the stars came out above us. After the day I'd had, it was good simply to have a quiet moment where nothing was required of me, where I could hang with my boy and breathe a little.

Wow. Dalvin's smile was so nice...

Yeah. Okay. But I could only afford to breathe so much. "I gotta go," I said, staring into his eyes, tripping a little as I backed away toward the bike rack. "Homework. And dinner. And more homework. And college apps! I gotta put in at least one college app tonight."

"You're still putting in college apps? I thought you got into the University of Chicago?"

Shit. Why did I mention the college app thing? "I did. I also picked up that Excellence in Academics scholarship."

"Bruh! That's what up!" He gave me dap. "But I don't get why you're putting in college apps this late in the game."

"I'm just...keeping my options open, man."

Dalvin shook his head. Smiling that smile. "Zeno Miles Anderson. When's that dude gonna come out and play again?"

"We'll hang, man. I promise."

"Oliver's gonna give our cast eight days to learn their lines and run rehearsals before we start filming. You think we can do the interviews in that time?"

What's a little more pressure on yours truly when it'll make things easier for my boy. "Sure man. After I get the questions down and line up a couple of victims for the camera, I'll text you, and we'll go for it."

"I like that plan." Dalvin watched as I unlocked my bike from the rack. "Hey, my moms is picking me up in a few. Stick around, and we'll drop you off."

My dad wanted to get in a little family time this evening. That was why he wanted me home for dinner. If I didn't leave now, I'd miss a big chunk of family togetherness. Yet I kept standing there, like a plant taking root. What the hell? "Appreciate the offer, but...I gotta move. Text ya later."

Dalvin's smile got bigger. His eyes looked kind of sad though. Aw.

I hesitated some more. Until my better angel snapped at me: *You'll disappoint Dad if you're late, idiot. Move ya black ass!*

Dalvin's lips parted as if he were about to say something, but I jumped on my bike so fast it wobbled and threw my friend a wave as I rode off.

Chapter Three

THE GARAGE STOOD open when I wheeled off the street into our driveway. Mom climbed out of her car, fresh off her latest stint driving long haul for Mednikow Medical Supplies. She'd arrived home a day earlier than expected. No wonder Dad had been all about me getting home for dinner on time. Mom wore stone-washed jeans, a red pullover sweater, and purple sneakers. Yeah, she looked more like a suburban shopper than a trucker.

As I sailed into the garage between her and Dad's cars, Mom looked at me and broke out a smile. "Zeno! Hi, baby boy. You're—" And just like that, the smile turned flat off. "Where's your helmet?"

Oh shit. I should've turned around the second I saw our garage door up. Usually, I kept the yellow and black helmet (which Mom gave me the same day Dad gave me the bike two years ago) with me when I rode. At moments like this, I could simply go, "Oh, I only this second took it off. It was hot under there." Or something like that. But I totally stopped carrying it weeks ago, lulled into believing I wouldn't get caught, I guess. You know, because neither Mom nor Dad ever saw me come or go on my bike.

So yeah. Oop. *Big* oop. I stood there like a dummy, straddling the bike, looking at my mom with this crooked smile.

"Son, I asked a question," she said, walking around the front of her car to confront me more directly. When she meant business, she always got in my face. She still managed the intimidation thing even though she was six inches shorter than me now.

"I heard ya, Mom. You must be so tired. Come on in and let me get you some tea with honey." I pushed past her, using my feet to paddle the bike toward the kitchen door.

She caught me by the backpack before I'd made two steps. And then she was back in my face. "Oh, hell to the yes, you're going to make me tea. But now let's talk about that helmet. Where is it?"

The crooked smile turned into a sheep grin. "In my closet. Under my duffel bag. Behind those boots Grampa gave me last year."

Mom folded her arms across her chest, one eyebrow arching up. "Why on earth is it there while you're riding through the streets on this bike?"

"Come on, Mom. That helmet messes up my hair! Nobody should walk around with jacked hair."

A beat. Then Mom laughed, which was definitely not the reaction I expected. "Oh, my son is *such* a narcissist."

"I'm not a... Okay, I'm a narcissist. So what? Is it a crime to want to look your best?"

"No, but you won't look so good with your brain splashed over the asphalt, either."

"Ugh, Mom."

"Did I paint too graphic a picture for you? Well, I've actually seen it, son. I've seen the head trauma bike and motorcycle riders sustain when they get into accidents without helmets." Mom was a paramedic with the Memphis Fire Department for eleven years before the stress got to her and she quit. "I don't care what the helmet does to your hair. That's what combs are for. Going forward, you will wear your helmet from the moment you get on that bike to the moment you get off. You will wear your helmet *every* time you ride your bike. Fail to do so, you'll not only be grounded, I'll take that bike from you permanently. I'll sell it and get new seat covers for my car. Are we clear, Zeno?"

"Yes, Mom. One hundred percent clear as polished glass."

"Now, for being so dunderheaded, get my satchel out of the car and haul it in."

I bowed low to her. "Yes, O' Queen of the Wiggle Wagon."

Mom scoffed and put her hands on her hips. "Please stop using trucker slang. You always make it sound X-rated. You've been watching porn again, haven't you?"

"Mmm. Smell that dinner, Ma! Let's get in there."

"Uh-huh. All I smell is that shea butter and manuka honey conditioner you use on your precious naps."

Dad was at the stove when Mom and I entered the kitchen from the garage. He wore a gray and green tank top over gray basketball shorts and bare feet. I wondered, not for the first time, what it would be like to have a father who dressed like an adult.

"There are my favorite people," he said as he finished painting hot melted butter over steaming ears of corn. He put down the basting brush, wiped his hands on his shorts, and shimmied—no, swear to God, I'm not making that up—his way toward Mom. "Hey, lady," he said in this low, slow voice.

"Hey, babe," Mom replied with a smile. She raised her arms, holding them out so Dad could slide his shoulders under them.

Mom and Dad latched on and locked lips like spouses who hadn't seen each other in four days.

I loved my parents. I loved that they loved each other. But I was not cool with overly expressive displays of affection between them. Certain aspects of their relationship should be kept private from their easily grossed out son. After I'd made my feelings clear on that subject, they naturally went out of their way to clown me every chance they got. When Dad, in the middle of their long slurpy welcome-home kiss, dipped Mom halfway down to the floor, and when Mom kicked her leg straight toward the ceiling— that shot me *way* past my comfort zone.

I dropped my backpack and Mom's satchel, pointed an indignant finger at the hall, and snapped, "Go to your room!"

*

I LAY NECK-DEEP in a tub of warm, sudsy, coconut-scented water. A fat, blue jar candle reminiscent of jasmine burned languidly on the rim of the tub. Eyes closed, I basked in the sweet, soothing sounds of tiny bubbles popping softly around me. After dinner, I'd started clearing the table, but Dad chased me off to finish my homework. I went to my room and did exactly that. With the assignments done, I submitted my latest college application and then did a few sets of crunches and chin-ups while watching an old episode of *black-ish*.

I liked the way my body felt after a good workout—the vibrant rush of endorphins, the tingling sense of power, all mixing together into a wonderful sense of tranquility. It was a great way to relieve stress and enable myself to chill. When my phone chimed with a text, I groaned. My little feel-good moment popped like a soap bubble. After drying my hands on a towel, I reluctantly reached for my phone.

The text was from Jemma: *What's up, helmet head?*

I replied with, *Bathtime.*

I should drop by. She added a smiling devil emoji.

Smiling, I responded with a throbbing heart emoji.

Party. My house. Fri nite. U R coming.

Okay, this was totally new for Jemma. In the time I'd known her, she threw two parties a year, one on her birthday and the other during fall break. This Friday night didn't fit either occasion. She plotted and planned her parties down to the last detail, ensuring good times for all with her parents and kid sister nowhere around. Impromptu was so not her. And what was I doing Friday night? Homework wouldn't be a problem; I'd get that done first thing after school. Did I have any carwash appointments? This was a rare three-day weekend off work for Mom. Had she or Dad planned any family time for Friday?

Jemma came back with: *Stop thinking so hard. Just BE THERE.*

Jeez. Talk about pushy. *Can I bring a friend?*

Girlfriend? She tacked on three spinning question marks and three throbbing hearts.

Just a friend.

Cool.

*

LYING ACROSS MY bed in a T-shirt and boxers, I wound down the day playing a Spider-Man video game on my phone. The room felt chilly, but I was way too involved fighting Mysterio to grab a blanket. My skin was still damp from the bath and a bit oily from the lotion I spread on to keep ashiness at bay. The tiny digital clock in the corner of my screen was closing in on 10:00 p.m. Despite the excitement of the game, my eyes were starting to feel heavy.

The knock came quietly, followed by, "Got a minute, Zeno?"

I paused the game, rolled over, and sat up in bed. "Come in, Dad."

He opened the door and leaned against the frame. "Hey."

"Uh-oh. You've got that hangdog look. Are you getting sick?"

"Your mom just jumped down my throat."

"Why?"

"She thinks I'm a bad dad."

"You're a great dad."

"I'm a dad who had no idea his kid's been riding a bike all over town for God knows how long without wearing a helmet. That's the way your mom put it."

"Oh. She asked you about that, huh?"

"Yeah. I thought you and I were good, Z-bo. I thought we were partners, and you left me hanging out to dry."

"I didn't mean to, Dad. I just—"

He held up a hand to stop me. "I really don't want to hear you say you put your safety second to a flesh 'fro."

I chuckled, picturing a fat, meaty head. "Flesh 'fro?"

"*Fresh* 'fro. You try saying that three times fast!"

"Fresh 'fro, fresh 'fro, fresh 'fro."

"Shaddup. On a serious tip, you realize this doesn't help your case for going off to the University of Chicago in the fall."

I heaved out a breath and let my head fall forward, chin thumping against my chest. "I realize, I realize." *Fuck.*

Dad came into the room and sat next to me. "You know how much I love you, right?"

Jeez. I raised my head a little. "Yeah."

"Well, I think your mom loves you even more. The hardest thing about her job is that it takes her away from home for days at a stretch. One of the things that makes it easier for her to be away is knowing that I'm taking care of you. Today, she's convinced I'm not doing a good job of that."

Dang. What the hell? I was supposed to be jetting along the path to manhood, but more and more it seemed I was rolling backward. What an idiot. It was one thing to impugn my own integrity, but I could've kicked myself for dragging Dad down with me.

Shaking my head, I muttered, "Sorry. I didn't mean for that to happen."

"Of course you didn't, but son, actions have consequences. You have no idea how hard it is to let you go out into the world every day. My main job is to keep you safe, something that's a lot harder to do once you leave this house. I have to depend on you to do everything you can to keep down the risks. You know? The things we talked about...how and when to use a condom, what to do if you encounter a cop. You have to take your well-being seriously, Zeno. I don't need you taking crazy chances out there."

"Like riding my bike without a helmet. I'm sorry. I won't do it again."

"Thank you." He reached over and squeezed my knee. "Hey, aren't you ready to trade up to a car? You're sixteen. You can get a learner's permit."

"I dunno. I never really thought all that much about driving. It's not, like, at the top of my wish list or anything."

Dad frowned, looking confused. "You don't want to learn how to drive?"

"Not really. I like my bike."

He patted my knee. "You're a strange kid, son."

"Thanks." I patted his knee. "You're a strange dad, Dad."

"Shaddup and get some sleep."

"As you wish, my Dark Sith Lord."

Dad stood, took a couple of steps toward the door, and

turned back to me. "Oh, by the way, your mom and I are going on a little road trip this weekend."

"You mean, I'm not invited?"

"Hell no."

Ohhh. "You're going to that cabin at Covington Lake."

Dad's smile was straight-up lascivious. "You know it. Just your mom and me, doing our do." He started swiveling his hips.

"Ew! Dad, stop! Get out!"

He laughed on his way into the hall.

I got up and shut the door after him. My eyes were actually burning. "God. I'm gonna have nightmares tonight."

*

SNUG BENEATH THE comforter, pillows fluffed under my head, lying on my side and curled like a cooked shrimp—that was my favorite sleeping position. The lamp still shone next to my bed, and random thoughts drifted lazily through my mind as sleep crept up on me. This was a kind of taking stock, a review of the day as to what went right and what didn't and what I could do better tomorrow.

Marvus Ahern. I thought of him a lot these days. Once, when we were twelve, I got my stupid butt in big trouble with Mom. Back then, I had this habit of playing catch in the house, tossing objects in the air and catching them. Mom told me who knows how many times not to do it. "You're going to break something, Zeno."

Well, I kept forgetting. And this one time, I got an apple out of the fridge, tossed it up, and it went straight into the ceiling fan. The blades, spinning on high speed, chopped the apple into two big chunks and fired them both straight into the kitchen window. The glass shattered into a thousand pieces, and the window screen got bent so badly it wouldn't fit in the frame anymore.

"What did I tell you?" Mom shouted.

"I'm sorry! I'll clean it up."

"No, you'll cut yourself. Get to your room. You're grounded. Seven days!"

"Seven days? But Marvus's birthday party is Saturday. That's three days from now."

"You won't be there."

"But I really wanna go. His dad's giving him this big new model. He wants me to help him put it together and paint it. And his mom's making everybody a cherry soda float—"

"Float your narrow behind into your room and stay there until I can stand to look at you again."

So, that Saturday afternoon, I was on lockdown in my room while Marvus and all our friends were having big fun at his party. And yeah, knowing what I was missing had me a little choked up. When I heard a soft knock, I wiped my eyes, slid off the bed, and started toward the door.

"No. Over here."

I turned. And my jaw dropped. Marvus was at my window, in a red polo shirt and red jeans (his favorite color then; you couldn't pay him enough to wear red these days), with a visor on his head that read, "It's My Birthday!" For a moment, the sight rooted me to the spot.

"Hey, hurry up," he hissed, urging me forward with backward jerks of his head. "My hands are freezing."

I rushed over and opened the window. "Marvus? What're you doing here?"

"I'm not celebrating my birthday without you. Come on. Let me in."

I raised the window screen, and Marvus shoved two frosty plastic cups at me. "Here, take these."

"What's this?"

"You know how you love my ma's cherry soda floats."

I grinned as I took the cups. "Oh man!"

"Keep your voice down. You want your mom and dad to come in here and kill us?" He pulled himself in through the window, a big red duffel bag strapped to his back, and closed it behind him.

"You're crazy, man. You can't duck out on your own party."

"Ah. Everybody's playing laser tag right now. They won't miss me." He sat on the floor and opened the duffel bag. Inside was the new model plane kit he'd wanted for his birthday along with everything we'd need to put it together and paint it. "Come on. Let's do this. Gimme one of those floats."

"Marvus, you're amazing."

"Nah, I couldn't enjoy myself knowing you're over here not having fun."

Yeah, Marvus was *that* kind of friend.

Since starting my senior year at MemTech, I hadn't seen much of him, even though he lived right down the street. I'd caught a glimpse of him this evening, getting off a city bus at the corner. I didn't stop to say hey or anything because, you know, I was trying to make it home for dinner. Yeah. Maybe tomorrow I should—

My phone chimed. I picked it up and got a FaceTime from Dalvin. His smile made me smile.

"My man," I said, eyebrows notching up, my spirits more jaunty than they were a moment ago. "Ain't it past your bedtime?"

His brown eyes were bright and alert. "Can't sleep. My folks are having a fight about where they're gonna vacay this summer."

"They're pretty loud, huh?"

"Yeah, but that's not really why I can't sleep. You're all tucked in, I see."

I rolled onto my back. Dalvin wasn't wearing a shirt. Some weird energy zinged up my spine. He stretched out his arms, and the tightening muscles in his chest and shoulders made me feel a little...I don't know...jealous? I folded my free arm across my chest, nudging my hand into my pit to keep from squirming. "Maybe you need to be tucked in."

He grinned at that. "Maybe I do."

"Hey, wanna go to a party with me Friday night?"

"Who's throwing the party?"

"Jemma. She said I could bring a friend."

"Cool. I'm in."

We grinned at each for about half a minute, saying nothing.

Then, slowly, Dalvin's smile dwindled, and I knew something serious was coming. "Hey, you ever thought about becoming a lawyer?"

"Heck no. Lawyers have to be ruthless and aggressive. That ain't me."

"Dude. You got that smooth talk down. You could charm a jury into anything."

"Sorta like you're doing with me now? You'd make a better lawyer than I ever would."

"It's something to think about."

"Wait a minute. You're thinking about becoming a lawyer? For two years, you've been all about how you're gonna become this big-time computer graphic artist. What's with all the lawyer stuff?"

"I meant it's something for *you* to think about. Did you get that college application sent off tonight?"

"Yeah. Christian Brothers University. My mom likes that one, for some reason. Oh, right, it's her alma mater."

Dalvin opened his mouth, paused, and then pressed his lips

together hard like they'd been permanently sealed.

"Okay, Dal. What is it you're not saying, man?"

"Z, you're the only person I know who's been accepted into a college and doesn't have a major."

"Okay. And what's the big deal?"

"Really, Z? What's the point in going to college if you don't have a goal? You know, a career goal."

Uh.

Dalvin waited another moment and then pressed on. "I want to go into computer graphics, so I've only applied to colleges that have computer graphics programs. Ollie's set on going into politics. Kipper wants to be an accountant. But you never talk about what you want to be. You need to figure that out first. How do you know the University of Chicago even has a program you want to major in?"

I never gave a thought to what undergrad programs UChicago offered. What sold me was the fact that Chicago was a big, fun, fast-living city. That sounded like a good place for a brother to be. I had plenty of time to figure out my future career. Then again, my parents had already made it pretty clear they expected me to get my shit together, and soon, or I wouldn't be moving to Chicago in the fall. That's why they were making me apply to local colleges.

I huffed at Dalvin, suddenly miffed. "Who're you now? My dad?"

"I'm trying to give you that friendly little kick in the ass you need. You gotta have a dream job in mind. You gotta have a passion about something. Like, I notice how you geek all the way out in chem lab."

"Yeah?" My face split into what felt like the biggest, toothiest smile. This guy noticed the little things about me. That made me feel really good.

"Yeah. So, if chemistry does it for ya, that could be your

college major. And maybe you go on to be a…pharmacist or a researcher who develops cures for diseases. And, like, the way you get epically pissed every time those crazy Tennessee lawmakers put up another bill to hurt trans people, if you're a lawyer with the ACLU, you can fight that stupid shit. I like that about you, by the way. You've never even met any trans people, but you're willing to stand up for them."

I pressed my head back into my pillow. "Wow. You…really know me."

He squinted at me, one corner of his mouth crooking up. "Yeah. That kinda happens when people are friends. Point is, man, you'll be awesome at whatever you do if you figure out what the hell you want."

I was suddenly so warm inside I couldn't even say anything. I could only stare, smiling, at my friend's earnest tan face.

"Why so quiet?" Dalvin asked after a moment.

"I…I appreciate the kick."

"You're welcome." He chuckled, his head dipping forward as his shoulders gently shook.

"What?"

"Nothing. Your hair's a mess."

"Dude! I'm in bed. I'm supposed to have bedhead."

"It's cool. I like seeing you this way."

Under the covers I wriggled my legs, squirming.

Dalvin sighed. "I wish…"

I waited a moment for him to finish. "What? What do you wish?"

"I dunno. That I could make things easier on you."

A sharp rap on Dalvin's door startled us both. A man's gruff voice followed the knock, calling, "Get off the phone, Dally. Go to sleep."

Dalvin rolled his eyes. "A'ight, Dad."

It was my turn to laugh. "Dally. That's cute."

"*Never* call me that."

"Time for you to go, boy. G'night. *Dally.*"

He grinned as I broke the connection.

The conversation left something in me buzzing. It was a while before I fell asleep.

Chapter Four

WITH A HOT mug of tea in one hand, Mom was rummaging through the pantry when I walked into the kitchen.

"Morning, Ma. I wasn't expecting to see you."

She was decked out in her fuzzy baby-blue robe and white polka dot pajamas, her home-all-day outfit. "Why not?" she replied, peering over her shoulder at me. "Last I checked, I do live here."

"I mean, I figured you'd be sleeping in."

"I got up to see your daddy off. Even offered to make him breakfast, but he only wanted cranberry juice." She stepped out of the pantry with a box of Cheerios clutched to her chest. "How about you? Breakfast?"

I plopped my overloaded backpack in a chair and placed my helmet on top of it. "I'll make us a real breakfast. Sausage and egg biscuits okay with you?"

"Sounds lovely." She put back the Cheerios.

I wasn't in a rush this morning and planned on walking out

of the house like a civilized person for once. Plus, it was great to have a little mother-and-son time. "Sliced oranges to go with?"

"Yum." Mom took a sip of tea as she sat down at the table.

I set the oven at 375 degrees and got a box of frozen sausage and egg biscuits from the fridge. (Yeah, like you thought I was actually gonna make that stuff from scratch.) "I sent off that application to Christian Brothers University last night."

"Hey, wonderful."

"I used your Mastercard for the application fee. I'll give you the fifty bucks after I get home this afternoon."

"You don't have to do that, Zeno. I know you're trying to help with the bills, but save your money for when you get to college. Believe me, that's when you'll be glad to have it. What about a major?" Mom frowned at me.

Uh-oh. I was positive "undecided" wouldn't go over too well with her this time. "Well, actually, I was thinking maybe chemistry. And then pharmacy school? And then maybe I'd go into research?"

Mom's face brightened. "Well! I like the sound of that!"

Great. Is there even such a thing as pharmacy school?

I arranged three of the big frozen sandwiches in a pan and returned the box to the freezer. "Oh, yeah, I'm going to a party tonight. At Jemma's."

"Good for you. You deserve a little time to enjoy yourself. Just do what you did at her other parties."

"Stay outta trouble and remember my curfew? Sure." I grabbed a bowl, two oranges and a knife and sat down across from Mom. "Hey, what was your major at CBU?"

"Biological sciences."

"So you majored in biology because you wanted to be a paramedic?"

"No, I actually wanted to get my doctorate and become a college professor and researcher."

Wow. That froze me for a second. "Why didn't you become a professor?"

"Life happened. Right after I got my bachelor's degree, I got married, and then I had a baby. I needed a job to help take care of my new family. One day, there was a six-car pileup on the expressway in front of me. I got out of my car and helped those I could before the police and ambulances got there. That inspired me, and I joined the fire department as a trainee."

"But you burned out, and now you're a trucker, and that's it? College was a waste?" I gulped, almost choking on guilt. Having me derailed my mom's whole career train.

"Oh, I still intend to finish my education and start my career as a professor. Once you're off to college, I'm going to grad school. I'm only thirty-seven. I can still do this."

"But you'd be finished with all that now, right?" Jeez, look at the years she'd lost! "You'd be teaching biology today if... I'm sorry, Mom, that you had to—"

"I made my choices, and I don't regret a single one. You and your dad mean the world to me. But now is the time for you to focus on getting yourself educated, trained, and established in whatever career you want to pursue. Do that now, son, while you are your only responsibility."

I nodded as I sliced the oranges into quarters. They went into the bowl, which I slid to the center of the table. Mom and I each grabbed a slice.

Casually, Mom said, "You and Jemma are kind of close, huh?"

"We're just friends, Mom."

*

LIPS, WARM AND soft, brushed against my shoulder. "Brought you something."

Taken by surprise at my locker, I shivered a little and almost dropped the book I was holding. "Dang. Do you have to sneak up on a brother like that?" I said, smiling.

"You know you love surprises." Jemma extended her hand, raising a candy apple so shiny with golden caramel it almost glowed. "Made it myself."

"Oh my gosh, Jem. This is awesome."

The treat was wrapped in clear cellophane and tied with a red lace bow. I was already thinking it would be lunch. My lips twitched. Jem's mom got her hooked on candy apples ages ago during a Halloween party. Her mom got me hooked last year when Jemma invited me over for our first sci-fi movie night.

"Thanks. I owe ya." I shoved the book in my backpack and took the treat.

"God, Zeno, it's only a snack. Don't make a big deal." Her glossy, wheat-colored hair was tied back in a ponytail, and it was obvious she had on her dancing togs under her khaki skirt and white turtleneck.

Not that her undergear was any of my business, of course.

I blinked a few times, scratched at my ear, and then squinched my nose. This situation was suddenly awkward as hell.

"You're adorable when you do that," Jemma said.

"Do what?"

She giggled, mimicked my moves, and said, "Look con-fused."

"I must be adorable full-time."

Jemma giggled again and leaned in, going for my cheek. I leaned down to her, and at the last moment, I turned my head and met her lips with mine. The kiss was soft and quick. We both blinked, and I realized I was as startled as Jemma was. Then she tiptoed up and planted another, longer kiss on me.

Oh, hell, that was nice. Exciting. Parts of me tingled. But we were in the middle of a crowded hall at school, and this was stuff for another time and another place. I cleared my throat and said, "Listen, I'm, uh, well...okay. It's... I kinda wanted to ask a favor."

Jemma clasped her hands coyly in front of her. "So. Ask."

"For our senior project, Dalvin and I have to film interviews of students talking about their greatest fear. Would you be willing to let me interview you?"

For a moment, Jemma's face twisted into a skeptical frown, which I thought was leading up to a big hell no. Then she said, "That actually sounds interesting. I'll do it."

Before I could reply, a thick arm slid around my neck, dangling down over my chest as if it belonged there. The warm scent of a citrus and spice soap gently filled the air as Dalvin's presence settled firmly next to me. My whole head heated up, and I suddenly couldn't look Jemma in the eye anymore. I kinda wanted to edge away from Dalvin, but something kept me standing right next to him. Oh, and he wasn't alone.

"Do what?" Richie drawled in a loud, obnoxious voice. "What're you gonna do for the Z man, Jemammary, and are you gonna do me next?"

"Here, do this first, Richie." Jemma offered up her middle finger. An unladylike move, to be sure, but I approved wholeheartedly with a braying laugh.

Richie smirked, absolutely shameless. Barely five-ten, he was a point guard on the basketball team, captain of the debate team, and chairman of the Young Republicans Club, the kind of guy destined to go from frat house to Wall Street in a single bound. Good-looking in a hawkish kind of way, he had long, wavy hair somewhere between deep brown and gold in color that topped him like a crown. He hung out with a fair number of people (apparently including Dalvin) but had a certain oiliness that I flat-out didn't like. He left me wanting a long hot shower every time I ran into him. Look up "smarmy" in the dictionary and you'll find a simple, two-word definition: Richard McMahon.

"I'll ride your purrty little finger," Richie cooed, "if you'll ride my—"

"Classy as always," I said, throwing Richie's chintzy smile back at him. "Your mom and dad named you perfectly, dude. They looked at baby you and knew right off you were a dick."

"Whoa. Was that a joke, Zero?" The corners of his mouth dragged down, an exaggerated pity party. "Were we supposed to laugh, Zero? Aww, poor Zero."

"*Anyway*," Jemma snapped, turning pointedly to Dalvin, "Zeno told me about the project you guys are working on, and I'll be glad to do an interview for your documentary."

"Cool," Dalvin replied, bumping my chest twice with his fist. "You're doing us a big favor, Jem."

"I'll do you a favor," Richie said, looking straight at me. "I'll be in your little documentary too. Just make sure you kiss up my best side." He turned his back to me, hiked up his jacket and started unbuckling his pants right there in the hall.

Dalvin rolled his eyes and growled, "Dude."

Richie stopped what he was doing, smirking again.

Jemma gave a little snort, shooting serious stink eye at Richie. "Come on." She grabbed me by the wrist and tugged me away from Dalvin and Richie, stopping only after we rounded the corner into the adjoining hall.

My hands were shaking. I blew out a breath with no clue as to why I felt so uneasy. In the other hall, Dalvin laid some choice words on Richie. Jemma still held my wrist, and her touch felt really good there. The kiss still lingered between us.

Jemma gazed into my eyes—*oh man, she's so pretty*—uhm... She stared into my eyes, all concerned and stuff, and it, like, made me feel fluttery in the head. And I think she saw what I was feeling because her eyebrows went up. She froze as if it surprised her, and then she rubbed her thumb over the inside of my wrist. I could've sworn she was about to say something.

Dalvin breezed around the corner. "Sorry about Richie," he said, half glancing back over his shoulder with a scowl.

He looked at us—looked at the way we were practically holding hands—and stopped abruptly. I quickly shook my wrist out of Jemma's grasp. The moment of silence that followed seemed to last about a decade.

"Oh, yeah." I forced a laugh. "That damn Richie..."

Neither Jemma nor Dalvin said anything to that. Silence started stretching again. The three of us exchanged looks, waiting.

Nope, not awkward at all. I scratched the back of my head.

What the hell was this?

"Forget Richie," Jemma said, breaking the tension. "I need a favor of my own. I'm in this recital at Saint Mary's next month, and I'm not sure which dance I'm going to perform. I've narrowed it down to three solos. I'd like to get some non-dancer input, if you guys would be willing to help me out. This afternoon, maybe?"

I looked at Dalvin, expecting him to beg off because of football practice. The team had made the playoffs for the state championship, and no one wanted our team to take this year's title more than Dalvin. I was surprised when he nodded and said, "I can do this afternoon."

Okay, that left only me. I had a carwash appointment, but that wasn't until five thirty, so I could spare an hour. "I'm there as long as it's done by five. We'll give you our opinion, for what it's worth."

"Great. Mrs. Ashton reserved the dance studio for me to practice. You guys meet me there after the final bell."

"You mind if I film your dance routines?" Dalvin asked. "It'll make nice footage for your part of the documentary and help show the audience who you are."

"That's fine with me. But don't make me look bad."

"That would be impossible," I blurted. And suddenly, I wanted to slap both hands over my face.

Fortunately, distraction arrived in a deep grunt, like the sound a wounded wildebeest might make, coming from the corridor where Dalvin had cussed Richie out. I turned that way as Richie himself slunk around the corner looking totally spanked.

"Yo Dal, let's go," he said. "We'll be late for homeroom."

"Catch you people later." Dalvin looked from Jemma to me, flicked a smile, and then disappeared around the corner with Richie.

Now it was Jemma and me again.

"Okay, then," I said, scratching at my ear as I looked down at my feet.

Jemma laughed. "*So* cute."

Chapter Five

I EXITED MY last class of the day—Global Studies—and nearly got bowled over by three hefty guys in green and white letterman jackets who were shoving, jabbing, and laughing at one another as they raced down the hall toward the gymnasium. Hm. That was odd.

"Hey," Dalvin said as he eased up behind me in his own varsity jacket.

"Hey." I watched as the three boys banged through the door into the parking lot that connected to the gym. "They kinda look like they're headed to football practice. I thought that was canceled or something."

"Nope. It's still on. We practice every Monday, Wednesday, and Thursday."

"Then...you're ditching practice?" That would be major. In the three and a half years I'd known him, Dalvin never ditched anything.

"Hell no, man. Yesterday, the coach showed the team video of three plays from our last regular season game and asked how those plays almost lost us that game. I was the only player who came up with the right answer, so Coach told me I could skip practice today since I already knew what he was about to drill into the rest of the team. He's gonna work the hell outta them."

"Bet you hate you're missing out on that," I said as we began ambling in the opposite direction toward the Arts wing. From my backpack, I pulled the chocolate bar I'd gotten out of the vending machine during lunch. I tore off the wrapping and chomped a huge bite. My eyes rolled up as I chewed. Pure heaven.

Dal was smiling when I looked at him again. I offered him a bite; he shook his head. His loss. Two chomps later, the chocolate bar was a sweet memory.

"You know," Dalvin said, "I make killer brownies."

What in the natural hell? I hesitated for a second in midstep. Was the dude into edibles or something? *Shit. Mom and Dad would kill my ass if I did edibles.* "Uh. What does that mean?"

Dalvin kept smiling, but his expression suddenly became unreadable. "It means I'm into baking these days."

"Like, actual baking?"

"There's another kind? Yeah, actual baking. My mom's got this side hustle where she does cakes and pies for people who want a homemade dessert without the trouble of making it themselves. She pulls in some serious cash, too, anywhere from twenty-five bucks for a sweet potato pie to four hundred bucks for a wedding cake. She got swamped this one time and asked me to help out, and I got hooked. I learned a lot from my mom, and now I bake on my own. I'm good at it, man."

I stopped cold in the hall, and three girls almost rear-ended me. They cursed as they ducked around and went on their way.

Dalvin turned back to me with this puzzled look on his face. "What?" he asked.

I pressed my lips together, covered my mouth with my hand, and wound up snickering through my nose. "I'm trying to picture it... You...in an apron...stirring up a batch of sugar cookies!" I burst out howling.

"Man, hell with you." Grinning, Dalvin swiveled sharply at the waist, shoving me away with his backpack. "You sound like my pops."

"Promise you'll bake me something. *Please.*"

He looked me square in the eye, his smile gone. "Anything for you."

Ooh. The serious vibe off him right now made my mouth go dry. I turned away for a moment, scratching the back of my head.

"So..." Dalvin blew out a breath. "Not exactly man stuff, huh, the baking?"

"Hey," I said, turning back to him, "my dad cooks most of the meals at our house. He always has, even before my mom started working shifts out of town full time. He makes desserts, too, and he's damned good at it like you. He *loves* cooking for his family."

"Yeah?"

"Definitely. I mean, I'd starve if it weren't for my dad. And I do most of the housework, laundry and cleaning the bathrooms and stuff. No such thing as women's work at our house."

This was a totally new side of Dalvin, a tiny crack in the armor of self-confidence he always presented. I liked this vulnerability in him, something he seemed to share only with me. I liked that I could back him up.

Dalvin smiled again. "Okay. I told you something embarrassing about me. Now let me hear something embarrassing about you."

"Dal, what the hell? Baking's your thing, and it's nothing to be ashamed of."

"Tell that to Richie or the guys on the football team. I'd never hear the end of it." He looked around anxiously at the kids passing by in the hall, maybe checking for eavesdroppers. They were wrapped up in their own business and paying no attention to us. "Uh, don't say anything about this to anybody around here, okay Z?"

"I promise I won't. And if it'll make you feel better, I'm into scented candles. And calla lilies."

Dalvin's whole face lit up. "Candles and calla lilies? Seriously?"

"Definitely. My mom lights candles and takes long baths. She says it helps her relax when she's stressed or feeling down or whatever. So, there was this time...something happened with this friend of mine, we stopped being cool with each other, and I was, like...really losing it. I lit one of my mom's candles and sank into a tub of warm suds and, dude, it mellowed me out. I swear. Sometimes, I just sit in my room in the dark with a lit candle, and I'm chill. Jasmine's my favorite scent."

The expression on Dalvin's face changed from amusement to concern. I knew immediately he wanted to ask about the friend debacle thing—*please, God, don't let him ask*—and I almost shook my head when he opened his mouth. Right away, he closed up again. Maybe he picked up on my dread, somehow, because he finally said, "So. Where do the calla lilies come in, huh?"

"Oh, right. Before I started elementary school, my parents used to leave me with my mom's mom while they worked. She loved calla lilies. In the spring and summer, I'd help her plant lilies around her house and take care of them. It became a thing for us that lasted until she died four years ago. When Mom sold her house, I transplanted some of her lilies into our yard, and I've been keeping them going since, as a way to remember her."

"That's a beautiful thing for you to do, man. Sorry about your grandma, though. Must've been tough, losing her."

"Yeah. I still have my dad's mom. She's a gangsta Spades player. Taught me everything I know about the game. When we partner up, we rule the table."

"I'm really close to both my grandmas too." Dalvin smiled. "I'm glad you told me this stuff."

I smiled at him. "Yeah?"

"Yeah. I was thinking today that you're really cool people. I can talk to you, always could, from just about the time we met. You have this way of making me see things for what they are."

"I can say the same about you."

"But we've been friends for over three years now, and it's, like, I know you but not really," Dalvin said. "There's a lot I don't know about you."

"Dude, you know a lot about me. I know a lot about you. Remember all those nights we stayed up late playing online video games? The way we marathon episodes of *Game of Thrones* on your phone? The way we play soccer and basketball after school? We're into a lot of the same stuff."

"But there's so much more. I've never been to your house, never met your parents. You don't even know where I live. Do you know my biggest fear? I don't know yours."

I looked away from him. There were a number of kids I hung out with at school whose homes I'd never visited and whose parents I'd never met. That didn't make them any less of a friend. Of course, I'd known Jemma about as long as I'd known Dalvin, and I'd been to her house a number of times. I played board games and watched movies with her parents and her sister. It was only fair that I invited her to my house for my dad's backyard barbecues. Did that make her more of a friend than Dalvin?

Dalvin massaged the back of his neck, a move that screamed nervousness. Or frustration. "I'm not trying to make anything major out of this, Z. I wanna know you better, that's all. Is it crazy to want that?"

I glanced up. The way he was looking at me...oh my gosh. There went that weird tingle through my body again. I liked the dude. He liked me. And I shivered.

Because Dalvin wanted us to be *closer*.

I tried to swallow and almost choked. "Hey. We can hang out more, no problem. Like my Grampa Nic says, ain't no thang but a chicken wang."

Dalvin laughed at my old school southern drawl. "Cool. I've got something I want to tell you—"

"At *last*. There you are."

We had arrived at the open door of the dance studio. Jemma leaned against the jamb in a green leotard, arms folded across her chest, fingers drumming impatiently against her elbows. She'd combed her hair back and tied it in a tight bun at the nape of her neck. Looking at her immediately formed an image of a lit fuse in my head.

"I thought you guys were never gonna get here," she said.

She grabbed Dalvin and me by the arm and pulled us inside.

*

I SURE AS hell was no dance expert and definitely not qualified to critique any such performance. But Jemma's obvious and extraordinary talent flat-out astonished me.

Seated on a padded piano bench, I watched closely as Jemma went through three distinct dances in time to music playing from a rather beat-up, old-fashioned boombox she'd placed on a metal folding chair at the back of the studio.

The first routine appeared to be a traditional ballet set to spritely classical music. She performed in an elegant, graceful, and at times flirty style, her movements embellished with a folding fan she opened and closed to playful effect. The second, a contemporary piece, seemed like something out of a glitzy Broadway show (not that I'd ever been to one), accompanied by an old-timey jazz tune. Bold and energetic, it had elements of tap thrown in for good measure. But the third dance really stood out to me—a combo freestyle/classical ballet done to a bopping hip hop beat, the moves sassy and passionate. Jemma's face shone with pride and power, and I could tell this performance blazed in her heart. While I liked the first two solid, beautiful performances, the third filled me with such joy I wanted to get up and dance with her. I barely even noticed Dalvin as he moved about the studio through it all, filming Jemma from various angles with his iPhone.

When she finished, Jemma glided over to turn off the boombox, grabbed a towel, and walked up to me. Glowing, she wiped her face and neck with the towel, inhaled deeply several times to steady her breathing, and then shifted her gaze slightly to include the still-filming Dalvin.

"Okay, guys. Opinions, please."

On my phone, I had a list of questions I'd prepared for her. My plan was to get to them at some point before we left the studio, and boom, that would be one interview down. Still buzzing from the intensity of her performances, however, I tucked my phone away, deciding to go with my gut.

"Personally, I think you should choose the third dance for your recital."

She brightened, clearly pleased. "What about you, Dalvin?"

"I'm with Zeno," Dalvin said without missing a beat on the camera work. "Do the third one."

"So why the third?"

"Before we answer that," I said, "can you tell us something about each dance?"

She wiped her face again and laughed. "Sure. The first is from a classical ballet, *Don Quixote*, third act, the character of Kitri, a spitfire in love with the town's barber. The choreography was by a ballet dancer named Marius Petipa. The second is from a suite called *Perks*, choreographed by my first dance teacher, Ms. Leweski, for her company. The third is an original, untitled piece choreographed by yours truly."

"I knew it!" I laughed, too, totally impressed. "I knew something about that third one was personal to you."

"Yeah," Dalvin added, "you gave a hundred percent to the first two, but you went above and beyond with the third. You *lived* that baby."

"I'm so glad to hear you guys say that. You're right. I really want to perform my own work. But the other two pieces were choreographed by professionals. Can my choreography actually compare to that?"

"You shouldn't be afraid to put your own work out there. Isn't it about how much of your heart you put into the dance," I said, "regardless of who created it?"

She thought about that for a moment. "Exactly, Zeno. You're absolutely right. More than anything, I want the audience to feel what my character is feeling. I want them to see what I bring to the stage."

"Have you always wanted to be a dancer?"

"Yes, from the time my mom took me to see *The Nutcracker* during the first Christmas season I can remember, when I was five.

Ms. Leweski's company did the staging, and by the time I was six, my parents had enrolled me in her dance school."

"Who's had the bigger influence on you, Ms. Leweski or MemTech's dance teacher, Mrs. Ashton?"

"There's no simple answer to that. I took lessons from Ms. Leweski until I started here at MemTech, so I learned more from her. But Mrs. Ashton helped me refine my technique, and most importantly, she helped get me into Juilliard. It took both teachers to get me this far."

It was as if I were truly seeing Jemma, the real Jemma, for the first time. I'd never known her to be this engaged before. Dance was obviously one of the most important things in her life. Her love of it shone from her eyes, from her very skin. And that, I announced, made this the perfect time to get into the final subject of the interview.

"Hang on," Dalvin said. "Let's change things up a bit. I wanna get more of the dance studio flavor in this. Jemma, let's get you to stand over there by that bar thingy on the mirror wall."

Jemma gave him a huffy smile. "It's called a ballet barre, Dalvin."

"Yeah, thanks. You can kinda lean back with your elbows on the bar thingy...or ballet barre. Z, grab that piano bench and set it up here, about ten feet in front of where Jemma's gonna be standing. I want you to sit there while we finish the interview."

Jemma and I hurried to get ourselves positioned as directed. Dal moved around with his phone, sizing things up from various angles through the camera lens. Once he seemed satisfied with the setup, he started the camera rolling.

"Okay," Dal said, "ready you two? Remember, don't look directly at the camera. Just focus on each other and pretend I'm not here. Go!"

Dang. Dalvin was really...something when he took charge. He'd trespassed on Oliver's territory, directing, doing it brilliantly. Who knew?

Posed against the ballet barre, Jemma smiled pleasantly at me. Mirror panels covered the entire surface of the opposite wall. In our reflections, Jemma looked like a superhero. I looked like a super tall toddler who had no idea what was going on. Jeez.

I took a breath to steel myself. "So, Jemma, what scares you most now?"

She stopped smiling. The shine left her eyes. For a moment, she seemed almost reluctant to answer. "What scares me most, now that I'm actually on my way to Juilliard, is that something will happen to stop everything. My parents think aiming for a career in dance is great, but they keep telling me I should have a backup plan. They say no matter how talented or well-trained you are, a single injury can ruin it all. I'm scared my parents will be right."

Wow. Mr. and Mrs. Haynes had been nothing but supportive of Jemma and her sister, at least as far as I had seen. And wanting your athletic, dancing daughter to have options in case of some career-ending trauma wasn't the same as intentionally blocking her dream. But it was enough to make Jemma doubt herself, a doubt I'd never known was there. I mean, I didn't think the girl was afraid of anything.

Jemma smacked her forehead suddenly. "Oh my God. I just realized how stupid that sounds."

"What do you mean?" Dalvin asked.

"Homelessness, police brutality, nuclear missiles in North Korea. And the thing I'm most worried about is whether I get to dance for a living? Stop filming, Dal. Maybe we should do this over—"

"Jemma," I said, grabbing the hands she'd raised to block

Dalvin's camera. "This isn't about who wins Most Sensitive. Any-body who half knows you gets that you're not a shallow person. And that's definitely not how you were coming across now anyway. You aren't the only senior in this place who's worried about their future career. This moment is about you. We want you to be real right now. You wanna reshoot and talk about something else, we'll reshoot. But I think what you did is great. I think *you're* great."

Jemma turned immediately to Dalvin. He gave her a thumbs-up.

She looked at me again, hands on hips, and smiled. "Okay, you guys. You made me a believer."

*

ANOTHER TEN MINUTES or so was all it took to wrap up Jemma's interview. Dalvin and I thanked her again for her partic-ipation, and she thanked us for the feedback on her dances. The three of us gathered up our gear and walked together to the main entrance. We stepped outside and stood on the steps in the warm amber slant of the setting sun.

"You're not driving today?" I asked Jemma.

She shook her head. "My mom's car wouldn't start this morning, so I told her to take mine. I texted my dad. He'll be here any minute." She poked a finger dead center in my chest and held it there. "Okay, Z, spill. Who's this date you're bringing to my party?"

"Excuse you." I firmly took her finger and pushed it aside. "I'm not bringing a date. I'm coming with my boy here."

Dalvin threw an arm around my shoulders and flashed Jemma the peace sign.

"Oh! Well, that's great. I'm so glad you're coming, Dal." From the glint in her eyes, you'd have thought she just won the lottery.

A dark green Audi SUV pulled up in front of the school. Through the windshield, Jemma's dad waved at us, friendly as ever.

I waved back. "Your carriage awaits, milady."

"Your British accent sucks subway tunnels, milord." Jemma fluttered her fingers in my direction and pulled away. "I'm outta here. Got some shopping to do and some family to get rid of," she said, bopping toward the SUV. "See you guys tonight."

"We'll be there," Dalvin said.

We watched until she climbed in next to her dad, and the two of them drove off.

"Speaking of tonight, Zeno, I'm picking you up. What time should I be at your place?"

"Oh, uh...I was gonna walk. Jemma doesn't live that far away from me, only a mile or four."

"Why walk miles when you can ride with me? What time am I picking you up?"

"Uhm, eightish, I guess?"

Dalvin bumped my shoulder with his. "Cool. Where do you live?"

Chapter Six

IT HAD BEEN a minute since I'd checked out any social media. There hadn't been much time for it lately. But Friday evening, having finished homework and gotten myself all suited up for Jemma's party, and with my parents hastily packing for their trip to Covington Lake, I found myself with a few minutes to kill. Dalvin had been prominent in my thoughts since school ended, so I figured I'd scope his Instagram while waiting for him to show.

Pics and videos of his football games, practice sessions, and workouts filled his pages. He'd been posting a lot of that stuff since starting his campaign to get the attention of college coaches. Scrolling through his more recent posts gave me a little shock. Tucked among all the gridiron shots was a pic of me, of the two of us, actually.

The pic showed us standing in the hall in front of his open locker, both of us in jeans and hoodies, our faces beaming hundred-watt grins. I held Dalvin's fist aloft as if he'd won a boxing championship match. That was a couple of weeks ago, right after the principal had announced over the PA system that Dalvin had ranked fifth on the soon-to-be-released list of the top ten high school football players in the state. The kids in the hall were crazy cheering, but the pic—which had over a thousand likes—only showed Dalvin and me.

We looked so happy. I was glad for Dalvin because the ranking would be a significant boost to his college recruiting prospects. And he was thrilled, of course, to make the list. What caught me by surprise was that Dalvin had slipped a caption across the bottom of the photo: *Forever*.

I stopped breathing for a moment. And then I stared at the caption for, like, a couple of years.

Was I crazy to think this meant something...more?

I looked out the front window for the umpteenth time and saw a shiny black sedan roll to a stop in front of the house. In the dim gray evening, Dalvin climbed out of his dad's car, looking like the perfect jock in blue skinny distressed jeans, a blue long-sleeved, formfitting T-shirt, and blue kicks. He paused long enough to double-check the address on our mailbox and came striding up the walkway.

Huh.

"Ma! I'm leaving." I grabbed the handle and pulled the door open.

"Slow your roll, fella," Dad called out. I turned as he and Mom stepped into the living room.

"I gotta go. What's up?" Oh my gosh. Were they trying to check out Dalvin?

And at that precise moment, Dalvin appeared in the frame of the door I conveniently held open. He raised a hand, flashed his killer smile, and went, "Hey everybody." As if he hadn't walked into the buzzing chainsaws of a parental ambush.

"Hey there, kid," Mom replied as cheerily. "We're Zeno's mom and dad. So you go to school with him."

"Yes, ma'am," Dalvin said. "I'm Dalvin Drake. Zeno and I are working together on a project for Film Club."

"Oh, you're *that* guy," Dad said loudly, "the one Z-bo says has a stick permanently wedged up his ass."

"Jeez, Dad! He's not that guy."

"No, babe," Mom corrected. "Dalvin Drake. He's been all over the Sports section. Remember? The wide receiver who helped get MemTech into the playoffs this year?"

"Oh, yeah. You know, kiddo, I was a star high school football player myself." Dad puffed out his chest at Dalvin. "Best quarterback in the state."

"Yeah, like fifty years ago," I grumbled.

"Twenty years, excuse you. And my baby's as fit and fine now as he was then." Mom pinched Dad's cheek.

Dalvin grinned like a toddler in a bouncy castle.

Daanng. "Okay, Dal, let's go."

"Hold on, now." Dad came forward, sticking out his hand.

Dalvin did the respectful thing and shook with him.

Dad winked at me. "We just wanted to meet your buddy. That's all."

"You see, Dalvin, Zeno doesn't have many friends these days."

"God, Mom. I have friends, okay?"

"Not that I can see," Mom said to Dalvin while cutting her eyes at me. "He used to bring friends home all the time, play dates, sleepovers—"

"That was in *elementary* school!"

"What about Marvus Ahern?" Dad said, "You and that boy

were thick as thieves until, what? About six months ago? Then POOF! No more Marvus."

Shit! Why don't you go ahead and cut me now, Dad?

"No more anyone. Oh, except for Jemma," Mom added, and then she smiled. "Do you happen to know Jemma, Dalvin?"

"Yes, ma'am. She hangs with Z a lot at school."

"Well, a guy needs more than a girlfriend," opined Dad.

"Oh my gosh. How many times do I have to say it? Jemma's not my girlfriend."

"We want Zeno to have good friends," Mom said. "Which is why we're so glad to meet you, Dalvin. Our son's a little high-strung these days."

"He hardly ever takes time to be a kid. Ya know what I mean?" said Dad. "He could use a little help pulling the stick out his own ass."

"Okay! We are *so* done here!" I grabbed Dalvin by the shoulders, spun him around, and bulldozed him through the door.

"Don't forget, Z," Dad yelled, "your mom and I are heading out around three in the morning. We'll check in on you before we leave."

"Yeah, okay, right!"

"Nice to have met you, Dalvin!" Mom sang out. "Hope to see you again soon!"

"Same here!" Dalvin called back.

I shoved him even harder, rushing him toward the sedan.

"Whoa. Go ahead and manhandle a brother." Dalvin laughed.

"Sorry about the crazy folks."

"Not a problem. They seem like cool people. I see where you get it now."

"Get what?"

"Your personality."

"Great. Why don't you stab me now?"

He laughed again. And despite feeling like my whole face had gone up in flames, a smile tugged across my lips. I liked hearing him laugh.

*

WE REACHED JEMMA'S at eight thirty, and the party was already stompin'.

The place buzzed with music and laughter. About twenty people crowded the great room, red cups in hand, some in loud, animated conversation, others dancing. More crowded in the dining room and in the doorway to the kitchen, all kids from school. Many of them greeted us as Dalvin and I made our way into the great room.

"What up, D!"

"Z man!"

"Drinks in the kitchen, dudes!"

Dalvin leaned in close to my ear. "Man. This place is lit."

"For sho."

"Want anything to drink?"

"Canned soda," I said, remembering my mom's admonition that I should pop my own tops at parties.

"Okay. Be right back."

I took up a spot near the dining room door, leaning against the wall. An old Chris Brown song that I liked was playing, and I kinda bopped my head to it while checking out the crowd. Jemma was nowhere in sight. Sooner or later, I'd track her down to let her know I'd made it.

"Look at you, cute as a big ole bumblebee." Macie Hicks sidled up to my left, hands tucked in the pockets of her skirt, looking up at me through the longest eyelashes in the world.

I was decked out in a lemon-yellow hoodie and black jeans. Mom clowned me about the bumblebee look, too, but hell, they were my favorite colors. One more weird thing about me, it seemed. "Hey, Macie."

"Dance with me."

"Uh-huh. Where's Elric?" Elric was her boyfriend. Her super jealous, fist-slinging, start-a-fight-in-a-minute boyfriend.

Macie smiled innocently. "What? You're not worried about Elric—big, tough guy like you."

I waved goodbye to her. "Catch you later, Macie."

She smirked and moved on.

I kept bopping.

A few moments later, Dalvin reappeared with two cold, ice-dappled cans of soda. "Here ya go." He passed one off to me.

"Thanks, man."

We popped the tabs and took swigs together.

"You like that song, huh?" Dalvin said.

"Yeah. I know Chris Brown got all cray-cray with Rihanna, but dude can make you feel a love song."

"Love song? 'Go Crazy' ain't no love song. He's singing about some girl riding him real good."

"Wait. That can't be right."

"Listen to the lyrics, Z."

"He says the girl amazes him. That's frickin' romantic."

"No, what he says is everything she does *sexually* amazes him."

I listened closely to the lyrics. Dal was right. I stopped bopping. "Dang. Everything comes down to sex. Ain't no love left in the world."

"Nah, there's love out there, bruh. You just gotta keep your eyes open and find it. Or let it find you." Dalvin took another swig and leaned against the wall next to me. "Hey, Z."

"Yeah?"

"The new *Zombie Killers* movie opens next week."

"Word? I can't wait to see that shit, man. Gonna be lit."

"We oughta catch it together."

Wait. *Did he...ask me out on a date?* The energy coming off him said that he had. Or was that me fooling myself? That *Forever* pic on his Instagram—maybe I should ask him what that meant. But he was smiling at me, waiting for my response to his movie invite.

"Hey, that'd be cool—" I started.

"Big Diggity D!"

I cringed at the sound of Richie McMahon's voice. The douche himself appeared moments later in a red muscle T and gray track pants, raising a fist to bump with Dal.

"Man, I didn't know you were gonna be here," Richie said.

"What're *you* doing here, Rich?" I knew Jemma hadn't invited his ass. Not on purpose, anyway.

"Jemma said the basketball team could come. That kinda includes me." He waggled his eyebrows my way. "D, come on. Sean and Jerk Dirk are out back getting their asses kicked at beer pong by a couple of girls. You and me can be next up and take those gals down. If ya know what I mean."

"I'm cool hanging with Z right now," Dalvin said flatly.

"Dude!" Richie grabbed Dalvin by the shoulder. "In an hour, you could be getting laid. You can't pass that up. Don't worry. Zeno will still be holding up this wall here when you're done."

"Fuck you, Richie." I felt way more disturbed than I should have. It wasn't as if that was the first time Richie ever took a dig at me. "Go ahead and check out the game if you want, Dal. I should find Jemma anyway."

"But Z—"

"I'll catch you later." I pushed off and wound my way through the crowd, scowling. Yep, I definitely felt hurt. What was up with that?

*

JEMMA. FINALLY.

After trips through the kitchen, family room, sunroom, and backyard, I circled back to the kitchen, and there was Jemma loading kernels and oil into the big kettle of her popcorn machine.

"Hey, girl."

She looked up at me. "Zeno." She came over and wrapped an arm around my neck in a quick hug. "I was wondering when you were gonna get here."

"I've been here. Looking everywhere for you."

"You know me. I stay on the move at these parties." She wore her hair tied back in a ponytail and sported a blue and red polka dot blouse over white pants. A simple look, but the girl was rocking it. She flipped the switch on the popcorn maker. "Can I get you anything? Snacks or something to drink?"

"I already had a soda. I'm good for now."

"Think twice." Jemma went to the fridge and pulled out a bottle of red punch. Straight-up red punch. She kept her drinks liquor-free so she could stay on top of things. I avoided liquor because I feared being drunk, a natural reaction after seeing a couple of guys and gals get stewed and make fools of themselves at the very first party I attended. For Jemma and me, liquid courage was any soda that gave us a sugar high.

"Think twice for what?" I asked, raising my eyebrows. "What're you up to?"

"I set up my karaoke system by the pool," she said as she

poured punch into a red plastic cup. "You're singing tonight."

"The fuck I am."

"Don't argue with me, Zeno."

"Jemma, come on. You know I can't sing."

"That doesn't matter with karaoke." She placed her cup on the table and raised the bottle of punch. "You sure I can't get you a soda or some punch to loosen up those vocal cords?"

I threw my head back, eyes to heaven. "Jemmaaa!"

"Stop the whining. It'll be fun." She placed the bottle back in the fridge.

"I'm not whining. And it won't be fun."

"Now you're pouting."

"I'm not... Okay, I'm pouting."

She laughed and pinched both my cheeks. "We can sing a duet if that'll make it any better."

"I can do a duet, I guess. What're we singing?"

Footsteps banged through the door that opened into the backyard, and Richie made his way into the kitchen. Sheezus, I couldn't get away from this dude tonight.

His gaze burned nastily when he saw us. "Well, what's going on in here?"

Jemma folded her arms across her chest. "Richie, what the hell do you want?"

He put on a look of mock offense. "Hey. Easy, babe. I smelled the popcorn and came to get some. That's all."

Kernels were still popping like bullets in the machine.

"Bags are by the machine," Jemma said to him snappishly. "Give it a minute to finish. And keep your mouth shut while you wait."

Richie saluted like a pro and then flipped us both the finger once Jemma turned her back to him.

God. If only there were an insecticide for assholes.

"My karaoke playlist has lots of everything, from almost every genre and every era," Jemma went on, returning to our conversation without missing a beat. "You can pick whatever song you're comfortable with."

"This is your big idea, so you pick," I said. "I'll go with whatever."

Jemma was almost as good a singer as she was a dancer. I intended to spare all and sundry the violence of my vocals by letting her sing while I mouthed the words along with her.

Her eyes gleamed. "Okay. You know me. I love a challenge—"

Whump! The whole table shook as Richie stumbled against it. Drops of punch splashed from Jemma's red cup, and he put out his hand to steady it. He looked up sheepishly at Jemma. "Oops. Sorry."

Fuck the bug spray. Just give me a giant asshole swatter.

In fine southern lady fashion, Jemma spat out, "Shit a mile!"

The popper had finished. She snatched up a bag, skipped the scoop, and used her *hand* to shove in popcorn. "Here," she snapped, slapping the bulging bag into Richie's hands.

Richie sniffed the hot popcorn, smiled, and rolled his eyes dreamily. "Ah. Seasoned with the delicate flavor of your pretty skin." He lifted her salty hand toward his face, sticking out his tongue.

"Ugh!" Jemma shoved Richie straight out the back door.

My twisted face said it all. "I am so grossed out right now," I announced. Because, you know, I'm Dr. Redundant.

"Forget that bag of dirt. It's karaoke time."

"Can a brother get another time slot, please?"

"No." She picked up her cup and held it out to me. "Here. Take a big gulp. We're doing this."

Well, dang. I drank down the punch, wishing I'd skipped the party, stayed home, and done something productive. Like watching porn on my phone.

Chapter Seven

DUMBASS.

To be completely transparent, I'd come to the conclusion I was a dumbass a long time ago. I'd done a lot of stupid shit in my life. In this instance, however, I was specifically referring to the whole duet thing.

Jemma chose "A Whole New World" from *Aladdin*. You know, with distinct parts for Aladdin and Jasmine. And there I was thinking "duet" meant we could just sing all the lyrics together with me lip-synching from beginning to end.

What a dummy.

Well, if that was the way things were gonna go, fuck it. Suddenly, I didn't give a damn anymore. Kids packed the area around the pool, some in bathing suits, some in street clothes. Kids filled the pool, again some in bathing suits, some in street clothes, and just about all nursing a beverage of some kind. For their sake, I hoped they were good and drunk.

The karaoke machine and projection screen were mounted on a stand overlooking the deep end of the pool. Great. That meant if things went too far south with my performance, I could always jump in feet first and drown myself.

Jemma mounted the stand, and I clambered up after her. Applause followed as kids began gathering in for the coming festivities. Jemma brought the mic to her mouth and made an announcement, but I couldn't make out a word of it for some reason. My head felt as if it were beginning to rise like a mound of bread dough.

The music started, eliciting more encouraging cheers from our audience. The screen lit up with lyrics, which appeared strangely fuzzy. I squinted, which only made them blurrier. Fortunately, I'd watched the animated movie enough as a kid that I knew the song by heart.

My part was up first. Right on cue, I opened wide and belted out the first verse with my entire heart. It was epically bad, not a single note in key, my voice loud and croaky as hell. Every kid around the pool groaned. Did I care? Oddly, no. I felt loose, free…bold. On the chorus, I frickin' doubled down, throwing my arms wide and punching the unmelodic words toward the mountains of east Tennessee.

What happened next was the strangest shit of all. My audience broke out in rowdy cheers, pumping their fists in the air. They actually celebrated my awfulness.

That's what I'm talkin' about.

Laughing, Jemma gave me a hearty pat on the back, bro style. I bowed to her, and she burst into her part. The kids around the pool lapped it up. They whistled and clapped and some even sang along.

It was beautiful. It was right. The night was magic. I reached out and took Jemma's hand because, of course. She swirled around me, and I turned with her. Then we were dancing as we sang to each other. The breeze seemed to lift us toward the heavens, stars sparkling icy white against the purple silk of the evening sky. A sky that suddenly whirled along with us.

Whoa!

"Watch it." Jemma caught me by the elbow as I tipped backward. She held on, steadying me as I tried to catch my balance.

My feet wouldn't cooperate. They seemed to stay tangled. I was still trying to sing, but...the words... I couldn't remember the words. What? What was I doing? Why was Jemma pulling on my arm? Cheering. Laughter. Why all this noise?

Jemma hugged up on me, her hands wrapped around my bicep, her head pressed tightly against my shoulder. "Zeno, what's wrong with you?"

I could barely hear her. She seemed very far away even though she was touching me. My head... The top of my head felt as if it was stretching up and up. The music was so loud. I really needed to sit down. I turned to look for a chair or something and staggered sideways, arms flailing. Jemma's grip disappeared, and I went down hard on one knee.

"*So* wasted!" someone shouted, and the cheers exploded.

I tried to lie down. I needed to lie down. Jemma caught me by the arm again. She pulled, urging me to my feet. But my knee refused to cooperate, failing to provide the necessary lift.

"Work with me, Zeno," she grunted.

A rush of movement on the other side of me was followed by, "Hey. Let's get him down from here before he falls and breaks his neck." Someone took my other arm.

That voice. I knew it.

I looked over into a slightly red, slightly sweaty face. "Richie.

What it be like? That'sh what my popsh used ta shay ta hish crew back in tha day." Huh. What was up with my voice? I went to pat Richie's face and wound up slapping him instead. Hard.

"Ow!" Richie barked. "Shit. What the hell kinda shine did he drink?"

"I gave him some punch," Jemma said, "but I don't know what he had before that. This is weird. Zeno never drinks at my parties."

"Wait. You mean that red punch you had in the kitchen?" Richie's mouth formed a perfect O.

That was funny as hell. I laughed and tried to smack him again, but he pulled his head out of the way.

"Come on, Rich. Help me move him."

They tugged and towed me off the stand to mucho applause, across the yard, through a screened porch, and into the house.

"Jesus," Richie grunted. "This guy's a lot heavier than he looks."

"Just a little farther," Jemma encouraged.

"Where are you taking him anyway?"

"My room."

"Oh. Hey, why don't we save ourselves some trouble and just dump him here in the kitchen?"

"That would be a douche move. By the way, you're the douchiest person I know."

"Why do people keep saying that to me?"

More pulling. More tugging. I could feel my feet dragging as I stumbled over the carpet. My head buzzed like a hornets' nest, but the buzzing seemed to be miles away. Wait. I couldn't see. Why couldn't I see? Oh, my eyes were closed. Hah. I tried to open them, but like my other body parts, the eyelids were on vacation.

"Here," said Jemma, "let's get him on the bed."

I felt myself lifted and dumped like a heavy duffel bag, and then I fell face forward and bounced twice on a fluffy something before settling in a prone position.

"Whew! Glad that's done," Richie heaved.

"No, turn him on his back."

"What? Why the hell?"

"Because he's barely conscious, and I don't want him smothering with his face in my pillow. Duh!"

Low grumbles from Richie as he stuffed his hands under one of my shoulders and hefted me over onto my back. "Okay. Zeno's fine now. Let's get out there and grab our own drinks."

"You go ahead. Thanks for your help."

"Seriously, Jemma, leave the deadweight and we can—"

"Get out, Rich."

A flounce of footsteps and then a door clicked shut. I still couldn't get my eyes open. Or maybe they were open and I just couldn't see. What? Where was I? My curfew...I should get my ass home.

"No, just lie back, Z."

But...home...have to go—

"I said lie down. You're in no shape to go anywhere right now."

A hand on my chest firmly pressed me back until my head settled into the pillows. My brain...full of fuzz. Couldn't think.

Couldn't...

*

WHAT WAS THAT?

Did I sleep?

Hair brushed gently against my arm.

"Jemma?" My voice was low, raspy, only a bit above a whisper.

"I'm just putting a blanket over you, Zeno. You'll be okay."

Her hands were at my chest, spreading the blanket, her hair brushing my arm again. I reached up, fingers sliding through the silkiness, and caressed her chin.

Jemma.

So pretty. Why is her skin so soft?

I took her chin between my thumb and fingers and held it. I couldn't see her face, but I felt it above me.

Kiss her. I want to kiss her.

This wasn't the first time I'd wanted to do that. But it was the first time I felt...I don't know...mellow enough to do it without being scared like a punk. Blindly, I raised my head.

My lips found her cheek first, teasing the warmth of her skin. I felt her hand on my chest once more, firmly trying to press me back onto the pillows.

"Z," she said quietly, "I don't think you know what you're doing."

"Yesh, I do."

I stiffened my back, refusing to be brushed off. Shifting my head, I kissed the tip of her nose on my second try. The lilac hints of her perfume made my head spin faster. I lowered my chin and touched my lips to hers. She didn't respond. I slid my hand into her hair, my fingers following the curve of her ear.

"I know I want this," I whispered between kisses.

The pressure of her hand against my chest vanished. Her fingers traced slowly over my collarbone in what seemed a questioning, searching manner. What did she want to know? I'd tell her anything. I'd tell her how awesome she was. I'd tell her how her bravery and her smile inspired me. I'd tell her how much I wished, when she gave me that homemade candy apple, that I'd asked her on a date.

So much to say! But I was getting lost in the lilac softness of her hair and her lips and her arms. Her hand stopped its tracing and cupped the back of my head, pulling me closer. She parted her lips a little, and finally, she started kissing me back.

God. Oh my God...

Chapter Eight

A HAND CAREFULLY rested on my forehead. My name, quietly called, floated into the fading dream.

"Dad?" I hummed.

"Zeno, it's me," Dalvin said.

Dalvin? His hand was big and hot. I pushed it sluggishly away, blinking my eyes open.

The room—*the fuck with the yellow walls and white lace curtains?*—was lit only by a bronze bedside lamp. I flinched, blinking rapidly, as even that soft shine hurt my eyes. The comforter had twisted into highly uncomfortable knots beneath me.

Dalvin leaned over the bed, looking down at me with a worried frown. "Hey," he said, "you with me now?"

I pushed up on my elbows. My brain and my mouth felt as if they'd been stuffed with plastic bags. A blunt ache began drilling its way into my skull an instant later. Twinges of nausea rumbled my stomach ominously. "The fuck, bruh?"

"You tell me, man. I was looking all over for you. Finally, I ran into Jemma, and she said she left you in here to sleep it off."

"Sleep? Was I asleep?"

"Shit. Like, out cold. You were starting to scare me. I had a hell of a time getting you awake." Dalvin sat on the edge of the bed, facing me. "I thought you said you don't drink, Z?"

"Drink what?"

"Yeah, that's what I'm trying to figure."

"My head hurts. And I think I gotta throw up."

"That's what happens when you get drunk, man."

"I don't know what you're talking about. Where am I?"

"Jemma's room."

"What? How did I get here? *Why* am I here?"

Dalvin slapped a hand to his face and shook his head. "Jesus. It's twenty minutes to midnight, and you are all fucked up."

"Midnight?"

He pulled his hand away. "You told me that was your curfew."

"What curfew?"

"Your parents want you home from the party by midnight."

"Wait. I'm at a party?"

"Dang. Zeno, what the hell happened to you?"

I tried to think. Music pounded mutedly through the walls like beats beamed from another planet. "Uh. Nothing? I don't know."

"Come on." Dalvin stood. "Jemma's making coffee. We gotta get you up and get your head straight so I can take you home without your folks kicking both our asses."

Dalvin slid his long arms around my shoulders and got me sitting on the edge of Jemma's bed. "There ya go, dude. Hang on a sec." He knelt, gathered my shoes, and slipped them on my feet.

"Okay. Slow and easy. Let's stand up."

He rose first and got his hands under my shoulders. He lifted me the way you'd lift a baby. When my head took a sudden spin around the room, Dalvin kept me from plopping back down on the bed. And when the vertigo passed, he stepped back and gave me the once-over.

"Hell. Let's get these clothes straightened up on ya. Looks like you slept in 'em, all right."

As he hitched up my jeans, tucked in my T-shirt, and pulled down my hoodie, Jemma came in with a steaming mug of black coffee.

"Right on time," Dalvin said, taking the mug from her.

He raised it to my mouth. The coffee went down hot and bitter. The two sensations sent a surge to my brain.

I scrunched my entire face. "Ugh."

Dalvin smiled. "You look better already. Think you can make it to my car?"

I nodded.

"Take the mug. I'll get it back later," Jemma said. "Get home safe, guys."

*

"WE'RE HERE."

I opened my eyes, lifting my head. We were parked at the curb in front of my house. The engine clicked as Dalvin switched off the car. Strident yips from some lonely pooch punctured the quiet night. The light by my front door glowed softly. The windows were all dark, the house settled in slumber.

"Doesn't look like your folks are waiting up." Dalvin sounded relieved.

"They aren't. They trust me."

"Well, you only got about two minutes of trust left. You better get in there."

"Right."

I opened the door, shifted on the seat, and practically fell out of the car. Grabbing the door's edge was the only thing that kept me from kissing the sidewalk.

Dalvin hissed in a breath and, in what seemed like two seconds, was at my side. "Yo. You okay?"

"Yeah," I mumbled, clinging to the door as I tried to get my legs under me.

Dalvin helped me to my feet. He took my right arm, hooked it over his shoulders, and slid his left arm around my waist. "Here. Lean on me."

I hung over him like a blanket. He pretty much held me upright the entire way to the front door.

I got out my key and fumbled it into the lock. "Thanks, Dal, for getting me home."

"You sure you don't want me to help you inside?"

"Nah. I got it." I pushed the door open and gave Dalvin a half-hug before pulling my arm off his shoulder. "Catch ya later, man."

"Yeah."

It felt good that he lingered until I stepped inside and shut the door.

*

NINE THIRTY-FIVE A.M.

I lay in my boxers, staring at the digital clock on my dresser, a gift from my mom. But who needs a clock when you have a phone? Filtered sunlight gave the room a cool, easy glow. Sleeping in on a Saturday morning wasn't a thing for me. That was usually when I handled my share of the household chores, driven by the motivating power of dirty laundry and dusty carpets. Today, I felt no incentive to move; I had all the energy of a brick.

What was Dal up to this morning? He'd definitely been on point last night, getting me home not only safe but within curfew. He was a great guy, the best. Thoughts of him were giving me a nice case of the warm fuzzies. Which meant...what? He'd edged up a notch or two on the friend-o-meter? I should maybe call him. Maybe we could hang later. We'd talked about that. Where the hell was my phone?

I rolled out of bed. The motion caused a note taped to the headboard to flutter. I grabbed the slip of paper and recognized Dad's spiky writing. The note read: *Hey, Sleeping Beauty. We stopped in to say goodbye, but you were down deep. Don't burn up the house while we're gone. See you when we get back, Love, Mom and Dad.*

Nice. I pulled the note off and tucked it in a book on the nightstand. My clothes from last night lay scattered across the floor. I grabbed my jeans and tugged my phone from the pocket. Dang, no juice. Where'd I put my charger?

The doorbell rang. I pulled on my black jeans and strolled up the hall to the living room. After a glance through the window, I felt my whole face light up. I opened the door. Dalvin stood on the porch in a snow-white sweatsuit over black kicks, his hands tucked casually behind his back.

"Hey, man!" I greeted him.

He beamed a smile. "Damn. You look happy."

"Funny that you just showed up."

His smile went down a notch. "Well, I tried calling this morning, but you never answered. I wanted to make sure you were okay after last night, so I came over. Sorry. I probably caught you in the middle of something—" His eyes drifted down to my bare chest for a second, and his face blanked. He seemed to lose the point he was making.

"No, it's okay that you dropped by. I only meant...I was just thinking about you, and boom, here you are. I was actually about to call you, but my phone died overnight."

He tried to hide it with a nonchalant shrug, but his eyes lit up. He seemed pleased to hear that he'd been top of mind this morning. It was a really cute look on him, those earnest, happy, puppy-dog eyes.

I had to smile at that. "Come on in."

As he walked in, he was obviously hiding something behind his back, angling his body so I wouldn't see it. He gave the living room a quick survey. "Nice place."

I looked around at the throw pillows stacked against one arm-rest on the sofa and the blue throw blanket that had been haphazardly folded and left on the coffee table. "It would look even nicer if my parents had tidied up after their little movie-streaming night."

"Dude, this is nothing. You wanna see a disaster zone, check out my house after my five-year-old brother has been loose in it for an hour."

"Glad I don't have to clean up after him. By the way, good looking out last night at Jemma's. I really appreciate what you did, getting me home and all."

"Anytime, Z."

"So. Whatcha hiding behind your back?"

Dalvin's smile tightened a second time. He lowered his chin, blushing slightly. "Made ya something." From behind his back, he produced a brown paper bag and passed it over to me.

"What's this?" I opened the warm bag and peered inside. "A chocolate muffin?"

"Chocolate with chocolate chips," Dal clarified. "I kinda noticed chocolate is a sexual experience for you."

"Oh my gosh, yeah." No shame in my game when it came to the greatest nirvana so far in my life. "This bad boy is about to become breakfast. You want some coffee?"

*

WE SAT AT the round wood table in the breakfast nook. The open curtains let in bright shafts of sunlight, bathing the little forest of Dad's houseplants lining the bay window. Dalvin watched happily—and a little amazed—as I devoured his homemade muffin in slow, savored bites.

"Damn. You make eating that look erotic," he said, blinking like crazy. "I'm almost embarrassed to be sitting here."

I finished off the muffin, followed by a swig of coffee heavily dosed with sugar and—what else?—chocolate-flavored creamer. "Dal, you just don't know how this hits the spot."

"Nah, man, I definitely see how." He took a sip from his coffee (black with two sugars) and gently set down the World's Best Boss mug (a gift from one of Dad's employees) I'd pulled from the cabinet for him. "It's kinda quiet around here. Your parents home?"

"No. They decided to rent a cabin on Covington Lake. That's about two hours northeast of here. They left early this morning and will be back tomorrow night."

"You got the place to yourself all that time? Nobody checking in on you?"

"Nope. Just me."

"Sweet. So, what're your plans?"

I shrugged a shoulder. Without Mom and Dad pressing me about college apps and acting like a man, I could relax for a minute. "Nothing really. I had an appointment to detail a customer's car this morning, but he canceled on me yesterday. My home-work's done, so my day is wide open."

I leaned forward a little, getting closer to Dal. "What about you? You wanna hang?"

A slow smile spread across his face. He leaned toward me. "Yeah. Let's hang."

*

I CLEANED THE kitchen, neatly arranged the throw pillows on the sofa, put away the throw blanket, and left Dalvin flipping through offerings on Netflix while I grabbed a quick shower.

Under the cold, pounding spray, my mind worked like an over-stimulated bee, buzzing around the void that was last night. Weirdest fucking thing! No matter how much I probed, I couldn't produce a single memory of an entire evening. However, as much as the miss-ing evening bothered me, the fact that Dalvin was in the house proved a major distraction. By the time I emerged from the bath-room, last night's mystery had been shoved to the bottom of my brain.

Since the folks weren't home, I walked naked back to my room. I dressed in blue track pants and a red jersey featuring the X-Men's Storm going toe-to-toe with the female version of Thor. Then I hurried up the hall to the living room where Dal was wait-ing.

"Hey," I drawled.

Dalvin sat on the floor, his back against the sofa. An episode of *Stranger Things* played on the widescreen, while he watched a video on his phone. (My dad called me weird when he saw me mul-titasking like that. Nice to know I wasn't the only weird kid in town.)

Dal paused the video, looked up at me, and cocked his head

to one side. "Hey. Who do you think won that one?"

"Won what?"

He nodded at the battle depicted across my chest.

"Oh." I clapped a hand over the image of the white-haired mutant. "Storm, definitely."

Dal squinted a skeptical eye. "Nah. Mutant versus goddess? Goddess wins every time."

"Female Thor ain't no goddess. Jane Foster is a human who lucked up on Thor's powers. Storm was born with hers, plus she's badass. Dude, that's not even a contest. Storm kicks Jane's human ass."

"Agree to disagree," he said with a shrug. "Come here and look at this."

I stepped over Dal's outstretched legs and sat on the sofa, close enough that my knee pressed against his shoulder. His Adam's apple did a bobble.

"Whatcha got?" I asked.

"This is Jemma's interview. I edited the footage yesterday and tweaked a couple of things. Tell me what you think."

He started the video over from the beginning. It opened with a montage of scenes taken from the dances Jemma performed for us at MemTech's dance studio Thursday afternoon. Then came the interview scenes. Jemma looked great and sounded even better, sincere, passionate, intelligent—all the things she was in real life. Thankfully, I didn't appear in any of those scenes, just my voice, asking the questions and commenting on her responses.

At the end of the video, Dalvin placed his phone on the coffee table and turned to me. "Okay. Your thoughts?"

"Dal, no shit. This is great. It's perfect. I like the way you framed the shots and used different angles. You even used angles of Jemma's reflection in the mirror. And I like how you kept the focus totally on her."

"That's where the focus is supposed to be. Which is a big part of why I didn't get any shots of you in there. Also, I got the feeling you wouldn't mind being excluded." He winked at me.

I took the situation a step further and nudged him with my knee.

"Okay," he continued. "After you write the narration to introduce this segment, I'll get you to record it and dub it over the dance footage. That'll be one interview down, at least one more to go."

"Uh, that recording thing...can you do something about my voice?"

Dalvin seemed puzzled. "What's wrong with your voice?"

"Ugh, I hate it! I mean, in my head, I sound cool. Listening to myself talking to you now, I sound like an intelligent, educated person. But when I hear myself in a recording, I sound so freaking *awful*, like I crawled out of a freaking backwoods swamp or something. It's like hearing somebody chew ice or scrape fingernails over a chalkboard. We can't have anything like that in our film—"

"Man, chill. Your voice is fine."

"Are you serious? Have you actually listened—"

He put his hand on my thigh. That shut my mouth cold. I looked into his eyes.

"Zeno..." Those cheekbones of his were high and mighty impressive. Those warm brown eyes didn't blink. "I like your voice. I like everything about you."

A long pause followed. His gaze wouldn't let me go. He kept his hand on my leg, a steadying, solid pressure, and I couldn't move. The space between us changed somehow, as if all the air had become electrified. My heart began to rush, my skin tingling. I wanted to...I wanted him to... Sheezus.

Too much. Too fast.

I jerked myself away from Dalvin, trying to cover the motion an instant later by yawning and stretching my arms over my head. Startled, Dalvin blinked at me.

Yeah. Awkward. *Great move there, Zeno.*

"Uh...you know, you're really good at filmmaking, Dal. All that video you made of your friends, the football team, the homecoming dance, Debate Club and now this bit with Jemma. You got an outta-this-world talent for that stuff. Maybe you should be, like, going to film school."

"Thanks. But I already know computer graphics is the thing for me. Besides, there's a lot of CGI involved in movies these days. Same difference."

He got to his feet, moved over to the chair across from the sofa and sat. "If we're gonna talk about somebody's career options, it should be yours, man."

I let my shoulders slump; suddenly, everything seemed to be weighing down on me. "Yeah, you're right. That's one of the things I need to figure out. Why don't we take a walk?"

"I got my dad's car right outside."

"I know, but I feel like walking."

"Okay, cool with me. Where are we going?"

"Convenience store about three blocks from here. We can head in that direction and maybe pick up some snacks."

"Dude. You just finished a big-ass double chocolate muffin."

"So shoot me. I get the munchies when I'm, uh...fidgety."

Dalvin rose from the chair and stood next to me. He reached down and gave my shoulder a squeeze, a gentle, intimate touch. He'd never done that before, and I didn't know what to make of it. Fortunately, I didn't have a lot of time to think about it.

Dalvin nodded, smiled, and said, "Let's go."

Chapter Nine

MY DAD HAD great taste in kicks, and unlike me, he could afford to indulge it. I plundered his closet for a pair of black-and-white canyon sandals. They were about two sizes too small for me—I was up to thirteens now—but *dang*, they looked good on my feet. Bunions be damned! I topped off with my dad's orange Denver Broncos beanie and returned to the living room.

Dal goggled his eyes at the Bronco orange and went, "Really?"

"This," I said, pointing at the beanie, "is my dad's. And yeah, he's into a scrub NFL team. But this color really pops on me."

Dalvin rolled his eyes and flashed a smile. "Can we go now?"

I opened the front door. "After you."

We set out at an amble, two dudes with nowhere particular to go and no particular hurry to get there. Scattered masses of fluffy white clouds drifted across the sunny blue sky, with a steady breeze that blunted the unseasonably warm edge in the air. Kids played here and there throughout the neighborhood, lending a nice, easy feel to everything.

Well, not everything. I side-eyed Dalvin, trying to gauge his mood. He'd been jokey enough before we left my house, but I couldn't shake the feeling that I'd messed things up with him somehow. That I'd maybe offended him or something.

That I was a big idiot.

"Hey. What is it, Zeno?"

"Huh?"

"I thought you wanted to talk. We've been walking for a minute, and you haven't said a word. I'm getting the feeling that you're pissed right now."

"Me? No. Nothing like that. Sorry. I guess I'm kinda worried."

"About?"

"What I'm gonna study in college is one worry, but I still haven't really thought about it. It's off in the future, and there's stuff happening now that bothers me. I don't know what last night was about. A lot of it is a blank in my head. I remember coming home from school, having dinner, doing homework, and then detailing a customer's car. I remember getting dressed for the party and you and me going to Jemma's. But that's pretty much it. The next thing I remember is waking up in your car and you getting me home, and even that's hazy. You were at the party. What happened?"

"After we got to Jemma's place, I got us each a can of soda. Then you went off to find Jemma while I was hanging with Richie. Eleven thirty rolled around, and I realized it'd been a minute since I had eyes on you. I started looking for ya, ran into Jemma. She told me you were drunk and passed out in her room."

"So I drank actual liquor?"

Dalvin shook his head. "Don't know. We popped the sodas

ourselves, so there's no way anything got slipped in those. I didn't see you drink any alcohol while I was with you. But you were blasted when I found you in Jemma's room and out cold."

"That's crazy. That's just not me. My big fear is losing control. I've seen what happens when people get liquored up—like this girl at one of Jemma's parties who flashed her boobs at a bunch of guys before yacking on herself. All of it on video and posted all over Instagram, of course. I don't drink alcohol because I don't wanna get drunk and do something I can't fix or take back. That's why it's so scary I can't remember last night. Sheez, I could already be on YouTube or something."

"Ask Jemma. Maybe she can tell you more."

"Yeah, I will." I clenched my jaw against the sudden cold, shuddery feeling in my chest. "Ugh. Let's talk about something else. What about you? Did you have fun last night?"

He chuckled and slipped his hands into his pockets in that laid-back way of his. "It was a'ight. Won a game of beer pong against two girls. Danced with this redhead named Peyton from my sociology class. Tried to school Richie on how to act human. Nothing major."

"So you drank beer?"

"One cup. That was the only bomb the other team landed."

"You like beer?"

"Hell no. Guys on the team hyped beer so much, they had me thinking my first taste was gonna be this sweet experience, but that crap was nasty."

I turned my face away from him.

"Hold up, Z. Did you just smile? You're glad I hate the taste of beer?"

I pulled in my lips, looked at him, and nodded.

"You do know that when you get to college, drinking beer is

gonna be a requirement, like Psych 101."

I kind of half giggled, and then I stopped walking and slapped my hand over my eyes. "Damn. I can't believe I got drunk."

Dal put his arm around my neck, pulling me into a bro hug. I leaned against him, my arm going around his waist.

We didn't say anything. We just held on to each other.

Moments later, I felt better. Then, an idea flashed in my mind, so stunning in its rightness, so totally on point, that I gasped. I gave Dalvin a firm squeeze and backed away from him. He shot me a what-the-hell look.

"Change of plan," I said brightly. My face positively glowed with cheer. "Convenience store is out. I've got a better destination in mind for us."

"Like where?"

Instead of answering, I grabbed his wrist and started pulling him along. "I'll show you. You're gonna love it. Come on."

We'd gone half a block before I realized I was practically holding Dalvin's hand. I let go.

*

THE SIGN OVER the door, in goofy red and yellow letters, read as follows: Fun and Games Family Play Palace.

Dalvin stopped cold when he saw it. "Are you serious?"

"Serious as global warming."

"You expect us to go in there and *play*?"

"Hells yeah."

"Z, I haven't been to a place like this since I was ten."

"Me neither. Which is cool because all that fun we've missed since then, we can catch up on it together."

At the register in the dim lobby (the lights were kept low because of the several video games spread around), I shelled out for twenty bucks' worth of tickets, which could be used to play any of the games within the palace. We entered a large courtyard lined with several doors leading off to the play areas. Signs over the doors listed the particular fun and games to be had therein. Lots of running, shouting, and laughter rumbled around us. The "Family" in the name implied you could expect to see some adult types kicking around with their little ones. But no, Dalvin and I were the only patrons over five feet tall. Except for the attendants, there wasn't a soul in sight older than twelve.

That didn't bother me at all. It felt good to be here. With Dalvin. It felt right.

Dalvin looked around dubiously. Scratching at the base of his frohawk, he said, "Where do we start?"

The last time Mom dropped me off here, I was eleven, and I brought Marvus Ahern along. Before she left to do some shopping, she reminded me that Marvus was my guest, and I should let him choose the first game we played.

I quickly brushed the memory aside and said, "You're the guest, Dal. You pick."

"Okay." He marched off toward the door straight ahead of us, and I followed.

*

WE WERE IN the tenth and final round of Bumpin' B-Ball, a sort of cross between Putt Putt Golf (formerly my favorite game at the Play Palace) and HORSE, essentially basketball on an obstacle course. Each round lasted five minutes, and each player scored ten points for every shot he or she sank.

Going into the tenth round, Dalvin had 210 points to my 130. It wasn't that I was a lousy baller (I'm pretty good at b-ball, actually) or that I was letting him win, exactly. I liked watching him in

action. Dal was having the time of his life, and that was like chocolate for my soul. Plus, his muscles in motion were a very beautiful
thing. Not making excuses, but the dude was distracting me.

The obstacles were inventive, and they got progressively more
obstructive from round to round. The first-round obstacle was easy,
a big traffic light that slid up to reveal the goal on green and slid down
to cover it again on red. It stayed green for a full ten seconds, plenty
of time to take a shot, and if you missed, there was a good chance
your opponent could get the rebound and take his own shot. The
fifth-round obstacle, a lighthouse, had the goal opening at its top
where the light would be. It spun the opening around every five seconds. The tenth round presented the hardest challenge: a red metal
picnic basket, open at the top, attached to a white-gloved hand at the
end of a ten-foot-long metal arm. The arm moved the basket *constantly*, up, down, side to side, round and round, in randomized pat-
terns. I was getting dizzy trying to follow the movements.

"Oh, come on!" I shouted at the gods of fun and games,
standing there with the ball in my hands and no idea what to do
with it.

Dalvin smiled at me, all cool and confident. "Hey, Z, we got
this."

No, we didn't. The damn thing had no pattern, and I couldn't
anticipate where the basket would be at any given point. All I could
do was lob the ball and pray. I took a hook shot. As the ball arced
upward, I prayed it would drop ten points on me. The mechanical
arm flashed in a downswing, swatting the ball away with what almost seemed an attitude of contempt. A human player would have
accompanied the move with a scornful, "Get that shit on outta
here!"

The ball ricocheted off the wall, and Dalvin got the rebound.
While he was, admittedly, more skilled at basketball than me, he

put up a jump shot with no better results. He got the same vicious mechanical smackdown. For five minutes, we went back and forth, taking turns putting up shots. When the round ended, neither of us had scored a single point, but we were grinning at each other as if we'd won a million bucks.

"Man, that was great!" Dal said as we headed for the exit. "We gotta do this again."

"You know it. But next time, we gotta bring more money. That twenty bucks went fast."

"Thanks for the games, Z. Next time's on me."

"Cool." I got my butt kicked at Bumpin' B-Ball, and I was crazy happy about it.

Weird, right?

*

WE AMBLED BACK toward my house, chatting about possible candidates for our little documentary on student fears and over-coming them.

"Maybe we can get one of the guys from the football team, or basketball...or soccer," Dal suggested.

"Do you really think guys like that will take this seriously?"

"They're not all dumb jocks, Z."

"I know. But a lot of them are assholes."

"True. But there are some decent jocks too."

"Yeah. Like you."

"And you."

We walked for a while, saying nothing, locking gazes with each other from time to time. It felt wonderful, as if Dalvin and I were alone in a boat drifting lazily along a quiet stream. If I were under an infrared camera, I was pretty sure my body would be blazing right then.

Swear to God, in another minute, I thought I was gonna start singing to dude. It was time to do something before I made a total fool of myself—and scared the hell out of Dalvin.

"I just don't want the doc to feature all popular kids doing spectacular stuff," I blurted, rushing suddenly to fill the void that had opened in our conversation.

"Like Jemma?"

"Well…yeah. I mean, at least one of the subjects oughta be just your average person."

"I agree with that. You want something to drink?"

We'd reached Jackson Foods, the neighborhood convenience store. Cheery as ever, with its big red awnings, the wide windows featured signs listing the day's specials. When I was six, a trip here meant one thing: candy, candy, and more candy. If Mom hadn't set limits, sometimes gently smacking my greedy little hands when I grabbed fistfuls of colorful jelly bean packs and fruit chews, I'd have been sporting an all-gums smile these days.

"Yeah, I'm kinda thirsty. I could do with some water. What about you?" I started toward the door.

"Hey, wait," Dal said, trying to step around me. "I'll get it—"

"No, seriously. It's on me. What do you want?"

"Water."

"Cool. Be right back."

I went inside, grabbed two bottles of water from one of the big refrigerated cases in the back, and walked up to the front counter. Mrs. Jackson, a dark-skinned, slim Black woman maybe a few years older than my mom, smiled at me.

"Zeno," she said, her voice light and pleasant, "long time no see."

"Hiya, Miz Jackson." I placed the two bottles on the counter and held on to the edge while she rang them up. "Yeah, I'm really busy these days."

"So your daddy's been telling me. School and running your little business. That's a good thing. Keeps you out of trouble and on track. I'm so proud of you. You're gonna make something special of yourself."

That was another metaphorical brick added to the load Mom, Dad, my teachers, and my guidance counselor had placed on my back.

"Thanks, Miz Jackson. I appreciate the vote of confidence." I paid her and grabbed the bottles. "See ya."

"Make sure you stop in and say goodbye before you take off for college."

"Yes, ma'am. I will."

I hurried my butt on out of there. Along the way, I told myself I wasn't going to allow my burgeoning sense of responsibility to suck the joy from what had so far been a great day hanging with my friend.

Outside, I handed Dalvin one of the waters with a smile. He said thanks and twisted off the cap. I opened my bottle and we both drank. Head tipped back, he let his eyes wander as he guzzled. I took a moment to close my eyes and tried to tamp down the little burn of anxiety still working its way into my head.

"Uh, Zeno...this dude is staring at you."

I opened my eyes and frowned. Dalvin's body was angled at me, but he'd turned his face toward the opposite side of the street. I looked where he was looking.

Shit!

Marvus.

He stood in front of the UPS store. His mother, slightly in front of him, clutching a brown leather iPad case, talked happily with a gray-haired woman in a yellow pantsuit who I didn't recognize. Marvus and his mom had small, slender builds, and they looked much alike, with tan skin, short, tight black 'fros, and dark brown eyes. They both wore blue jeans and pullover sweaters that were maybe a little too much on a steadily warming afternoon. Marvus stared at me across the wide, busy avenue as if he feared my body would combust at any second. I immediately got the impression he wanted to cross that busy avenue but perhaps was unsure whether he should.

"You know that dude, Z?"

"Yeah." I raised my hand in front of my chest and waved it a little. Marvus waved back. I hoped that would keep him from coming this way. "He lives down the street from me, on the next block. His name is Marvus Ahern."

"Okay. That's the guy your moms mentioned." Dalvin studied Marvus for another moment and then turned to me. "He looks like he really wants to talk. You going over there?"

"No! Uh...no. That lady in the brown sweater is his mom. They're busy. Out running errands and stuff. I'll catch him another time."

I put a hand on Dalvin's shoulder and gave him a little push. "Come on. Let's get back to my place."

Chapter Ten

"DUDE. YOU HAVE a lot of toys."

We were in the family room off the kitchen. Dalvin was referring to the air hockey, pool, and ping pong tables that lined the rear wall along with a vintage pinball machine and (I kid you not) an Atari Arcade game console.

"Those aren't mine. They belong to my pops."

Dal gave me side-eye.

"For reals, man. My dad bought those games when I was a little guy. I grew up playing against him."

"You must be a helluva player by now." He faked a punch at me, touching his fist gently against my abs.

"Yeah, I'm pretty good. My dad's better. He still wins more than he loses."

Dal's eyes got a little distant. "Your dad's cool."

"An overgrown kid is what he is." It was nearly one o'clock, and my stomach was cussing me. "Lunchtime, dude. Wanna share a frozen pizza? We can shoot a little pool or something after."

"Sounds good, but I gotta bounce. I got practice in an hour."

"Since when does the football team practice on a Saturday?"

"First game of the playoffs is next Friday. Coach is paranoid and wants us to have an extra workout. It's overkill in my opinion, but hey, I'm not the coach." Everybody involved in Tennessee high school football was paranoid these days. The championships ordinarily started around the end of November. Due to a sudden extreme Covid outbreak, those games got pushed back, squeezed in around the start of the boys' basketball tournaments.

"What're you doing after?"

"Studying for this history test I've got on Monday."

"Why don't you come back here and study? You could even sleep over. We'll stay up late, pop popcorn, and watch horror movies."

Dal's eyes lit up and narrowed at the same time. "A sleepover. Like you used to have in elementary school."

"Yeah." I almost panted like a happy dog.

"And this is gonna be cool with your folks?"

"Remember what my mom told you about wanting me to have more friends over? She'll love you for it." I could see the hesitation in his face now, in his vanished smile and the sudden interest he'd taken in the big black sneakers on his feet. "Is this gonna be cool with *your* folks?"

"I have to ask. Sometimes, my mom and dad do this date night thing on Saturdays. If they do it tonight, I'll be on babysitting duty. And I have church tomorrow."

"You go to church? That's one thing you and I definitely don't have in common. I think the last time I set foot in a church was for my aunt's wedding, and that was eight years ago."

He raised his head, looking at me again. "I've been going

with my dad for as long as I can remember. He's always been big on church, so big he's head of the Deacons Board, a Sunday school teacher, and a member of the men's chorus."

"You and your dad really love the church, huh?"

"My dad does." Dalvin shrugged. "Me, I just sing in the youth choir."

"You *sing*? Dang, is there anything you can't do, man?"

That got a little smile out of him. Wow. A blush crept across his face. "I'll check with my folks after practice and get back to ya about the sleepover. That okay?"

"Cool with me."

He wished me a good lunch. I wished him a good practice. Then I walked him to the door.

*

I TOOK THE frozen pizza Mom left for me, a medium Chicago-style deep dish from the one and only Lucia, proprietor of Lucia's Pizza Porium (may the pizza gods forever smile upon that woman's dough-tossing hands), and cleaved it right down the middle. I stuck half in the oven, set the timer for thirty minutes, and returned the other half to the freezer. While my lunch was heating, I changed the sheets on my bed, cleaned the bathrooms, and set out fresh towels from the linen closet. By the time that was done, my phone had finished charging. I left the pizza to stay warm in the oven and grabbed my phone to check for text messages.

There were three from customers wanting appointments to have their vehicles detailed. One from this tenth grader I occasionally tutored who wanted help with an English assignment. And this from Ollie Gates: *U say u r camera shy, and u do this! WTF?!!!*

There was an attachment. From YouTube. I opened it and saw Jemma and me on some kind of little stage by her pool under a deep purple night sky. We held mics in hand as we belted out a Disney tune in front of a rowdy crowd of half-dressed kids, most of whom went to MemTech. My on-screen screeching tore through my head like a spike. WTF indeed.

It got worse. Moments into the song, I was making goo-goo eyes at Jem, slurring my words and stumbling around like your basic drunk. Jemma actually had to prop me up at one point. But wait, that wasn't bad enough. *Richie* jumped in to help my intoxicated ass off the stage while the kids all around us cheered.

Oh. My. Gosh.

The doorbell rang. I certainly did not want to answer it. How many people had seen this stupid video? I couldn't look anyone in the eye right now. The bell rang again, and again, an impatient, I'm-not-going-away sound. Sheezus.

I went to the front window and sneaked a peek through the curtains. A familiar powder blue VW Beetle convertible was parked at the curb. Ah. The very person I needed to see most. I went to the door and opened it.

"Hey, Jemma."

"Hey, Zeno." She wore a plain pink jersey that was a size too big over blue jeans that fit like a second skin. Her hair draped down her back loosely. "Sorry to just show up. I called three times, but you never answered."

"Yeah, my phone died. I just got it charged."

"Are you okay? After last night, I mean?"

"I guess. I'm not hurt or anything."

"Come take a ride with me. I wanna talk."

"I've got pizza in the oven. My folks aren't here if that's the reason for taking a drive."

She nodded and stepped past me into the living room. I closed the door as she made herself at home in a corner of the sofa, tucking one leg under and folding her arms across her chest. She was clearly in a mood—and not a good one. Had something happened to her? Was that why she was here?

Dumping a barrage of questions in her lap didn't seem the right thing to do at the moment. This required delicacy.

"The, uh, pizza is ready. Have you had lunch?"

"No. I haven't had breakfast either."

Uh-oh. This is hella serious. "Come on. I'll share."

I led her to the kitchen. She sat at the table while I gathered glasses, flatware, plates, and peach iced tea (homemade and sweetened to perfection by yours truly). I set the table for two, poured the tea, and brought over the hot-from-the-oven pizza. I cut a big slice for each of us.

We ate in silence. When we were finished, Jem wiped her mouth and asked for a tea refill. I obliged, refilling my own glass as well. After I seated myself across from her again, Jemma took a sip of tea and sat up straight.

"Do you remember anything about last night?" she asked.

"No. I don't remember the party at all."

That deflated her. Her spine caved, and she slumped back against the chair. "I was afraid of that."

"But thanks to the illustrious president of Film Club, I already know what I did at your place." I grabbed my phone and held the screen out to her as my YouTube debut played again. "I can't go back to school after this. I can't show my face anywhere after this, ever. So if this is what you came to talk about—"

"It isn't. Not really." She shook her head at me. "God, you are such a drama queen."

"Are you looking at this video? I'm not drama-queening. I..."

Shit. She was right. I was not only a drama queen, I was a *selfish* drama queen, making this about me when it was supposed to be about Jemma.

Before I could correct course, Jem—ever the good friend—tried to comfort me. "Relax, Zeno. That video's not as bad as you think. If you read the comments, you'll see most of the people who watched it actually liked what you did. They thought the whole thing was a gag or something, you doing a wasted version of Aladdin. Check out the title on the vid."

I checked. It read, *Give This Guy the Best Actor Oscar*. "Oh."

"Yeah, 'oh.' Now, will you please chill?"

Something about all this didn't make sense to me, but the video was so not the point now.

"Are you okay, Jem?"

"I don't know. I did something last night, and I think it was wrong."

She paused. I said nothing, giving her whatever time she needed. She sipped more tea, tucked a loose strand of hair behind her ear, and folded her legs under her lotus style.

"Zeno," she said, looking straight into my eyes. "Why have you never asked me out on a date?"

Well, color me totally blindsided. I sat there for a good thirty seconds, my mouth a little *O*.

"Do I need to repeat the question?"

"No, I got it. I mean, we've been friends forever—"

"But that's not why you haven't asked me out on a date. I've been getting this vibe from you for months now, that you were into me."

Dang that sharp perception of hers. She wasn't wrong, but I still didn't know what to say.

"You flirted with me," she continued in the face of my

stunned silence. "And I flirted back. We've been doing this for months, and I started getting into you. Then, I gave you that apple at school, and we kissed. You turned from a slightly nerdy under the surface, funny semi-jock into this tall, good-looking guy who was going to take me out and become more than just a friend. Only that never happened. Was I wrong about how you felt? Did I make this up in my head?"

"No, not at all." I cleared my throat, stalling. If Earth was due for another apocalyptic asteroid strike, now would be a good time. "I did get into you. You're nice, we're into a lot of the same things, you've been a real friend to me, and you're hot. I thought about asking you out a few times, but I...I was afraid you'd say no. Also, if you said yes, I kinda thought your dad would come after me with a baseball bat."

"What's that supposed to mean? My dad's not a racist. He wouldn't have a problem with me dating a Black guy."

"That's not what I meant. Your dad seems like he would go after *any* guy who tried to date his little girl. Either way, that's what it comes down to. It's hard to ask somebody out when your heart's stuck in your throat." *And isn't it kinda risky to fall for a friend?*

"Okay. Well, now you know I wouldn't have said no. And you don't have to be afraid of my dad. *I* decide who I go out with, not him."

There it was, laid out on a platter with a complete table setting. All I had to do was man up and ask. But I couldn't. I didn't want to ask her out, not now. I loved Jem, admired her, and at some point, all of that had started growing into something more. She was as attractive to me as ever. Yet something had changed in what I felt for her. I didn't know how or when that had happened, and I sure as hell couldn't explain it, even to myself.

Jemma leaned back in her chair, the expectation fading from her eyes. "Sorry, Zeno. I know I'm putting you on the spot, and maybe this is too much pressure."

"Jem, I don't think it's a good idea for us to date right now." She lowered her eyes.

Quickly I added, "I just don't want to change things between us."

"Even if it's for the better?"

"But what if it's not?"

"Okay. Got it." She drew in a breath and sighed. "You saw in that video how out of it you were last night. Richie and I took you to my room. I put you in bed to sleep off whatever that was, and you kissed me."

"What?"

"I didn't think you knew what you were doing. I told you that and pushed you away. You said you knew what you wanted and kissed me again. I wasn't sure about you...it didn't feel right to me. I should have followed my instincts."

Uh-oh. Honestly, I would have rather stuck my head inside a nest of killer hornets than ask my next question. "What happened?"

"I kissed you back, and we made out."

I shot to my feet so fast the chair flipped with a bang to the floor behind me.

"I know, Zeno, I know." Jemma sank even lower in her chair, looking absolutely miserable. "My mom always told me a girl can't consent to or control anything when she's drunk or unconscious. I get it now...that applies to everybody."

"Oh shit, Jem. Did I force something on you last night while I was drunk?"

"God, Z, you're not listening! *I* took advantage of *you*. You kissed me a couple of times and started passing out. I kissed you back. I kissed you back when you couldn't even stand up on your own. I should have never responded at all, but I kept thinking about the flirting, the way we kissed at school, the way I'm starting to feel about you..." She groaned, her face twisting as if sharp pains were blazing through her. "It was just plain wrong for me to do that."

The cogs in my brain ground to a complete halt. For the life of me, I couldn't think of a single thing to say or do in response to that. I didn't even know how I was supposed to feel at the moment.

"And you can't see us being anything more than friends. Right?" she asked.

Say something to her, dammit. Don't just stand there like a dumbass. Say anything!

Jemma answered her own question. "Right."

She swept her long hair back and twisted it into a ponytail. Her face seemed to freeze over. It was as if some invisible shield went up between us. "Well, I apologize for taking advantage of you. I have to go now. Thanks for lunch. You don't have to see me out. I know the way. See you around."

She walked out like someone who'd just fought a major battle and lost.

*

"WHATCHA DOIN', Z?"

I jumped like a twitchy lap dog (dang, make a little noise when you walk up on a brother, okay?) and looked over my shoulder.

"Oh. Hey, Dalvin. You're back." I resumed swinging the electric hedge trimmer.

"Yeah. Whatcha up to?"

"My dad's been after me to prune this shrub."

"Dude, the way you're swinging that blade, looks like you're murdering it."

He had a point. "Yeah, well…" I shut off the trimmer and backed away. If shrubs could sigh in relief, I was sure this one would. "Guess I'm on a spree. I cleaned the kitchen after I had lunch, took a three-mile jog, weeded my mom's flower garden, and then I started pruning—"

"Are you emotional right now?"

Amazing how Dal could read me so well. And borderline scary. "Yeah."

"So instead of eating your feelings, you work them to death."

"Pretty much." I wiped the sweat out of my eyes with the back of my hand. The trimmer suddenly weighed a ton. Either that or I was exhausted. My free hand shook. Standing still made me want to scream and cuss.

"Want to talk about your emotions?"

"No, actually."

"Want a hug?"

He looked at me with big, soulful, sincere eyes. A calming, I-got-you gaze topped a small hopeful smile. Was this dude perfect or what? And me? I was a big, needy nerd baby who couldn't even give one of his best friends a pat on the back when she needed it most. I didn't deserve Dalvin's comfort. But…I lowered my head. And shut my eyes. And nodded.

Dalvin closed me in his arms, a tight hug, exactly what my heart needed. His firm body was warm and strong around me. For the first time since that disastrous lunch with Jem, the inside of my head stopped boiling. My hand quit twitching, and when I breathed out, some of my anxiety went out as well. The bright afternoon sun lit up my relief.

After what seemed far too brief a time, Dalvin let go and stepped back. I remained still for another moment, head down, letting the soothing vibe from the hug soak into me. Raising my head, I finally noticed the bulging backpack strapped over Dal's shoulder. I pointed—something which would have, if Mom had been there, earned me a smack on the hand.

"What's up with the backpack?"

"History book," he answered, "and a change of clothes for church tomorrow."

"What do you need with— Oh, right. Sleepover. It's okay with your folks, huh?"

He smiled so wide I could count all his teeth. "As long as I make it to church on time."

"That's great, Dal. Come on."

I took him in through the garage, where I stopped long enough to return the trimmer to its spot beneath Dad's work bench. We stepped into the house and past the laundry room into the kitchen. As I went to the sink to wash my hands, my head started whirling again with the sense that I'd done something horribly wrong, something I urgently needed to fix. But Jemma wasn't here, so fixing the problem wasn't possible now. Even if she were here, how would I fix a mistake on the supersized scale she'd described?

I mean, I think she said we had sex. Didn't she say that? I was so out of it I could have done anything to her. Why did I have to hurt her of all people? You can't take back sex. Did she feel used? Did she hate me now because I wasn't into her the way I once was? Oh God, did I use a condom? I didn't have one on me when I went to the party because I wasn't expecting to smash anybody. What if I got Jemma pregnant? Oh my gosh. Would she still be able to go to Juilliard? Would there be an abortion? Her dad would kill me. My mom would kill me first.

Gah! I gotta stop thinking about this!

"So how was football practice?" I called out way too loudly.

The outburst got me raised eyebrows from Dalvin, but he followed up with a pleasant smile. "Our kicker fell and bruised his tailbone, and a lineman stepped on our quarterback's throwing hand. Other than that, it was great."

I laughed, and it sounded forced even to me. "You said extra practice would be overkill. Think Coach got the message today?"

"Doubtful. He's not the kind to ever admit he was wrong about something."

"Well, you can always hope." I dried my hands on the back of my pants, the knees of which I now noticed were damp with bright green grass stains. "Are you glad you don't have to babysit your kid brother tonight? What's the little guy like, by the way?"

"He's great, actually. He was a big surprise. I was an only child until I was twelve. You get kinda used to having things a certain way, having all of your folks' attention. Then *boom*, suddenly you're sharing your room and everything else with a screaming infant. But I'm kinda used to him now."

His eyes lit with what was obviously big brother love. "His name is Eli, and we have this routine. The folks start their workday really early, so I get him up every morning, and we play these little word games while I'm getting him dressed and making his breakfast and taking him to kindergarten. Thunderstorms at night scare him, so he crawls in bed with me, and we pretend the thunder is explosions from us shooting down enemy spaceships. He watches my football games and gets so excited. It's like I'm a superhero to him. I actually like the little man...most of the time."

"Sounds like you're gonna make a great papa someday."

Shit. If Jem has a baby, what kinda father would I be? I'm too weird to raise a child.

"If I ever have a kid, I'm damn sure gonna be the best father I can be." Dalvin looked like a guy swearing an oath in court. Then, one moment later, he looked like a guy who was lost. "It's a crazy scary world. That's what Eli's growing up in."

I knew what Dal was feeling and clapped a hand on his shoulder, pulling in close to him. "Come on. Let me show you where you're sleeping. Then I'm taking you to my dad's air hockey table and opening up a big can of whup ass."

He grinned in a slightly disgusted way, his nose wrinkling. "You might wanna shower first, man. I didn't say anything before, but you smell kinda ripe."

Truth. I sniffed one of my pits, and it was straight eau de horse's ass with hints of vintage mildew. I aimed the pit at Dalvin's face. He shoved me away, both of us laughing.

"Come on." I took him down the hall, past Mom and Dad's room.

As we passed mine, Dalvin stopped, peering in. "This yours?"

"Yeah."

"Damn. That room is like something off a magazine cover. It doesn't look like anybody's ever even breathed in there."

"I like things neat."

"Well, I'm kind of a slob, so you and I may not get along." He slyly cocked an eyebrow as if playing the thought over in his head. "Or maybe we will. Opposites attract and all that." He winked.

This weird sensation hit me, and I found myself smiling as my cheeks burned. Dalvin was in my house, looking into my bedroom, spending the night. How epic was that? I stank like a dirty locker room, but he moved close to me again as if to snuggle. I could feel the heat coming off him and smell the citrusy-spicy scent of his soap. I wanted so much to touch his skin. Trace a finger over those majestic cheekbones. Stroke through his dark, kinky frohawk. Take his hand.

Kiss him.

Dang. What was I thinking? I was into guys as much as girls, and I was cool with that. I'd felt a connection building between Dalvin and me from the day we met, jolted perhaps by the fact that we were tall, skinny semi-nerds striving to navigate high school. And while I'd always thought he was attractive, the vibe I felt had been strictly platonic. When had I gone from liking the guy as a friend to whatever *this* was? Why were these feelings continuing to build, and what if they suddenly changed? That had happened with Jemma, and now, I wasn't sure if we were even friends any longer.

Also worrying me was the fact that, since meeting Dalvin, I'd never before picked up a hint that he was anything other than straight. The last thing I needed was to fall for a hetero dude, especially when he was a friend. Over the course of the day, however, Dalvin had definitely been flirting with me. He was doing it this very moment, standing close enough I could practically feel his pulse, close enough to electrify my whole nervous system. Was he just clowning? Or was he actually letting me know he was into me?

Casually, Dal plucked an errant leaf from my hair. Then, as he tucked the leaf into my pocket, he smiled at me. Ah, that smile. Those eyes. Sheezus. And happy hummingbirds suddenly filled my chest. What would it be like to cuddle with this dude? What would it be like to take him on a date and dance close with him and...WTF?

Oh shit, I shouldn't let this happen. It could be great or it could be a big fat disaster. Emotionally, I couldn't afford to lose another friend. I should pull up on this thing with Dal, let my feelings cool. But...he was so nice, so playful, so supportive, so funny, so sensitive, so creative, so cute, so ripped, so *here*.

At the end of the hall, we turned into the guest bedroom. "You can toss your backpack there," I said, gesturing at the bed. "I left some towels on the dresser, hoping you'd get a chance to stay over. I'm gonna grab that shower. You need anything right now?"

"Nah. I'm gonna study for my test. Might as well get that outta the way."

"Okay. See you in a bit."

I took a change of clothes into the bathroom with me, which was exactly what I would've done if my folks had been home.

Chapter Eleven

GOOGLE "FALLING IN love with a friend" and you get some interesting stuff—songs, TV episodes, movies, and books, all on the thrill and wonder of going from friends to lovers. Cute stuff. Not so cute were some of the vlogs and blogs with posts of personal experiences. The posts detailed a slew of complications leading to ex-lovers and ex-friends. Those vloggers and bloggers all offered the same advice: *Don't do it.*

Encouraging. Right?

That sealed it for me. I wasn't going to risk Dalvin's friendship. I was going to put a stop to the flirting. I was going to stop staring at his broad shoulders, stop doing the heart-fluttery thing when he smiled at me, stop thinking about that *Forever* pic he put on Instagram, and certainly stop the fantasy make outs. We would just be boys, dedicated to having each other's backs. Most definitely.

That left Jemma. I already missed her teasing, her big

cheerful laugh, her constant pushing for me to take chances and try new things. I would have to talk to her at some point if there was to be any chance of salvaging our friendship. But what the hell was I going to say to her?

"Hey."

The softness of Dal's voice sent a warm rush through me. Naturally sexy vocals. God, it was so not fair subjecting me to that right now. I'd spent the hour or so after my shower seated at the kitchen table, mulling over everything about my life that was driving me crazy. At least I'd decided how to deal with my Dalvin problem. I deftly clicked off the Google search, pushed away my phone, put on a neutral face, and turned to him.

"Hey, man. How's the studying?"

Dalvin stood in the doorway, leaning against the jamb, holding his phone in his hands as he watched me. "I'm done and ready for the test, but I'll do a quick review tomorrow night for a little insurance. Can I ask you something, Z?"

"Sure."

"I wanna take some pics of you while I'm here, maybe shoot some footage. You may or may not see me doing it because I like to get people being real. You know what I mean?"

"I think I do."

"So, would it be okay with you if I do this?" He switched to camera mode, raised his phone my way, and paused.

"Wait. You take pictures and film people all the time at school without asking them anything."

"That's in public. This is your home, dude, and I'm here as a guest. It doesn't feel right to snap pics in your house without asking you. Also, my dad says it brings bad luck to the picture taker. But main thing is I'm a courteous guy, and I'm not about disrespecting people where they live. Which brings us back to—is it okay for me to take pictures of you while I'm here?"

"Yeah, it's cool. Can I see the pics you take?"

He smiled, raising his phone. "You know it. Tomorrow before I leave, we'll sit down and look at everything together." He snapped the pic and immediately slid the phone into his pocket.

"Hey, I'm curious about something, Dal."

"What's that?"

"There's this picture you posted on Insta, you and me, at your locker—"

"Wait." He pulled out his phone again, thumbed at the screen, then held it up to me. "You mean this one?"

There it was, staring back at me, the post that still made a mess of my mind.

I sighed. "Yeah. I was wondering. It says 'Forever.'"

"Right. Actually, it says 'Bros Forever.'" He turned the screen back to himself, swiped it with his finger, and turned it to me again. The pic had blossomed into a wider shot that included more of the hall and several cheering students around us. And the caption read exactly as Dalvin had just said.

So, the pic wasn't some grand romantic gesture. I let my shoulders slump.

"This dude Aaron snapped the pic and sent it to my phone," Dalvin was saying with a fond smile. "At the time, it was the only shot I had of you and me together. You really look good in it. I put in the 'Bros Forever' before I put it on my Instagram so everybody would know I wanted us to always be friends. Only thing is that when I cropped the picture down to just the two of us, it chopped off the 'Bros.'" He shrugged. "Either way, you get the message, don'tcha? I'm glad to have you in my life."

Well, that was a real mood lifter. Grinning, I said, "I like the way you put things, man."

Dalvin suddenly marched right up to me. It made me a little nervous, but in a good way. I tingled all over, wondering what he was about to do. Dang, what happened to my conviction?

"Turn around," he whispered in my ear, a sexy command.

Okay then. Can't wait to see where this is going.

I turned my back to him and closed my eyes.

Oh my God! His thick, powerful hands landed suddenly on my shoulders. His fingers worked magic, sending sensations down my back and arms so intense I had to bite my lip to keep from calling glory hallelujah to the heavens. Where the freak had the dude learned this stuff?

"How does this feel?" he asked softly.

"Mm. Like downtown heaven."

"Good. Now tell me, Zeno, what's got you so worried?"

Eyes flicking open, I made a dismissive shushing noise with my lips. (I also shuddered as Dal concentrated on my left shoulder with both hands. Mercy!)

"You know, you remind me so much of Eli right now," Dalvin said sagely. "He does this thing where he stresses so hard over something that he crawls into a corner hugging a pillow, but ask him what's wrong, and he's all 'nuthin,' like, little Macho Man. You've got something heavy on your mind. I saw it the minute I walked back in here. And this shoulder of yours is tense as fuck. You don't have to talk about it if you don't want to. But anything you need, your boy is right here."

"It means a lot to hear you say that. But really, don't worry about me. I'm okay."

"Cool." There was this hesitancy in his voice, the word drawing out in a doubtful rolling sound.

Those magic hands of his kept working the tension in my left shoulder. I closed my eyes again, letting my head roll forward until my chin pressed into my chest. Another minute and my entire left arm felt as loose as overcooked spaghetti.

"Come on, man," Dalvin whispered above my head. "Relax."

He moved on to rub, knead, and tease the muscles in my neck, my right arm, and my back. It was like having my body liquefy; a few minutes more and I would probably ooze right out of the chair and down to the floor. Man, his touch...it melted my defenses as well. They crumbled one after the other, leaving only the raw pain and confusion I'd been trying to hide.

"Dalvin...I'm not okay."

He leaned in, sliding an arm around my chest, and hugged me. "I'm sorry to hear that. How can I help?"

*

I MADE A new pitcher of iced tea, peach flavored with an infusion of fresh lime juice. Dalvin took a couple of mugs, some flour, cocoa powder, a few other ingredients, and, inside of three minutes, baked two perfect chocolate cupcakes in the freaking microwave oven. Amazing! I didn't even know such a thing was possible. We sat down across from each other at the kitchen table and consumed our way into a nice sugar high, the perfect condition for difficult conversations.

After pouring tea refills for the two of us, I jumped in with both feet. "At the party last night, while I was drunk or whatever, I had sex with this girl."

Dalvin froze with a forkful of mug cake halfway to his open mouth.

I closed my eyes. And then covered them with my hand. It was the only way I could continue.

"I just found out today. I had no idea. I mean, I lost my virginity, and I don't even remember it. How stupid is that? How do you think it makes...this girl feel? We had sex, and then I just brushed her off like she was lint on my shirt collar or something."

There was a clink, followed by the scrape of the mug across the tabletop as Dalvin pushed it away. "Z, you were drunk. You didn't know what you were doing."

"That's the whole problem, man. I got drunk and did something awful to a good friend."

"Zeno, look at me."

Jeez, am I a little kid or what?

I pulled my hand away from my eyes.

"I'm not playing down what happened between you and...this girl—" Dal said.

"I don't want to put her name out there."

"I know, and that's cool. But think about this. You can't blame yourself for something you did while you were wasted."

"Really? If I get my ass behind the wheel of a car while I'm wasted, I'll go to jail for drunk driving. I screwed up big time. Shit! What if my mom and dad find out?"

"They'll understand. I'm sure of it. But what I mean about not blaming yourself is, you don't drink, right? You told me you stay away from alcohol at parties because you want to keep control of yourself. So, I'm having a hard time believing you intentionally got yourself drunk."

"Maybe I did. *I can't remember.*"

"Well, what did the girl you had sex with say? She accuse you of forcing her or something?"

"No, but her feelings are hurt because I...just used her and threw her away after. Like a candy wrapper." I smacked myself in the forehead. "She told me she liked me, and she asked me if I felt that way about her. But I don't. Dalvin, I couldn't lie to her, so I didn't say anything, and that made it even worse."

"Okay, I get it. You're worried about this friend, and you should be. What you have to do is sit down with her and talk all of this out. Find out if you can do anything to make it up to her. But, dude, you gotta stop kicking your own ass over this. It doesn't sound like you knew what you were doing."

"I didn't, but that doesn't make it okay."

"I know. All I'm saying, Zeno, is that you gotta put things in perspective here. I've known you since freshman year, and I've never seen you do anything to deliberately hurt anybody. I wouldn't hang with a dude who dogs out girls. Believe that. You're a good person. That's one of the reasons I like you so much." He reached across the table, took my hand, and held it.

Which, okay, is so not the kind of thing guys do with one another. But it felt good. Not in a flirtatious or romantic kind of way. Just good. It felt right, necessary. It was as steadying as an anchor.

I held on.

*

USING A TRIPOD mount, Dalvin had set up his iPhone on the counter to film the whole grubby process.

It felt like I was up to my elbows in dough. And the dough was winning without a doubt.

"Dude, come on," Dalvin said. Standing next to me, watching carefully, he laughed. "Ease up. You're supposed to knead the stuff, not abuse it. You keep that up, and you're gonna make rubber."

"Okay, Duncan Hines." I tried being kinder to the dough. "Ya know, it would be easier to take that half a pizza outta the freezer and chuck the bad boy in the oven."

"Yeah, but it wouldn't be anywhere near this much fun."

Admittedly, I was having a pretty damn good time.

Satisfied that I was behaving appropriately with the dough, Dalvin returned to his sauce-making. He tossed chopped onions, bell pepper, and garlic into hot melted butter, lightly sautéed them, and then added cans of crushed tomatoes and tomato paste. He tossed in a bunch of Dad's herbs from the cabinet. In fact...

"You remind me of my dad."

Dalvin cocked his head to one side. "Is that a good thing?"

"Yeah. I think I mentioned a time or two that he's a hellacious cook. You didn't say you can do other stuff than just baking."

"Well, it woulda been remiss of my mom to show me how to make pizza dough without going all the way to making a whole pizza. Remiss. See how I snuck in that SAT vocab?"

"Smooth, dude. It's good that your mom didn't obnubilate anything when she passed on her recipe to you."

"Whoa. Did you just out-vocab me?" He chuckled.

I liked watching him do his thing. He was a messy cook, with flour on his face and big orange tomatoey smears on his shirt. Empty cans, spills, and wadded paper towels littered the countertop he worked at. I couldn't stand disarray, but this was all somehow adorable to me.

"Okay, that's good," Dalvin said, eyeing the white gluey mass in front of me. "You can put your dough in the bowl now. Cover it with a towel, and let it rise."

I put the dough to bed as instructed. By that time, Dalvin had brought his pizza sauce to a nice, even simmer.

"Now we just have to let everything percolate for about twenty minutes," Dalvin said.

"Cool. While we're waiting, I'm gonna clean up a bit." I looked my friend up and down. "Starting with you. Come here."

He walked over to me, and I guided him to the sink. There, I filled the sink with warm, sudsy water and proceeded to carefully wash from his hands up to his elbows. He kept his eyes closed, smiling, clearly enjoying every minute of the attention he was getting. I took a towel and dried off his hands and forearms, then wiped his face and rubbed the smears out of his shirt.

"There ya go," I said when done. "You don't look so much like a dirty street kid now."

"Okay. Thanks...I think."

"Sit down and relax. It'll only take a few minutes to tidy up the kitchen."

He grabbed his phone and circled slowly around me, filming as I put away bottles of spices and seasoning, tossed empty cans and used paper towels in the trash bin, washed the flour-covered cutting board, and wiped down the countertops.

"Man!" Dalvin remarked from behind the lens of his phone's camera. He moved in for a closer shot. "Check you out, so freakin' domestic. That's cute. You're gonna make a good husband one day."

Yeah, he slipped and said the quiet part out loud. There went that fluttery feeling in my chest again. Followed by the heat in my face, along with the tingle on my lips.

I. Want. To. Kiss. Him.

Damn. *Think about something else. Idiot.* "Uh...Dalvin. What's up with your name? Anything in particular behind it?"

"I'm not named for an ancestor, if that's what you're getting at. I'm named after one of the members of Jodeci."

"Jodeci?"

"Yeah. That's one of those old-school R&B singing groups. My dad was really into them back in the day. He claimed the right to name his firstborn, and that's what he came up with. My mom hasn't forgiven him to this day." Dal shifted to my left, still filming. "What about you? Tell me the story behind 'Zeno.'"

"Eh, that's nothing interesting, not like yours. I'm named after my great granddad. He ran this ice cream shop, the first business owner in our family."

"Sounds interesting to me. When was that? Like in the sixties?"

"I guess so. Maybe the fifties."

"See, those were Jim Crow times. Your grandpa had to have guts to run his own business then. And you're following in his footsteps with your car detailing business. Your folks knew what they were doing when they named you."

Dalvin abruptly shut off his camera. He put the phone aside and hoisted himself onto one of the barstools. "I make you nervous, don't I?"

I started to lie, but I was sure he could see right through me. "Sometimes."

"Do you want me to go?"

"No." *Hell* no.

"Okay."

About a minute of silence followed. We avoided looking at each other, yet all the while, I knew Dalvin was thinking as hard about me as I was about him. We were definitely building toward something. I didn't believe Dal knew where this was going any more than I did, and that probably scared him a little, just as it did me.

Maybe he *should* leave. The longer he was here, the more I was becoming attracted to him. I enjoyed sharing a space with the brother, teaming up on a pizza recipe while we were shut away from the rest of the world. He had this calming effect on me. If he weren't here, I'd be roaming around the neighborhood like crazy or pushing myself through a hectic workout to escape my worries. His being here was a pretty good thing.

Except there was no way Mom and Dad would let me have a girl over to spend the night, especially while they were out of town. If they knew what was going on now between Dalvin and me, they'd roll his butt out of here with—as my dad would put it—"the quickness." I didn't want to do anything that would make my parents think they couldn't trust me.

Most of all, I didn't want to lose Dalvin as a friend.

Just as I was about to rescind my sleepover invitation, Dalvin slid off the bar stool and stood. "Well, our dough and sauce oughta be ready now. Let's build that pizza."

He flashed a chiseled-cheek smile, bowed like a true gentleman, and extended his hand in a you-first gesture. It was a heavy-duty dose of pure charm.

Heck. Who could say no to that?

*

WE TEAMED UP again, clearing away our dinner dishes, loading the dishwasher, and stashing leftovers.

"That was awesome pizza, Dal."

"Must not have been all that awesome. You only ate one slice."

"It was a biiig slice."

"Dude."

"For reals, though, that tasted great. I never had pizza with grilled shrimp and catfish bites on it."

"Me neither. It was the only meat your folks had in the fridge. I had to make it work."

"My dad does that too. He calls it being creative in the kitch."

I tossed a jar of red pepper flakes to Dalvin, and he put it away in the cabinet. While he wiped down the stove, I set the dishwasher cycle and started it. With the cleanup done, we kinda stood there, wiping our hands on our pants and, at least on my part, waiting to see what would happen next.

"Wanna play some air hockey?" Dal suggested.

"Oh yeah. I'm ready to spank that ass."

Dalvin gave me this look.

"Dang, man! You know what I mean." I laughed a little too loudly.

My phone dinged, alerting me to a text message. I hadn't heard from my parents since they left and figured they were finally checking in.

"Hang on a sec," I said as I crossed to the table, grabbed my phone, and pulled up the message.

It wasn't from Mom and Dad.

"Something wrong, Z?"

"Uh, no. It's just a customer. She wants to know if I can detail her car." I texted a response, agreeing to the job.

"*Now*? It's almost night."

"Yeah. It shouldn't take long." I was already moving toward the door to the garage, stiffly, as if my joints had suddenly rusted.

"Let me get my keys. I'll drive you."

"You don't have to do that."

"Z, you said you work outta your dad's auto shop. That's miles away—"

"I'm meeting this customer somewhere else. It's not far, walking distance. I've got some cleaning supplies in the garage."

"Well, I'll go with ya. Pitch in. That way you can get done faster."

I shot him my gangsta look (which, to be honest, is not all that intimidating even when I want it to be). "Hey. You trying to cut in on my profits?"

"Nope. I'm trying to get you back here ASAP so you can

spank me at air hockey. I wanna get that shit on film."

I blushed for probably the thousandth time that day. "Dude, sit your big football-playing, pie-baking ass down somewhere and chill. Okay? Watch a movie or something. I won't be gone long. Promise."

I exited the kitchen so fast I nearly tripped on my way out the door.

*

I WORKED ON the car—a dark gray Acura TLX sedan—in the customer's driveway as the final rays of daylight faded from the sky. I took my time polishing that bad boy, being careful not to miss a spot or leave streaks.

The side door creaked open. I didn't look up at the sound of the approaching footsteps. "Well, Zeno," my customer said. "It looks like you're just about done."

"Yes, ma'am. Only a few more minutes."

She studied me for a while. I could feel it. I wanted to run off somewhere.

"Again, I thank you very much for doing this on such short notice," she said. "I've been trying to reel this doctor in for three weeks, and today, completely out of the blue, he calls me up and wants me to take him to brunch tomorrow to go over the deal I offered. I can't take him out in a dirty car."

"No, ma'am."

She was in pharmaceutical sales and very good at the whole schmoozing thing. So, I was expecting something a little more diplomatic from her than what came next. "I should smack you right upside your rude head."

She was absolutely on the mark, however. I deserved a smack to the head. "Yes, ma'am."

"I can't believe you stood right across the street from Marvus and me and didn't so much as wave a hand."

I did wave a hand, actually. She just didn't see it. Still, I'd more than earned the rebuke. "I'm sorry."

"As well you should be. Your parents raised you better than that."

I gave the lid of the trunk a final swipe and stepped back. Even in the semidarkness, the car bore an impressive sheen. "I'm all done."

"Great job, young man. You have a wonderful work ethic. I wish some of that would rub off on Marvus. The bum."

"He's a good guy, Mrs. Ahern."

"You think so, huh?" Her voice hardened.

"Is he home?"

"He's out with his girlfriend." Mrs. Ahern still wore the jeans and sweater she had on when I saw her earlier across from the convenience store. She pulled three bills from her pocket and passed them to me. "Here you go, Zeno. Thanks again. Say hello to your parents for me."

"I will." After tucking my payment away, I loaded my cleaning supplies back in the big plastic bucket I used as a carrier. "Tell Marvus I said whassup."

"Tell him yourself the next time you see him," Mrs. Ahern said, her voice hardened again.

*

I QUIETLY LET myself in through the back door. Chatter filtered into the kitchen from the television in the family room. A quick glance that way revealed no sign of Dalvin. I returned my supplies bucket to the garage and then went to the fridge.

"You're back. You get the job done?"

Dang. I barely managed to keep from flinching at the sound of Dalvin's voice behind me. Dude must be a ninja. I never heard so much as a footstep.

"Yep. Want something to drink?" I reached for a bottle of water.

"What I want is you and me and air hockey." Dalvin had taken off his kicks and his socks. He stood in the doorway on a pair of big, tan, nicely manicured feet. The sight of his toes embarrassed me for some reason. Three years I'd known him, and this was the first time I'd taken a good gander at his bare toes. Then it hit me: I was embarrassed because I wanted to touch his feet, to hold them in my lap and massage them—

What the fuck kind of freak am I?

Back to business. I looked Dalvin in the eye and curled my lip. "Come on, then, and take this ass-whuppin'."

*

MY HEAD WASN'T in the game.

I was damn good at air hockey. That ain't bragging, just a fact. Trying repeatedly to beat my dad had honed my skills sharply. But I couldn't get anything past Dalvin's defense. He seemed to anticipate my every move, always getting his paddle in place to block in the same moment I took my shot. On the flip side, I was always a step behind him, sweeping in with my paddle an instant after he sent the puck sluicing in cleanly for a goal.

Any other dude would have talked big smack over my weak game. Dalvin stopped in midplay and said, "Z, your head's a million miles away. Come on. We're gonna try something else."

"Like what?"

He moved around to my end of the table, took the paddle from my hand, and put it aside. "I'm about to show you."

He opened the back door, and we went out onto the wooden deck. A wide splash of rusty gold hung over the trees on the western horizon. Above that, twinkly white dots, the first stars of the night, spangled the deep magenta sky. Faint sounds of traffic mingled with the chirps of lonely crickets. The soft, steady breeze carried a pleasant, early spring chill and the crisp scent of freshly cut grass.

"Just in time to catch the last of the sunset," Dalvin said quietly. He sat on the steps that led down to the yard and held out his arm, beckoning me to join him.

I sat close beside him, and he slipped his arm snugly around my shoulders. The thick warmth of his muscles, though a direct contrast to the enticing, heavenly softness of a girl, somehow seemed just as inviting to me. I leaned into him as we looked out over the shadowy backyard.

"This is my favorite time of day," Dalvin said, his voice even softer than before. "It's like the world is settling down, snuggling in. Everything is so calm, and you can feel yourself settling down too."

He gently rubbed my arm with his hand. The motion, along with the gorgeous evening sky and the stillness surrounding us, gradually took effect on me. The sting from my conversation with Mrs. Ahern, my fear and confusion, slowly began to...not fade, exactly, but to wind down. My mind cleared, and a pressure seemed to lift off my heart. Everything focused on this dude sitting next to me, the magic of his presence. I needed this quiet moment, and he knew it. He knew it before I did.

I turned my face to him, his profile as serene as the violet evening. I watched him, surprised that I couldn't feel my own heartbeat now. It should have been pounding. Maybe it was. Maybe I couldn't sense anything at the moment but him.

"You want to kiss me, don't you?" Dal whispered.

"Yeah."

"And you're scared."

"Yeah."

"You don't have to be scared, Zeno. I've been wanting to kiss you since I got here."

Then he did the perfect thing. He turned his face to mine and leaned in.

Chapter Twelve

WE KISSED ON the steps of the deck, his arm around my shoulder, my hand on his big thigh. We kissed while the moon rose, its pale glow turning the night air silver. We kissed until we were out of breath and giddy, and when we finally pulled apart, we looked at each other in bright-eyed amazement.

"Damn, dude," Dalvin gasped. "I think I might be gay."

I grinned. And laughed. "Nah, man. Not you."

We hugged each other. Then we sat for a while, arm in arm, watching the moon do its slow surf across the sky.

Like your typical degenerate teen, I wanted more. I tapped Dalvin on the shoulder and went, "Hey." When he turned his face to me, I kissed him again. And kissed him some more. Some things in this world are simply right—the sun coming up in the east, the tides flowing with the moon, the trees budding in the spring. Kissing Dalvin Drake was like that. Emotions on my part were getting pretty high. From the way Dalvin squeezed me, his feelings were mighty worked up as well.

I pulled back. "Let's take this inside."

"Hells yeah," he groaned.

*

IN THE FAMILY room, we cuddled on the floor and skimmed through the multitudinous offerings on Netflix. We settled on *Malcolm X,* a Spike Lee biopic from the early 1990s starring Denzel Washington.

"It's one of my favorites," Dalvin said, which was all it took to get me on board.

"I never heard of it."

"That, sadly, is not surprising. This is one the best movies ever made, and it's so underrated. It got no love at the Oscars when it shoulda easily taken Best Actor, Best Director, and Best Pic."

The movie certainly lived up to Dalvin's hype. At least the parts of it I saw did. We sneaked in a few kisses at the beginning. That led up to more kisses midway through. Things started percolating between us in a most distracting way.

I broke away for the third time. "We're not giving this movie the attention it deserves."

"No, we're not. What do you suppose we oughta do about that?"

I grabbed the remote control and hit the Pause button.

"That works." Dalvin smiled and came at me again.

It turned into a spectacular make-out session. He kissed my ears, my neck, squeezed my shoulders, back, and waist. I couldn't stop caressing the muscles in his chest and arms, couldn't stop pressing my body against his. My heart was doing burpees in my throat. What the heck took us so long to get to this? We were barreling like hell toward the fully involved stage—Dalvin reached for my belt buckle—when my body tensed up.

Dalvin paused. "Is this okay with you?"

"Uhm...I think this is enough for now." I rolled off him and lay on my back. "I'm sorry. I've never done this before. With a dude, I mean. Sorry."

"No worries. Neither have I. It'll be fun figuring this out together."

"Can we watch the rest of the movie?"

Dalvin drew in a breath and sighed. A vein pulsed crazily in his neck. He was still able to give me a sweet smile. "Sure, Z. Anything you want."

I pressed the Play button. Malcolm X's life unreeled before us once more. We settled together on the floor, side by side. The movie pulled us back in, making us laugh and fume at the appropriate points. But this wonderful new dynamic kept buzzing between us, pulling like a magnetic force. I reached out, brushing my fingers against Dalvin's. He reacted instantly and in kind.

We held hands through the end of the movie.

*

"WANNA WATCH SOMETHING else?" I asked as the credits began to scroll.

"It's getting late. I gotta roll out in the morning and make it to church on time."

"Right." I switched off the television.

Dalvin got up from the floor. I followed suit. We stood there, face to face, as several charged moments of silence passed between us.

"Zeno," Dalvin said in his quietly earnest way, "I like this, you and me together. It's not a one-time thing for me. I hope it's the same way for you."

Even after all our kissing, that hit me right between the eyes. I blinked. "Are you really that into me?"

He laughed. "Yes! Isn't it obvious?" He ran both hands over his frohawk. "It's killing me right now, standing so close and not touching you."

"How long have you felt this way?"

"I think it started sometime last spring. You remember the last day of school? They cut us loose at noon. You and I got sodas outta the vending machine and went to the parking lot. We sat on the hood of my dad's car and talked until you had to go. I got in the car, watched you ride off on your bike and...this is gonna sound stupid... sitting there, watching you go, I cried a little when it hit me that I wouldn't get to be with you again for three fucking months."

I was breathless. "Wow."

"That's when I realized that I was crushing on you."

Damn. I'd spent most of June, July, and August hanging with Marvus or Jemma. What I had with Dalvin today, I could have explored for the past nine months. "We texted a lot over the summer. Why didn't you tell me how you felt?"

"I didn't think you were gay. You talked about girls a lot. You flirted with girls a lot. I've had crushes on dudes before, and they always went away, so I figured I'd get over you. But I didn't. When we came back to school, the feelings were even stronger. By the time winter break rolled around, I was ready to find somebody to brainwash me so I'd stop thinking about you that way."

"I'm sorry you went through that, Dal."

His face was practically glowing. "It's okay, man. The past two days more than made up for it. Outta the blue, you started flirting with me. I thought you were, like, kidding around or something at first, but then I picked up this sense that you were actually getting into me. Then today, you asked me to sleep over..." He closed the distance between us and took both my hands. "I thought that meant you wanted to get closer to me."

"You're right. I did want that. I still do."

"So." He gently pressed his forehead to mine, holding my gaze. "Here we are. Close."

From his tender expression, I knew what Dalvin wanted. I also knew the next move was totally up to me. That left the question: What did *I* want?

"Dal?"

"Yo, Z?"

"It's time for bed."

Holding Dalvin by the hand, I led the way down the hall. At the door to my room, Dalvin stopped. A gentle tug got him moving again. I guided him into the guest bedroom. There, we both stopped, and I turned to him. He looked at me with eyes so full of trust I almost broke down in tears. A smile trembled on my lips. I was happy. Excited. And I couldn't stop thinking about what had happened with Jemma.

I didn't trust myself.

I kissed Dalvin, a quick brush on the lips. Then I leaned into his ear and whispered, "Good night."

He looked surprised only for a moment. "Good night, Zeno."

I closed the door on my way out.

*

"WHAT? DID YOU just forget that you have a son?"

It was the perfect way to start a video chat with my clowning parents. On my screen, Mom pursed her lips while rolling her eyes, and Dad smirked.

"Hmph," Mom snorted. "As if you wanted us checking up on you."

"Hey, son, I remember the last time your mom and I came to the cabin. We called just to let you know that we'd made it, and you acted as if we'd committed a felony. On and on you went, whining that we didn't trust you by yourself for five minutes. We figured this time we'd give you your space."

"I'd say we did the right thing, babe, not calling his spoiled butt," Mom said, nudging Dad with her shoulder. "He looks mighty damn happy."

"Yeah, you're all aglow there, Zeno." Dad tossed in. "What's up with that?"

I rolled over on my bed, lying on my belly as I struggled to keep the heat from rising to my cheeks. "Nothing's up, and no-body's glowing. Come on."

"No," Dad shot back, "there's something going on with you, son. Something had to put that shine in your eyes."

Mom squinted at me, drilling in with a long, discerning look. "Have you got a girl over there?"

"No!" I scowled, faking indignation. "Unbelievable. All I wanted was to say good night to my mom and pop, and this is what I get for reaching out to two people who were obviously too un-concerned to call me. Jeez."

Dad looked at Mom. "Sara, I think our boy is pouting."

Mom twisted her mouth skeptically. "No, Marco, our six-foot-three, almost grown-ass son wouldn't pout—"

"Yes, I'm pouting!"

Mom waved me off. "I'm glad you enjoyed your day without us, Zeno. Your father and I certainly enjoyed our day without you. We did a little fishing, took a nice hike through the woods, played ping pong, ate a delicious fish dinner, and streamed a couple of good movies."

"And now we're signing off," Dad said. "It's past our bedtime."

"Past your bedtime? It's just ten thirty."

"Sweety pie," Dad called loudly, as if Mom were in another room instead of sitting right next to him, "you got the handcuffs ready?"

"Sure, sweetpea," Mom called back to him. "You just make sure you bring the whipped cream and strawberries."

"Really, you guys? This is child abuse, you know. I should call the cops right now."

"You go right ahead and do that, son. Your mom and I have some more catching up to do." Dad slid his arms around Mom's waist.

Mom blew me a kiss. "Good night, hon. We'll see you tomorrow. Have a good night."

"Good night, Mom, Dad."

Mom's hand grew giant-sized as she reached for the phone, and then the connection terminated.

I'd hoped for a longer conversation. I truly wanted to talk with my parents, but it was also a stalling tactic. Sooner or later, I'd have to reach out to Jemma. Sooner would be better, but I was maybe not the bravest dude in the world. Ah well…

I sent a text. *Are we still friends?*

Her reply came within moments. *Of course.*

Whoa. Thank God. My heart started beating again. *OK. Talk later?*

A thumbs-up emoji came in response.

I plugged my phone into the charger, stripped down to my boxers, and snuggled under the covers. Sleep took me over in minutes.

*

TYPICALLY, I WOKE in stages, keeping my eyes closed through the first few minutes of consciousness, burying my head under a pillow for a few minutes more, and finally curling into a defiant ball before throwing back the covers. That Sunday morning, I was out of bed in an instant, clearheaded and ready to go even though the sun was just beginning to rise. Dalvin's presence in the house was like smoke; I was alert to it, charged and ready for action. There was no sign he was up yet. Except for the rush of heated air moving through vents in the ceiling, the house was quiet. I made my bed, gathered a clean set of clothes, and poked my head into the hall. The door to the guest bedroom was closed. Perfect. I tippy-toed my way to the bathroom and quietly emerged fifteen minutes later freshly showered and dressed. The door of the guest bedroom was still closed.

I started up the hall, practically cackling like an over-the-top movie villain. I was gonna surprise my boy big-time. As I approached the living room, a luscious warm aroma hit me. What the hell? I hurried through the living room into the kitchen.

"Dalvin!"

Standing by the fridge in his Sunday best (black slacks, white shirt, blue paisley tie), he smiled at me. "Morning, Z. You've got perfect timing. Come on in, sit down. I'll have hot blueberry pancakes on the table in two minutes."

"Dude. I was gonna make *you* breakfast. And bring it to you. In bed."

That raised Dalvin's eyebrows. "All right. Next sleepover, I get breakfast in bed. Right now, I'm serving you. Take a seat."

"If you're gonna cook, messy man, don't do it in your come-to-Jesus clothes. Look at yourself. You got flour all over your pants."

He looked down sharply. "Oh shit."

I laughed. "Hang on." I crossed to him, grabbed a towel, and cleaned the white, dusty patches from his slacks. "There ya go.

Now you look like you're ready to FaceTime the Lord."

"Thanks." He added a grateful kiss to my nose."

"Hey!" My indignation was so thick you could cut it. "Lower."

"Okay, okay. Sorry." He smiled. And kissed me on the lips.

"That's better. Now, where are those pancakes?"

*

WE ATE PANCAKES and syrup, topped off with fruit salad. "Man, Dal. Great breakfast. Lotsa carbs."

"Yeah. I double down on protein before football games and load up on carbs before church. Keeps everything balanced." Dalvin pushed his plate aside and picked up his phone. "You ready to see the footage I got yesterday?"

"Oh, yeah, right. Let's see that."

He pulled his chair around to my side of the table and sat next to me. As I watched, my mouth slowly dropped open. Wow. He'd captured portions of our pizza-making, eating dinner together, cleaning up the kitchen afterward, the air hockey game, and then edited them into a beautiful short film set to Frank Ocean's "Thinkin Bout You." That was followed by still shots of us together and of me solo, reflecting all my moods from the day before.

"This is great, Dal. You must be able to turn invisible or something. I don't even remember seeing you shoot half this stuff."

"Not invisible. Just unobtrusive when I have to be."

"You do this every day with your camera?"

"Nah. Yesterday was special." He leaned his shoulder into mine. "It was our first day together. I want to remember that."

There went that little shudder in my chest again. "Me too."

"Zeno?"

"Yeah?"

"I'm not out or anything..."

"I'm not either, not about being bi."

"I want us to go on a date. I want to go on lots of dates with you."

I looked into his eyes. Everything he was feeling at the moment was there, deep enough that I could take a dive. "And...you want to keep this on the low?"

"Yeah, for now. See where this is going. Is that okay with you?"

I slid my arm around his waist, smiling. "It's cool. I kinda like the idea of having you all to myself. But I have this fantasy of the perfect date."

"Word?"

"Oh yeah. Funny thing. I did roller blading when I was a kid, but I've never been on a pair of ice skates in my life. Yet somehow, I got this vision of me and my date, ice skating on a frozen lake. There's music, and there's other couples on the ice, but me and my date are circling around to this slow love song, arm in arm, totally lost in each other."

"Man," Dalvin breathed in, long and slow. He sighed and kissed me.

"Will you send me a copy of your film?" I asked.

"Already did. I texted it to ya as soon as I finished it."

"God, you're perfect." It was my turn to kiss him.

Dalvin leaned into me, lifting an arm around my shoulders. His soft, warm lips tasted of syrup, which was fantastic. Then, out of the blue, he yanked himself away.

"We keep this up, and I'll be late," he said, getting up from his chair. He backed up a few steps, watching me closely. Then he grunted out a loud burst of frustration and came rushing toward me, arms outstretched. The next moment, he wrapped around me like a python, the side of his head pressed to mine. "Oh man," he moaned. "I wanna stay here with you."

"So stay. It'll be great."

"Ugh. I can't."

"Hey, I'm not trying to block your blessings or anything, dude, but I can see you're really not feeling church today. If your heart's not there, what's the point?"

He shrugged, nodding. "You're right."

"So? You're staying?"

For a moment or two, he pursed his lips, and I would've sworn it was gonna be a yes.

He shook his head sadly. "It's better that I keep the peace, man."

I decided not to touch that one. "Do what you gotta."

"I gotta clean up your kitchen and get outta here."

"Leave the kitchen to me. We can't have you showing up in church wearing food stains."

"Right. I'm gonna brush my teeth again and grab my stuff."

Dalvin hurried out of the room. I sat there, basking in the lingering aroma of pancakes and a heady mishmash of emotions. What a weekend! My confusion, embarrassment, and fear had taken a definite back seat to the sheer excitement and wonder of what I'd discovered in this boy of mine. There was, too, the wonder of what I'd discovered about myself. It was nothing new that I found some guys very attractive. I had no idea, however, that kissing another guy would be so crazy amazing.

I was still sitting there, minutes later, when Dalvin reappeared in the kitchen with his backpack in his hand. "Z? You okay?"

"Yeah, I'm good."

"You looked out of it there. Is something wrong?"

I got up and went to him and took his hand. "Everything's good, man. Come on. I'll walk you to the door." We crossed the living room, our grip tightening with every step. "Am I gonna see you later?"

He bit his lip ruefully. "Nah. My parents have this thing they're hosting at Orange Mound Community Center this afternoon. I'm watching baby bruh while they're gone. But I'll see you at school tomorrow. Wanna meet me at the cafeteria for breakfast?"

"Sure. I'll treat you to coffee and a granola bar."

We reached the front door and stopped there, facing each other.

"Keep Saturday night open, okay?" Dalvin said. "We're gonna have our first date. I'm taking you out, dude."

"You're making me shake here, man."

"Yeah, I see you shaking."

He took my hands gently, and I could feel the tiny shivers going through his body, so like the ones going through mine. Part of it was sheer elation at what was happening. I returned his tender gaze and tense smile. The unspoken message was clear: we were both afraid, but we were each other's rock.

I raised my eyebrows, surprised. My tremors were gone, yet the fluttery sheen of excitement remained with me. Dalvin's face relaxed into a purely happy smile.

"There. That's better." Dalvin planted a soft kiss on my forehead. "Text ya later," he said, and then he was out, striding down the walkway to his car.

I watched him go, in a daze again.

*

THE SHEETS SMELLED of Dalvin's soap. I wanted to spend the rest of the day wrapped in them like a burrito.

Oh my gosh. Did I have to wash them?

My continued freedom to go about my life as I chose deeply depended on removing all evidence of my unsanctioned overnight visitor. I stripped the bed in the guest room and shoved the covers into the washer. With the laundering underway, I went to the kitchen, washed and dried the breakfast dishes, put everything away, and then took out the garbage. The countertops got a wipe down, the stainless-steel appliances got a good polishing, and I finished the kitchen with a thorough mopping. I wiped down Dad's air hockey table, including the paddles and puck, removing all traces of fingerprints. (Paranoid much? You bet.) I vacuumed the carpet and dusted the tables in the family room. Once the bed-covers were clean and dry, I took them to the guest room and re-made the bed.

Whew!

Mom and Dad got home shortly after noon. I met them as they came in from the garage, Dad carrying their overnight bags.

"Hey, let me take those," I said, smiling as I grabbed the bags. "You guys have a good time at the lake?"

"Yes, we did," said Mom. "I don't have to ask if you had a good time here. You're still glowing all over the place."

"Mom, come on. I'm just glad you're home."

Dad was checking out the kitchen. "Hm."

"Your dad and I decided we're going out for dinner this afternoon. Do you want to join us, or do you have other plans?"

"It sounds like you guys are still on your date thing, whatever. I'll just eat leftover pizza."

Dad snorted. "Ya don't want to go to dinner with your mom and me? I guess you're not that glad to have us home after all."

"That's so not cool. I'm gonna take your bags to your room."

Dad snorted again. He checked out the family room as I led the way to the hall—and the man snorted a third time.

"Hey, is something stuck in your nose?"

"You know, son, most parents who leave their kid home alone for the weekend come back to a big mess. This place actually looks cleaner than it did when your mom and I left."

There it was. Guilt. Burning on my face like a heat rash. Dad was fishing, still stuck on the not erroneous notion that I'd fooled around with someone while he and Mom had been away. It was time for me to do what I always did when he started one of his expeditions: plow right through it.

"What? You think I threw a wild-ass party while you were gone, tore the house apart, and then put everything back together?"

"No, that's something a normal teenager would do. You, my boy, are one weird kid."

"I think we all know where he gets it, Marco," Mom added.

"Ha. Thanks, Mom."

I placed their bags in their room.

Dad fell face forward across the bed, sighing, "Ah, it's good to be home."

"Well, thank you, Zeno, for welcoming us," Mom said. "I'm going to unpack and get changed. Your father doesn't know it yet, but he's treating me to a movie before we have dinner."

"Of course I am, Sara babe," Dad mumbled into the mattress.

"Okay, well I'm going out for a jog. I'll see you guys later."

"Oh, wait. How was Jemma's party?" Mom asked. "Did you have a good time?"

The unexpected shot of pain cut deeply through my belly. I managed to keep a straight face. "Yeah, it was great."

Chapter Thirteen

I ARRIVED AT school early on Monday morning. The eastern sky had just begun turning pink ahead of the rising sun as I locked my bike in the rack and headed into the building. Before meeting Dalvin at the cafeteria, I wanted to dump off my helmet and backpack. I entered through the south entrance and started up the stairs two at a time. Upon reaching the second-floor landing, I pulled up so sharply I almost fell backward down the steps.

A couple stood, backed up against the wall. The girl had her hands in the dude's back pockets, and the guy held on to the girl's butt while they kissed passionately. And by "passionately," I mean it looked as if they were snarfing each other's faces off their heads. Usually when I blundered across a make-out session, a typical high school scene, I'd just look the other way and keep moving. The thing that stopped me short this time wasn't the "what" but the "who": Tish Cooper.

And Ollie Gates.

I mean, *seriously?*

Ollie Gates and Tish Cooper? Doing the bump and grind thing? For reals?

Tish, though barely five feet even when you threw in her Bantu knots, had the whole hot and sexy vibe going. She was sorta snooty with guys, the kind of girl who would brush off any flirtatious offerings as if unworthy of her attention. To be honest, a lot of guys suspected she was all the way lez. And Ollie...well, again, just being honest, I personally didn't think the dude even had any hormones. You never saw him leer at, flirt with, or wax bodaciously about girls (or guys). He was all about keeping his grades up and his life on schedule, scoffing at things like parties, pep rallies, and dating as distractions. He seemed to totally devote himself to shoving bigger and bigger sticks up his ass.

So. What the hell was this?

I was, to borrow again from my SAT vocab studies, gobsmacked. I stood there with my hand over my mouth, gawking as my scandalized brain cells tried to make sense of it all. Was it simply that Tish only went for skinny, anal retentive, vicious nerd boys? Could it be that Ollie was actually human? My mind fairly boggled. Like any hormone-crazed couple worth their salt, Tish and Ollie didn't so much as come up for air, let alone note the presence of a potential voyeur.

It turned out that I'd gotten a bit ahead of myself on that point.

Ollie abruptly lifted his mouth from Tish's, shot me a hellaciously pissed off look, and snapped, "For fuck's sake, Anderson, are you waiting for sloppy seconds or what?"

Uh. *I think he just called me a creep.*

Ollie's rage ticked up a notch. "Oh, did I stump you there?"

Tish flipped a scowl my way over her shoulder.

I raised my hands in a "my bad" gesture. "Sorry guys, I didn't mean to...I just...okay. Yeah. See you later."

I hung my head and slunk on up the stairs.

Embarrassment nagged me all the way to my locker. As I dialed in my combination, somebody behind me went, "Yo! Drunk Aladdin!" I turned to see this white kid with a scruffy red goatee and slicked back blue hair passing by. He gave me an appreciative smile and a double thumbs-up.

Okay. It was gonna be *that* kind of day.

I stowed away my backpack and helmet and walked to the other end of the hall, where I descended the north stairwell to avoid my lusty fellow Film Club members. On the first floor, I reached the cafeteria just as the door closest to me swung open.

And there, of course, was Jemma.

"Oh. Hey." I could have sunk right through the floor into quicksand and it would've been all right with me.

"Hi, Zeno." She seemed just as uneasy as I felt, her hand clutching nervously at the straps of her backpack, but she still had the guts to look me in the eye. Her hair, tied in a ponytail, draped over her shoulder. She wore a blue leotard with black ballerina shoes and carried an ice-speckled, pint-size carton of OJ in her hand.

"You...you're here early, huh?" I asked.

"I'm using the studio to practice some dance steps."

"Aren't you overdoing it with the practice?"

"When I'm stressed, I practice. It's how I deal."

"Oh."

Her gaze intensified. And her strong, athletic body suddenly slumped; she seemed totally miserable. "Are you okay, Zeno?"

"Me? Yeah, I'm fine." I hated that I was making her so fucking unhappy right now. I'd hurt her feelings. What kind of friend does that? Sheez.

"Do you want to have that talk now?"

"Oh. Not now." I peered past her, into the cafeteria. There, across the room near the cashier's station, stood Dalvin, Richie, and three more of the school's jocks. "I promised a friend I'd have breakfast with him."

She took in a breath and held it for a long moment. Then she exhaled and said, "It would mean a lot if you came to my recital."

"Sure. I want to be there."

"I'll get a pass for you. Is there anyone you want to bring?"

"Uhm, yeah." I looked past her at Dalvin again. Jemma went on, saying something else about the upcoming dance recital, but I was caught up in what I saw unfolding in the cafeteria.

Richie said something, laughing, bragging to the three jocks, who in turn gawped at Jemma and me, their mouths tight *O*'s as they crooned, "Whoooah!" Dalvin's eyes bugged in shock for all of two seconds, and I knew what was coming next. I knew when I saw the cop in uniform standing at the beverage station with one of the food service workers. I knew, and it sent a cold bolt of dread through me.

I put a hand on Jemma's shoulder, gently but urgently pushing past her. At almost the same time, Dalvin grabbed Richie by the shoulder and turned the loudmouth to him, Dalvin's face one big twist of fury.

I shouted "Stop!" at the same time Dalvin punched Richie in the mouth.

Richie's grunt was eclipsed by the meaty *thock* of Dalvin's fist against his jaw. The three jocks with them jumped back, mouths wide open, looking horrified. Jemma gasped behind me. The blow was so solid, Richie hit the floor and slid several inches before coming to a rest, knocked out and as limp as a wet blanket.

Mr. Corning, one of the history teachers, dropped his cup of coffee as he spun toward the melee, too late to see what happened. Dalvin stood over Richie, fists clenched, eyes blazing away, unaware of the cop rushing in to grab him.

*

I COULDN'T REACH Dalvin.

The cop and Mr. Corning hustled Dalvin off to the principal's office while another teacher attended to Richie. They apparently confiscated Dalvin's iPhone; every call I made to him went directly to voicemail. I went to my morning classes but couldn't concentrate on anything. During lunch period, I went by the office, and Dalvin was still in there with Mrs. Ghoudry, the principal, a tall, bearded Black man in a business suit (Dalvin's dad?), and a lean, tough-looking woman in blue jeans and a black blazer who resembled one of those lady police detectives from *Law and Order:SVU*. Two other people were in there: Richie, huddled in a chair with a cold compress to his jaw and, sitting next to him, Jemma. Jemma looked ready to throw some punches of her own, and from the way she kept scowling at Richie, her ire was entirely for him.

WTF?

*

I HAD MY head down, my hands crossed on my desk, and my history textbook propped open in front of me. My mind was a vault, locked around this new central worry.

"Zeno!"

What? Why was Ms. Parson shouting at me? I looked up, and it immediately became clear from her frown that the woman had been calling me for some time now. "Yeah! I mean, yes, ma'am?"

"The principal wants to see you in her office now," Ms.

Parson said. "Go straight there. Mrs. Ghoudry made it clear this is urgent. Take your things with you. We have only fifteen minutes left in the period, so I doubt you'll be coming back here."

I gathered my stuff, shoved it in my backpack, and left the room. Ms. Parson was strictly phones-off during her classes. I pulled out my phone, turned it on, and checked for missed calls and messages. Three calls from Jemma. Six texts from Dalvin. All asking to meet with me ASAP.

Hells. My heart began thumping. What was going on here? I started to contact Jemma and Dalvin, but this thing with the principal, I needed to get that out of the way first. I shoved my phone back in my pocket and rushed to the office.

The moment the secretary saw me coming, she got up from her desk and stuck her head through the principal's open door. "Mrs. Ghoudry, he's here." Then, she waved me forward. "Come on in, Zeno. She's waiting."

I wasn't sure just how Mrs. Ghoudry's secretary knew me by name and on sight, considering I'd never been in the principal's office, but whatever. I entered the office, and she closed the door behind me.

Mrs. Ghoudry sat at a small conference table that occupied the middle of her office. She was in her forties, tall, slender, and brown-skinned. Glasses shaped like cat's eyes framed her pleasant, intelligent face. The woman in the jeans and the black blazer sat across from Mrs. Ghoudry. She also appeared to be in her forties, her skin pale, her short black hair showing strands of gray here and there. Her no-nonsense expression softened completely once I'd entered the room. Up close, I could see the police badge clipped to her belt next to the buckle.

"Zeno Anderson, please sit down," Mrs. Ghoudry said, in full poker-face mode. "This is Detective Marcia Hanson. She wants to talk with you."

"Uhm, hi," I mumbled as I put my backpack on the floor and sat down.

Detective Hanson looked at me like a doctor about to deliver devastating news to a patient. Was I in trouble? Did the police think I'd done something wrong or committed a crime? Usually, the police only come at the Black community one way, like a bulldozer. Somehow, this cop's demeanor was even more disturbing. Oh, my jeez. Mom was gone, back on her trucking route. Dad was at his auto shop. Picture a naked baby bird alone in a nest with a cat on the branch.

"Uh," I said, "do I need my dad here or, like, a lawyer?"

"If you want your father with you, Zeno, you can call him and we'll wait until he gets here to talk," Detective Hanson said, her tone soft and concerned. "But you're not a suspect. I think you may have been the victim of a crime."

"Me? Nobody's done anything to me."

"Zeno, just listen to the detective," Mrs. Ghoudry said, "and answer her questions."

Detective Hanson didn't take her eyes off me. She had a small spiral-bound notebook in one hand, open to a page of hastily scribbled notes, but she didn't refer to it. "You attended a party at Jemma Haynes' house this past Saturday."

"Yeah, I was there."

"And during that party, you became incapacitated. I've seen the video of you being helped away from the pool and into the house—"

"I didn't get drunk. I mean, maybe I was, but I didn't drink any kind of alcohol, for sure. I don't drink, and I don't know what happened. I blacked out and woke up the next day, and I can't remember much of anything about the night before."

"I don't think you were drunk, Zeno," the detective said, leaning forward. "Have you ever heard of GHB, gamma-hydroxy-butyrate?"

"Gamma hydroxy-what?"

"It's more commonly referred to as the date rape drug. Typically, at a bar or a party, the drug is slipped into an unsuspecting person's drink. The sedative effects incapacitate the victim and can also cause amnesia, leaving the victim vulnerable to sexual assault."

"Wait. You think somebody did that to me?"

"From what I've seen and heard, it's very likely." The detective paused for a moment. "I want you to think hard, Zeno, about this. While you were at the party, did you ever leave your drink unattended, or did anyone bring you a drink?"

"I don't...I can't remember."

"Did anyone make sexual advances toward you?"

"No." But Jemma told me we had sex. Did she tell this detective too? "I don't remember anything like that."

"Try to remember, Zeno. Think. Any details you can recall could be helpful."

I went back in my mind to Friday night. Beyond my getting showered and dressed, that time was mostly a void...except for Dalvin and what he told me.

"My friend Dalvin came by my house. We went to the party together, got there around eight thirty, I guess. We hung out, then we went separate ways for a minute. I don't know what happened after that. It's like there's this black hole in my memory."

"So, you arrived at the party with your friend. Did you drink anything when you got there?"

"I had a can of soda. But nobody put anything in it, I'm sure. I popped the tab on it myself."

"What happened after you finished the soda?"

"Dalvin said he went off somewhere. And I...I went looking for...somebody, I think... I don't know. Maybe somebody at the party saw me drink something else."

"Did you ever feel lightheaded? Nauseated?"

"I don't remember."

"Okay," Detective Hanson said, nodding. She raised her little notebook and consulted her notes. "Jemma says the two of you talked about doing a karaoke song together. She poured herself a cup of punch from a bottle, but you drank it instead, and the two of you went to the pool where you did your karaoke bit. That was when the video shows you became disoriented and had to be helped into the house. Jemma says you passed out, and she left you in her room to 'sleep it off.'" Detective Hanson looked at me again. "Does any of this ring a bell with you, Zeno?"

I shook my head, feeling like the biggest idiot on the planet. "No. I saw the video on YouTube, but I don't remember actually doing any of that stuff."

"When you woke up in your room Sunday morning, did you have any bruises, scratches or hickeys? Were any of the clothes you wore gone or torn? Anything indicative of a sexual assault?"

"No. No. I'm telling you, nobody did anything like that to me."

"Will you submit to a medical exam to confirm whether there's evidence of rape?"

Rape? How the hell could anybody rape me? If there was any evidence that I'd had sex, it would be from Jemma. "I won't do that. I don't have to. I told you, nobody hurt me."

"Okay, Zeno. There's one other thing I'd like to ask. Will you consent to a urine test to check for traces of GHB in your system? It's a long shot, considering the party was almost forty-eight hours ago, but I'd still like to give it a try. Is that okay with you?"

Well. There couldn't be any harm in that. "Sure. I'll do it."

The detective stood. "Mrs. Ghoudry says we can use the school nurse to collect the specimen. Come with me to the nurse's office. I'll take the specimen to the police lab for testing. If you give me your phone number, I'll call you with the results."

I kept my seat. Something was bugging me. "If the results are negative, then what?"

"You're done. My investigation involving you is finished."

I already knew I wasn't gonna like the answer to my next question. "And if you find traces of GHB?"

"Then I will be having a long talk with your parents."

Yeah. Exactly what I was afraid of.

Shit.

*

IN A SMALL bathroom at the back of the school's clinic, I took care of business while the nurse and detective stood guard outside the door. I handed off the specimen to the nurse, who turned it over to Detective Hanson, who dropped it in a plastic evidence bag and departed with dispatch. After washing my hands, I slung my backpack over my shoulder and dragged my butt back to the principal's office.

The secretary didn't even ask why I'd returned. She just waved me on in.

Mrs. Ghoudry looked up from her computer screen. "Hi, Zeno," she said with way too much sympathy in her eyes.

"Mrs. Ghoudry, I'm not feeling so good. I really need to go home."

She reached over and picked up an already completed dismissal slip. "I thought you might."

Chapter Fourteen

I'D JUST PULLED my helmet from my locker when my phone chimed. It was a text message from Mom.

On a break in Marked Tree. Thought of u. Have u done any more college apps?

Man. I really didn't need this. There were weightier things on my mind. Mom texted Dad and me from the road whenever she made stops—meal breaks, refueling, whatever. "Touching bases" she called it. I liked that it kept her close when she was a thousand miles away, but I couldn't even think about college right now. Luckily, this was just past the middle of the school day, so it wasn't as if Mom was expecting a response right away. I stuck my phone back in my pocket.

"Zeno..." Jemma came down the hall at me like somebody on a serious power walk, her tan-and-white flats slap-slap-slapping along the floor. She'd changed into a brown skirt and white blouse and carried her backpack in her hand. Her loose hair flared over her shoulders like flames.

"Jem, I'm about to head home. I got an early dismissal from—"

"I'm ditching," she said. "I'll give you a ride. We're gonna talk now."

*

MY BIKE WOULDN'T fit in the trunk of Jemma's cute little VW. The front wheel and handlebars protruded below the partially closed lid, making it look as if the Bug had just chomped down on an unlucky biker. We tossed our backpacks in the backseat. Jemma slid behind the wheel and slammed her door so hard I winced. I got into the passenger seat. She gripped the steering wheel in her fists for probably a solid minute. I got the impression she was choking back a scream—and that any second now, the steering wheel would snap into four pieces.

I kept my mouth shut.

"Fucking Richie McMahon," she growled between her teeth. Then she relaxed her grip, dropping her hands from the steering wheel. Sighing, she smoothed her hair back from her face. Her eyes didn't seem ready to shoot fire beams anymore.

"Okay," I said cautiously. "Did you get all of that outta your system?"

She turned my way and scowled anew. "God, Zeno. You look like a pretzel. Let the seat back."

"I'm good."

Jemma lunged at me, reaching across my lap. She tugged at some lever on the side of my seat, which shot backward so fast my head snapped forward and almost hit the windshield.

"Agh!"

"There," Jemma said, eyeing my expanded legroom. "Isn't that better?"

"Aside from the whiplash, yeah." I massaged the back of my neck. "What happened with you guys in Mrs. Ghoudry's office? And why are you so pissed at Richie?"

She started the engine, backed out of the parking space, and drove across the parking lot into the street before she answered.

"I'm angry with Richie for the same reason Dalvin punched him out. He told those friends of his that he brought 'love potion' to my party. He brought *GHB* to my party and tried to fake me into drinking it."

I grabbed the door handle. My immediate impulse was to make her stop the car so I could climb out and…I don't know. Run away.

"He got you instead, Zeno."

Don't stick your fingers in your ears and do the la-la-la thing, idiot. Don't do it.

Jemma watched the road. And waited. "Zeno? Did you hear what I said?"

I closed my eyes.

"You bugged out and passed out at the party because you were drugged. And that means I *did* take advantage of you be-cause—"

"Stop, Jem."

"Things are weird between us, and it's my fault."

I spewed out a long, slow sigh. "Please stop doing that to yourself. What happened at the party was not your fault. You said I started it. You said I kissed you first. It's not taking advantage if the other person is a willing participant, and obviously, I was will-ing."

"Oh—" Her sigh devolved into a groan. She briefly rolled her eyes upward. "You're not getting it. You were under the influence the whole time. The drug took away your consent. Why can't you see that? You kissed me first, yes, and you said you wanted it, but even though I didn't know it was GHB, I knew something had you out of it. And I still went ahead and responded. God. I can't believe I did that. You're the victim here, Zeno. It's really starting to suck that, between the two of us, I'm the only one bothered by that."

I raised my hands, a helpless gesture. "I don't know what you want me to do here."

"Dammit, stand up for yourself! Get mad at me. Get mad at Richie. Stop acting as if nothing's happened to you."

"Jemma, tell me for real. If I didn't force anything on you, why are you so mad at me?"

She sighed, the blaze vanishing from her eyes. For a while, she didn't say anything. She just drove, staring straight ahead. Then her lower lip trembled. "I'm not angry with you. I'm totally furious with Richie, but aside from that, I'm angry at myself."

"For what happened after I got drugged. But you shouldn't be. I kissed—"

"It doesn't matter that you kissed me first. How do I even know that was something you wanted to do? I want a guy to want me for me, not because he's out of his head on drugs. I wish I could take it back. I wish I could take it all back, everything, including the kisses at school and the flirting. But here we are. I like you a hell of a lot, the feeling's not mutual, and I don't know what to do with that."

"I'm sorry. I wish there was something else I could say."

"You were honest with me, and I can't ask for any more than that. You don't have any reason to apologize."

She pulled to a stop at the curb in front of my house and shifted the gear into park. Her eyes glittered in the bright daylight. She rubbed her hands over them, clearing away the tears. "Have you talked to Dalvin?"

"Oh..." I blinked hard. The one-eighty change in subject hit me like whiplash all over again. "No. Uhm, he texted me after he got out of the principal's office, but I haven't heard from him since, and my calls went to voicemail. Why do you ask?"

"Mrs. Ghoudry called Dalvin's dad. The man came to the office, and he was *pissed*. I think Dalvin's in serious trouble with his dad. You should make sure he's okay."

"Gotcha. But let's go back to what we were talking about before. I may not *like* like you, Jemma, but I still want us to be friends. You mean a lot to me; you always have."

"Right now, this whole thing makes me want to lock myself in my room and never come out. I have to deal with this. I have to get rid of..." With her hands on the wheel, she froze up, staring through the windshield in a daze.

"Uh? Jemma?"

She moved so suddenly I flinched. Foot firmly on the brake, the girl made an elaborate show of shifting the gear into drive. "I have to go."

"But—"

"I'm gonna need some space. Okay? Please. I'm sorry. See you."

What the hell? I grabbed my backpack, got out, and retrieved my bike from the trunk. What else could I do? Jemma took off so fast her tires actually chirped on the asphalt. I stood there, watching until she disappeared around the corner. Then I rolled my bike into the garage and let myself into the house. Usually, I'd dive into a big snack the first thing after coming home from school. I dropped my backpack and helmet on the floor, walked through the kitchen and lay down on the sofa in the family room. Curling against the backrest, I closed my eyes.

Damn. Jemma wanted me to understand what had happened

between us. Hells, I didn't even remember it. But I certainly under-
stood one thing: I'd gone too far with a friend.

And now I was losing that friend.

Chapter Fifteen

I COULDN'T REACH Dalvin.

I tried more texts and calls and got nothing. And I couldn't go by his house, having no idea where he lived.

I already felt bad when I curled up on the sofa. Now I felt worse. I hated feeling like that, sick but in a nonspecific way. Not a headache or queasy stomach, just an overall sense of lousiness. Simply BLAH.

I lay on the sofa, eyes closed, phone clutched in my hands, listening to the vague hum of the house breathing around me. For a good long while, I vegged there, one terrible thought after another sliding through my mind as to why Dalvin wasn't responding.

Dammit, why didn't I get the dude's address when he was here? And Jemma! If she's pregnant, she might want to get rid of it, and I don't know how I'm supposed to feel about that. Or what I'm supposed to do. She says she wants space, but shouldn't I be there for her? What kind of guy gets a girl pregnant and doesn't stand by her? A bum, that's what kind. A total and complete bum.

There were five solid knocks at the door.

The only reason I dragged myself off the sofa was that the knocks were at the back door. Who the hell does that? Moving across the kitchen, I could see a big silhouette looming against the curtains. I unlocked the door and tugged it open.

"Hey," said Dalvin.

*

MY MOUTH WASN'T working for the moment, so I reached out, took him by the arm, and pulled him into the kitchen. His smile was small and tight, his arms rigid, one hand clenched into a fist around his wallet and a set of keys. He flung them on the counter, went directly to the table in the nook, pulled out a chair, and sat down.

My hands were shaking. Why were my hands shaking? Was it because he seemed pissed and stressed and just a little sad? Or was it because he looked so good in his gray sweatsuit, and I was glad to have him here again? He sat there staring at the tabletop, his brow tightening, and I couldn't find any words. A dozen questions boiled through my head, and still, I couldn't speak.

Dang, fool, say something to him!

"Dalvin, why'd you come to the back door?" Okay, totally irrelevant question, but it was better than nothing.

He didn't look up. "I tried the front door, and there was no answer. The garage door is up, and your bike's in there. I figured you must be home, so I came to the back."

"Oh. Okay."

Note to self: at the end of this conversation, close the garage door before someone takes off with your bike. Now say something that matters to your friend.

"Jemma said your dad was really pissed at you in Mrs. Ghoudry's office. Are things cool with you at home?"

"I wouldn't say things are cool." He kept his head down, his voice soft but steady. "My dad can't stand to look at me right now."

"Because of that thing in the cafeteria this morning?"

"Yeah. Mrs. Ghoudry suspended my ass for three days and kicked me off the football team for Friday night's game. My dad wasn't happy about any of it. He grounded me for a week, and he's gonna have me doing manual labor around the house for a month."

I gasped, almost choking on the sharp intake of breath and the burning sense of outrage. "Are you for real? All that for swingin' on Richie?"

Dalvin finally lifted his head and looked at me. He smiled, grimly cocking one corner of his mouth. "Well, I gave the fool a concussion and knocked out one of his teeth. But it could've gone worse for me. When Richie's mom showed up, she wanted to press charges."

I grit my teeth, my jaw clenching.

Dalvin dropped the smile. "Everybody's pissed at me. My dad thinks I'm straight-up crazy, doing something like this a few months before graduation. He's afraid I just blew my chances at starting college anywhere come fall. The coach flat cussed me out, and half the team wants to kick my ass for fucking up our playoff chances. Ollie flipped because he thinks I'm throwing off his Film Club schedule." Dal shrugged. "Gotta admit, though, in spite of everything, it felt pretty good clockin' Richie."

I took a seat across from him. "Why'd you do it, Dalvin? Why hit Richie?"

Dalvin met my gaze, his brow crushing down on itself. "He

thought it was funny, Z. He told those guys you wound up drinking the 'love potion' he put in Jemma's cup, and he laughed about it. I don't regret knocking the sucker out. He bought that fist in his face."

"I wish you hadn't done it, man. Richie's not worth it. I don't want you to miss out on—"

"All the crazy stuff that happened to you at the party, the whole mess with that girl you mentioned, was because of Richie. You're acting like that—doesn't it piss you off even a little?"

"Yeah, I'm not exactly happy Richie turned me into a freak show. But really, I'm more worried about the friend I slept with, and about you. I texted, called, and you never got back to me. I thought maybe...your dad..."

"He took my phone when he grounded me. I told him I needed it for the Film Club project, but that didn't mean shit to him. Wait. You thought my dad—what? Beat me?"

"Or had you scrubbing toilets with your toothbrush. Or packed you off to a monastery in Mexico." I sorta ducked my head as a sheepish expression tugged the left side of my face. "I was thinking all kindsa crazy things."

Dalvin smiled, which was a relief because, amazingly, it seemed he wasn't offended at where my brain had gone. "Dude. My pops is probably the strictest man on the planet, but abusive, he ain't. For sho, we have our battles, but they're all verbal, and even then, we keep our respect for each other. If my dad and I ever got physical, believe me, you'd know it. Big as the two of us are, there'd be some real mountain-moving."

"Yeah, bet. Yo, you want something to drink? I'll make us some iced tea." I started to get up.

He reached across the table, taking my hand to stop me. "I can't stay, Z. I'm on my way to pick up my mom from her music lesson. She's learning how to play the trumpet, of all things. I detoured because I have to tell you something, and this is the only way I can talk to ya right now. The one thing I regret about popping on Richie is that I can't take you out this weekend. I'm sorry, man. I was really looking forward to that first date."

Aw. "So was I. But it's cool. We'll get there." I squeezed his hand. "I'm just glad to know you're okay. Uh, that thing you mentioned about Richie's mom... Is she actually gonna press charges against you?"

"I don't know. She got distracted when she found out the cops are investigating her precious baby for drug possession. And assault."

"What? Who'd he assault?"

Dalvin's eyebrows arched, and he froze for an instant. His smile was slow in coming back. He patted my hand. "It's a good thing you're so dang pretty."

I laughed out of relief because the whole vibe from him was suddenly goofy and tender, which was perfect. Hells, the dude had gone all southern gentleman at school this morning, fighting to protect my honor without a thought as to what it might cost him. This big, beautiful guy really cared about me.

Another instant and Dal's expression changed again, his gaze achingly merging with mine. He caressed my knuckles with his thumb. A wave of warmth tingled through me, swelling out from deep in my center. My hand trembled a little in his. God, what was this pull between us? I'd never felt anything like it. I wanted more for him, with him, from him. He blinked several times, revealing the new swell of fear he carried.

What do you need, Dalvin? How can I help?

Maybe it was telepathy. He seemed to know what I was thinking. He got up and came over to me, and I pushed my chair away from the table because I saw now what he needed. He threw one leg over my knees and straddled me, wrapping his arms around my neck. We were two tall, strapping dudes, and I thought that would make this awkward, but it didn't. He settled in my lap like we were made for it, resting his chin on my shoulder. I grabbed him around his waist, pulling him close, keeping him in place.

And he held on to me for a good while.

*

HE SPOKE SOFTLY, his lips against my ear. "I gotta go."

I released him from my arms, and he stood. Then, Dal took my hands and pulled me to my feet. I reached for him, ready to linger a bit more, but he moved over to stand beside me. He threw an arm around my shoulders and started us on our way toward the front door.

"I freaked when that cop grabbed me this morning," Dalvin said quietly. "I didn't know what he was gonna do to me."

"Did he hurt you or anything?"

"No. He took me straight to Mrs. Ghoudry's office and waited with me until she got there. Turns out he's married to the cafeteria manager, and our principal is their neighbor."

He still looked shaken, his eyes downcast and uncertain. This was a first for him in my experience.

"It's gonna be okay, Dal."

"Thanks, man."

I took his hand, the one dangling off my shoulder, and changed the subject. "What're you gonna do while you're suspended?"

"I have to complete my class assignments for those three days, and my dad's making me prune our trees and shit. I'll be plenty busy." He hugged me around the neck. "But I'll still have time to think about you."

Corny. And just what I needed to hear. Picture me cheesin' like a fool. "I'll be thinking about you too."

We reached the front door. He pulled his arm off my shoulders and faced me, stepping in close.

"I'm glad I stopped by. You made me feel better."

"So I won't see you or talk to you again until you come back to school on Thursday?"

"Probably not. Hold on to this until then." Dalvin leaned in and kissed me for what seemed like an hour. When he pulled away, he stared into my eyes and said, "You got a pen?"

"Hang on." I rushed to the kitchen, grabbed a black pen from my backpack, and hurried back to Dal. "Here ya go."

He took my right hand, turned the palm up, and wrote carefully across the base of my thumb. Then he handed the pen back to me. "My mom and dad don't get home until five most days. Come see me if you get a chance."

He gave my hand a squeeze, opened the door, and walked out. I watched until he got behind the wheel of his mom's car and, with a casual wave, drove off.

Dang. I hated to see him go.

I looked at what he'd written on my hand: an address. His address.

*

"HEY. HEY!"

I jumped a mile and looked up as Bobbo stomped across the pavement at me from the rear door of the auto shop. A big smear of black grease stretched across the front of his gray coveralls, his whole brow knotted, and his goatee more frizzed than usual. He stopped when I made eye contact.

"What the hell, kid?" he snapped. "Didn't you hear me yelling at you? You been polishing that one section of that car for fifteen minutes. Your customer's gonna be back here anytime now. Better get your ass in gear if you wanna get paid!"

"Yeah, okay, Bobbo." I revved up my polishing, moving on to finish the rest of the sedan, shivering with every motion. I'd only worn a T-shirt and jeans. The sun was low in the western sky, the late afternoon air cooling by the second.

"And answer your damn cellie," Bobbo continued. "Your old man's been trying to call ya. He says for you to wait here until he gets back."

My phone was on vibrate, but I'd been so deep in my head while working I must not have felt it. "Dad left? Where did he go?"

"He told me the principal at your school asked him to come in so they could talk."

The can of wax squirted right out of my spasming hand. *Oh holy fuck.*

*

THE TELEVISION DRONED on with a game of *Jeopardy*. The refrigerator hummed, occasionally going *clack-clack* as it cranked freshly made ice cubes into the collection bin. The sounds echoed in the emptiness of the break room. I sat (slumped, actually) at a table in the back, near the vending machines. There were homework assignments I should have been doing, but I hadn't brought my books or anything with me because I'd planned on being home now. So, I sat and listened and waited.

And cussed Mrs. Ghoudry over and over in my head.

The door swung open. Dad walked in. He'd changed from his coveralls to the blue sweats he'd worn to work. I met his eyes for about two seconds and then looked down at my hands spread flat against the table.

"Zeno." He spoke my name as if it pained his whole mouth. Even in my peripheral vision, I could see the drastic way his shoulders slumped, as if all the air had been let out of his chest. Why couldn't he just yell at me and make graphic threats on my life? I hated for people to be disappointed in me, especially my mom and dad.

I knew I should say something, apologize. Hopefully, that would save us both a long, awkward conversation and more deeply hurt feelings. I wasn't sure exactly what Mrs. Ghoudry had told Dad, however, and it didn't seem too bright an idea to go apologizing for something Dad may know nothing about.

"Dad, I—"

"No, not here. Come on."

We went upstairs to his office, which was pretty basic: desk, three metal chairs, file cabinet, desktop computer, phone. The only standout was the pinball machine in the corner. Dad and I had played a lot of games on that thing. I drifted toward the machine, hoping to distract him, but he pulled out a chair in front of his desk and pointed at me.

"Sit down, Zeno."

I sat. Dad perched one-hipped on the edge of the desk. He reached out, took my chin, and turned my wandering eyes to meet his.

"Son, why didn't you tell your mother or me that something happened to you at Jemma's party?"

"I'm sorry about that. Really sorry."

"I accept the apology, but I still want to know why."

"Dad, come on. It wasn't, like, a major thing."

He rocked back on his hip, brows scrunching. "Getting

drugged into unconsciousness is a major thing!"

"Don't be mad at me. I didn't know about the drug until to-day."

"I'm not angry with you. I'm worried, very worried. You lost consciousness, and you never said anything. You know your mom and I are on the fence about letting a sixteen-year-old go out of town to college in the fall. This doesn't help your case, son."

Going away to college was something that actually mattered. I could just as well attend the University of Memphis or Christian Brothers U and get a fine education. But attending college in an-other part of the country, being exposed to other cultures, other ways of thinking, would make my education, my life, so much richer. Not to mention that the idea of being totally independent and calling my own shots was pretty exciting. More and more, it just didn't seem that Mom and Dad were ever gonna be down with the whole thing. Shit. My only option could be the U of M. Which I had not applied to. Which maybe I should. Maybe I should take a gap year.

I threw up my hands, frowning at Dad. "It's not like I'm some kid. Sheez. I'll be seventeen in October."

"You'll still be underage. And don't change the subject. Your health and safety are important to your mom and to me. What's puzzling the hell out of me is why it's not important to you."

Now I was the one scowling. "You make it sound like I'm out there doing crazy stuff, running drugs or something."

"No, you just go riding your bike in traffic without a helmet. You go peddling off in the rain without a coat and then walk around school sopping wet. You work way too many hours wash-ing cars and then stay up late to finish your school assignments and get way too little rest."

Excuse you. I just had a very *leisurely weekend with a*

fantastic friend who...okay, stuck his tongue down my throat. But still...

"Zeno? Are you listening to me?"

I blinked at him. "Yeah, Dad." I opened my mouth and shut it again.

"What?"

"I don't see why Mrs. Ghoudry had to say anything to you. What happened to me had nothing to do with school. And I'm okay. What's the big deal?"

Dad closed his eyes and pinched the bridge of his nose, sighing heavily. "Do you have any more customers today?"

"No."

"Good. This boy who slipped you the GHB, does he have anything against you?"

"We never had any real tension. He's just your average high school asshole. He was gunning for Jemma. I don't even wanna think about what he would've done if she drank that crap. Better me than her."

Dad let his head fall back as if looking for strength from heaven. "Jesus." He stood, hands on his hips. "I want you to go straight home now and stay there. If you have any homework, do it. I'll be home in about an hour. I'll make dinner, you'll eat, and then I want you in your room."

"What, you're grounding me?"

"I want you to get some rest. I told Mrs. Ghoudry you're gonna miss your morning classes tomorrow. I made an appointment for you with Dr. Durwin so she can make sure that GHB didn't do any lasting damage."

With my pointer fingers, I turned up the corners of my mouth in a mechanical smile. "Once more with feeling, I am okay."

"I want the doc to tell me that. Now get outta here."

I got up and made it halfway to the door before I stopped. "Dad?"

"Yeah?"

I turned back to him. "You're not gonna make a big thing outta this, are you?"

"I don't know what I'm gonna do until the police finish investigating this mess."

"Are you gonna tell Mom?" *Please, please don't.*

He didn't even take a moment in answering. "Not while she's on the road. I don't want her to worry."

Whew! Okay, cool. One freaked out parent at a time, thank you very much. "I'll see ya when you get home."

Chapter Sixteen

*WHATEVER OUR SOULS are made of, his and mine are the
same.*

That quote ran on a loop in my mind as Dad drove us from
the Murphrees Medical Arts Center the next day. He dropped me
at home to retrieve my bike. The quote was still with me when I
arrived at MemTech's student parking lot just as the bell rang end-
ing third period. When I'd gotten assigned *Wuthering Heights* last
year by my Classic Lit teacher, I seriously wondered what the man
had been thinking. I mean, how exactly was a Black teen guy living
in twenty-first-century Midtown Memphis supposed to relate to a
novel written by a nineteenth-century white Englishwoman? This
was despite the fact of its possibly Black protagonist, Heathcliff.

I couldn't remember which character spoke the line, but it
resonated with me now. Took a year but, lo and behold! I started
thinking of Dalvin while Dr. Durwin and her staff did their poking
and prodding. Our friendship had grown stronger over the years,

but in a single weekend, my feelings for the guy had jumped off the charts. I thought of him often. I wanted to be with him, couldn't wait to kiss him again. This was starting to worry me for a variety of reasons.

Was this just super sexual attraction, or was I on my way to falling? Was Dalvin falling too? In our years-long friendship, why had this only happened in the last few months of our senior year? The colleges Dalvin had been accepted to were all out of state. Come fall, he'd be gone. Meanwhile, I wasn't sure if my parents were gonna let me go out of state or make me attend a local college until I turned eighteen. And that was assuming I ever actually figured out what I wanted to study. So where was this thing with Dal even going? He was confident, supportive, focused, and artistic. Didn't he deserve a guy who brought as much to the table as he did?

These thoughts were so thick in my mind I barely noticed as I stepped through the school doors into the main hall. Kids were streaming every which way, chattering, laughing, shouting as they changed classes. Wading into all this with a clouded head was not unlike riding a bike blindfolded into traffic. My brain cleared instantly when someone bumped my shoulder, or maybe vice versa.

My fellow bumper was also guilty of distracted walking. The book his nose had been stuck in hit the floor with a slap. He was a skinny Black dude in blue jeans and a great, fashionable green-and-black striped sweater. I didn't know him; he was maybe a tenth grader.

"Dang, fool," he growled as he reached down to retrieve his novel. "Can you see?" He looked up—*way* up—at me, and his mouth dropped open. "Yow. My bad, man!"

Ten pounds underweight (per Dr. Durwin), and I was still intimidating. Whatever. I walked around the skinny dude and went on my way, heading for my locker.

I really wasn't feeling school right now.

"Anderson!"

Oh, now what?

Ollie came storming up as I turned to him. He looked more frazzled than usual, with actual circles under his eyes, which made his raging peepers seem as wide and white as dinner plates.

"What the hell?" he said. "You weren't in geology this morning."

"Yeah. I was in my doctor's office. Couldn't do the whole two-places-at-once thing."

"I've been trying since last night, and I can't get in touch with Drake. What's going on with him?"

"Well, he got suspended—"

"I know that! Why the hell won't he answer his phone?"

"Why are you asking me?"

Ollie sucked in a breath and made a fist. The fist shook. I got the impression he was trying not to punch me in the face. "Because you're friends with the guy." Dude was gritting his teeth. For reals, somebody needed a deep chill.

"That doesn't make me his personal assistant."

Ollie raised both trembling fists. Yep, he seriously wanted to strangle me now. "Anderson, I swear to God, I am not in the mood. I will cut you right here."

"Sheez, Ollie. Dalvin's dad grounded him and took his phone. The dude *can't* call you back, okay?"

"Well, that's just grand! I start run-throughs with our actors tomorrow after school, and Drake's supposed to have the props ready for them. You get those props from him, Anderson. You get me those props tomorrow morning. *Are you listening to me*? Get me those props! I'm telling our faculty adviser that's your assigned job, and if I don't get my props on time, I'll be doing my fracking best to get you *and* Drake kicked out of Film Club."

He spun on his heels and marched off, the kids in the hall parting before him as if he were Moses waving a staff full of heavenly power.

"By the way, Oll," I called after him. "That doctor visit I mentioned? I'm okay, clean bill of health and everything. Thanks for your concern."

Dude didn't even bother to flip me off as he vanished into a classroom.

So not feeling school today.

If only the floor would open up and swallow me. I started down the hall again. At least I only had half a day left to endure. Oh, and then a Film Club meeting. Almost forgot about that. Should be fun.

Ahead, Jemma emerged from the stairwell with her friend and fellow swim team member Amanda Miller. They were talking, laughing, just a couple of happy kids. My smile popped on automatically. Amanda spotted me first. She was tall for a girl, almost six feet, and slender, which is probably what gave her the ability to torpedo her way through water. I'd danced with her a few times at parties, cheered her on at swim meets. We could carry on fairly interesting conversations about biking trails, rap artists, and NFL games. She waved, which drew Jemma's attention.

I waved back to Amanda. Jemma glanced at me and her smile faded.

My backpack suddenly got heavier, my shoulders hunching forward. I forced my smile to go bigger. As we drew abreast of each other, I said way too casually, "Whassup, Jemma."

"Hey, Zeno." No smile. No pat on the shoulder. No stopping for a quick chat. Just a brush-off like she would do with some rando trying to hit on her. She swept past me so fast I caught a chill all the way down my back. I turned, staring after her, hoping she would look back, give a wink, smirk, do anything to let me know we were okay.

But she just kept moving away.

Walking beside her, Amanda turned her head and gawked at me, like: *WTF?*

It was as if Jemma hated me. Why was she cutting me out of her life like this? She was stuck on this idea that somehow, she'd taken advantage of me at her party, but I sure as shit wasn't sweating her about that. I told her to just forget the whole thing, but it was as though she couldn't let it go. Why was she so determined to keep dragging this around?

Hang on a sec. Pregnant. She had to be pregnant.

Sheezus! With everything else going on, I'd almost forgotten that. And she was dealing with it all alone. No wonder she was so pissed at me.

My head felt like it would explode. I couldn't stay in this school for one more moment. I reversed course, fast-walking back down the hall and plunging right through the door into the late morning sunshine. Once outside, I broke into a run.

In the parking lot, I went straight for my bike. Someone had placed colorful stickers all over the bike and my helmet, but my brain was so frazzled I barely noticed them. After stuffing the helmet over my head, I hopped on the bike and took off like a shot.

I didn't slow down until I was four blocks away.

*

"YOU THERE. STOP."

The heavy, robotic voice was followed by the staticky *click click* of a police car PA system. Since I was rolling down the street on a bike, I paid no attention to it, my thoughts focused on other things. I mean, I'd never heard of police pulling over a bicycle. When the white, blue, and yellow Memphis police car swung sharply to the curb ahead of me, I braked to a halt, my head snapping up. The fog in my brain cleared instantly.

The cop who climbed out of the driver's seat was Black, in his midthirties, with a thick build filling out his dark blue uniform. His holstered stainless steel, black-finish service weapon rested firmly on one hip while a clunky-looking yellow taser rode on the other. Before exiting the car, he'd apparently grabbed a police baton, which he slid into a slot or something on his thick brown holster. I gulped, almost choking. This two-legged armory came directly toward me, his face ten shades of grim.

Okay. This had to be more fallout from that GHB crap. Wonderful.

The cop got right up in my face. That made me pull back. He had an inch or so on me, which made him distinctly *tall*. Despite his ferocious expression, the cop spoke with a light, casual voice. "What're you up to?"

"I'm just...riding my bike. Sir."

"What's your name?"

"Zeno."

He made a face. "Zeno?"

"Zeno Anderson. Sir."

The cop curled his lip just the tiniest bit. "Well, what the fuck kinda name is Zeno?"

"'Zeno' is Greek. It means 'gift from Zeus.' It was my great grandfather's name. Now it's mine."

The cop shook his head. What the hell? Was he disputing everything I'd just told him? This obviously had nothing to do with the lady detective's investigation of Richie's love potion. The cop looked me over with a sneer, as if I smelled rotten. He studied my helmet for a long moment and then made eye contact with me again.

"Okay, Zeno, am I supposed to hug you or kiss you?"

I pulled back even more, feeling completely stunned, and gasped, "*What*?"

He reached up and jabbed his finger at my helmet. "I'm just trying to figure out these fucking stickers on your head."

I pulled the helmet off to see what the hell he was talking about. Four big stickers had been pasted there, each bearing the colors of the trans flag, strips of blue, a strip of white, and strips of pink. They read, "Hug a trans girl. Kiss a trans guy." I looked down at my bike and saw the same stickers were stuck on its frame.

Oh. Right. This was Trans Awareness Day at MemTech. I just had to explain that to the cop.

He didn't give me the chance. "So, what are you, Zeno? A trans guy or a trans girl?" He laughed and shook his head again. "That shit always confuses me."

"I'm not trans—"

"Oh, you're some kinda he-she person, aren't ya? Flashing all these rainbow colors, you've got to be some part of that L, G, P, and Q party, right?"

Right. "Officer, why did you stop me?"

"Wait. You're not going to answer me? I thought you were out and proud."

Don't you have something better to do? A life to protect and serve?

"Please, just tell me why you stopped me. Did I do something wrong?"

The smirk vanished from the cop's face, and somewhere deep in my head I went, *Uh-oh.* "Show me some ID," he snapped.

"My ID's in my wallet, and my wallet's in my back pocket. Sir. Is it okay if I take out my wallet?"

"Yeah, yeah. Hurry it up."

I held my left hand out in front of me while reaching very slowly to my back pocket. I carefully held the wallet up with my thumb and forefinger.

"Stop stalling," the cop said. "Take out the ID. Show it to me."

I opened the wallet, pulled out my MemTech ID, and handed it to the officer.

He studied the ID for a moment, frowning. "What the hell's this?"

"My student ID card."

"I'm not asking for this crap. Where's your state-issued ID?"

"I don't have anything like that."

"You don't have a driver's license?"

"No, sir. I haven't taken any kinda driver's training, so I don't even have a learner's permit."

"How old are you?"

"Sixteen, sir."

"Bullshit. You're as tall as I am."

Okay. I didn't exactly know how I was supposed to respond to that.

The cop studied my face for a long moment. My left eye twitched.

"Just where are you coming from, fella?"

Now that he knew my age—even if he didn't quite believe it—and the school I attended, the officer had me dead to rights on truancy. "I was in my doctor's office this morning. My dad wanted to make sure I'm not sick."

I felt myself tensing for the expected grilling as to why, having finished at the doctor's office, I wasn't in school at this moment. The cop went in a totally different direction.

"Get off the bike," he said. "Put down the helmet."

I didn't hesitate, immediately dropping the helmet along with my wallet, putting down the kickstand and climbing off my bike in slow, measured moves. As I did so, I checked out the badge on the cop's uniform and memorized the number: 223.

"You got any drugs on you, Zeno? Any weapons?"

"No." The question electrified the hair on the back of my neck so badly I wanted to scratch my scalp. I didn't so much as twitch a finger though. What the hell was this guy fishing for?

"So, if I search you, I'm not gonna find anything that'll land you in jail?"

"I don't have any drugs or guns."

"Is it okay if I look in your backpack?"

"Yeah. Sure." Anything to get this over and done. I slipped the backpack off my shoulder and handed it to him.

The cop unzipped the top of my backpack, flipped it, and then I heard the thuds as my books fell to the ground. He flipped through the books. He pawed through every compartment and pocket on the backpack. Then, he casually tossed the backpack and my school ID at my feet. Just to be thorough in his assholiness, he yanked up my helmet, giving it a once-over before throwing it down, and poked around my bike, twisting and shaking various parts as if he expected to find a hidden panel.

Finally, he looked at me once more. The smirk was back. "So, you're really not going to tell me what you are, fella? You don't want me to know where you stand with the L, G, Ps and Qs? Come on. Aren't you people supposed to be out and proud?"

I lowered my head and said nothing. Not because I was ashamed but because I was shaking all over from a mix of emotions I couldn't even identify. For what seemed a very long while, there was silence between us.

"Okay, Zeno Anderson," the cop said cheerfully. "We're done here. You have a nice day now."

He strolled back to his car, got in, and drove off. Jaw clenched, I bent down to gather my stuff. It took several minutes to get everything put back, slip the backpack on my shoulder, and put on my helmet. I climbed on my bike.

And then my eyes burned, my vision blurring. It was another minute before the tears stopped, and I was able to ride on.

Chapter Seventeen

DALVIN LIVED TWO miles east of MemTech in the historic Central Gardens section of the city. And by historic, I mean it's on the National Registry of Historic Places (according to the big plaque mounted on a brick wall at the neighborhood's entrance). The imposing houses there had been mostly built in the early 1900s, and towering trees, at least a century old, lined the streets. Being the middle of a school and work day, there weren't a whole lot of people around; the ones I saw puttering here and there were elderly and white. They didn't pay a lick of attention to me as I wheeled along the street. I wouldn't have had it any other way.

Dalvin lived on a nice corner lot in a grand old stone-and-stucco Craftsman house in tones of brown and white. Maybe a half dozen trees of varying heights surrounded it. Soft breezes swam through the treetops, making the branches wave languidly and the leaves whisper a welcoming hello. Something about this place was very calming and...well, homey. I strode along the walkway, rolling my bike beside me with the helmet dangling from my handlebars, heading for the front door.

"Hey. You came."

I jumped a mile at the out-of-nowhere voice, stumbling over my big blue kicks. I did a quick look around, first to make sure there were no witnesses to my embarrassing shuffle (there weren't), and second to see who had scared the shit out of me in the first place. No sign of the speaker. Until, that is, he spoke again.

"You look good, Z."

Got it that time. The voice came from the big, dark green, supersized-leaf magnolia tree on the right side of the lawn. Beneath its mountainous canopy lay a scattered pile of snipped baby branches. And a ladder leaned against the trunk. A pair of brown steel-toed boots appeared, thumping down the rungs of the ladder, followed by blue-jean-covered legs, a brown jersey with cutout sleeves, and finally, Dalvin stood there with his big shoulders and awesome cheekbones, smiling across the lawn at me.

The only thing keeping me from rushing over to grab him was the humongous, formidable pair of lopping shears dangling from his left hand.

I took a breath instead. "Hey, Dal. You look dirty. I mean that in a hot way."

Yeah, my friend definitely had the whole hotness thing going strong. He *was* a mess though, with twigs and a leaf stuck in his frohawk, sticky yellow streaks (tree sap?) across the front of his jersey, and gray flecks of bark caught in the frayed knees of his jeans. His laugh was as warm and easy as his big brown eyes.

"I promise I won't dirty you up, man. Come on in."

Rolling my bike beside me, I followed him along a cobblestone driveway that led into the backyard. He carried the shears over his left shoulder, rifle-style.

"How long has your family lived here?" I asked.

"We moved here when I was thirteen," he answered. "My dad always wanted a house in Central Gardens, and he pounced as soon as one went up for sale."

"Nice neighborhood."

"Your neighborhood's nice. This one can be a pain. Our association is serious about trees. They tell you what kind of tree you can plant and where you can plant it in your yard. They even give the trees checkups to make sure they're healthy. That's why my dad keeps our trees pruned so they'll grow strong and pretty."

"Okay. I got a headache just listening to that."

Another wonderful laugh. "Welcome to Dalvin World. You cut class to come here?"

"Sorta. I had to go to my doctor this morning. She gave me a statement to cover my absence. I got to school in time for fourth period, but I figured I'd skip that and lunch and turn in my statement when I go back for fifth."

"Well. That makes me feel special."

"Dude, you *are* special." Saying it set my face tingling.

A few feet ahead of me, Dalvin abruptly stopped. I stopped too. His loose jeans sagged a bit. In the space between the top of them and the bottom of his jersey, a strip of black-and-white checked boxers was visible. Wow. Nice. Good to know we were both boxer dudes.

But I digress. Dalvin stopped. I stopped. He reached back, holding out his hand to me. I hesitated only a second or two, long enough to see that we were between the house and a wooden privacy fence. A long gate stretched across the driveway ahead of us, and when I glanced back, my view of the street was cut off by the corner of the house. I realized I wanted to make sure Dalvin was comfortable. But then, he had to be, or he wouldn't have reached out. Maybe I was the one who was uneasy.

That whole thing with the cop was still eating at me.

I leaned my bike against the wall of the house, put my helmet on the seat, and took Dalvin's hand. It was sticky with sap, in which little bits of bark were stuck.

I didn't mind one bit.

I'd watched a few porn videos with Marvus who, unlike me, didn't worry about what someone might stumble across in his phone's search history—even if it's wiped. Nothing I saw in those videos excited me the way holding hands with this sweaty, grungy guy did. There was something electrifying about the moment. As we resumed walking, Dalvin's face was calm, peaceful, as if everything was the way he wanted it to be.

At the gate, he put down the lopping shears instead of releasing my hand. He pulled a little device from his pocket that looked like a key fob and thumbed one of its buttons. The gate slowly swung inward. He picked up the shears and towed me into the detached garage at the end of the driveway.

He slipped the shears into a rack on the wall. "You said something about going to the doctor." He bit his lip, making the angles of his cheeks even sharper. "Are you okay?"

"Mrs. Ghoudry told my dad about the GHB thing."

He gave a crooked smile. "Oh. That must've gone over well."

"The man wanted me to see the doctor to make sure I'm not poisoned or anything. And the doc said I'm fine—"

"Glad to hear that."

"But get this. The doc says I'm underweight. Can you believe that? My too-tall ass is underweight?" I laughed. He didn't. "What?"

"You have lost weight," Dalvin said. "Since August. I noticed but didn't say anything. I thought you were going for lean mean muscle machine or something."

"Nah. There's so much I have to do every day, keeping up with school, my job, and all that. You know how it is. Sometimes, I forget to eat."

"Not good, Z."

"Tell me about it. This is one more thing my dad is stressing about. I hope he doesn't tell my mom. Between the two of them, they can lay down a guilt trip strong enough to make a grown man cry. So you know what they can do to me. And all over nothing."

Dalvin took my other hand, smirking. "Have you had anything to eat today?"

"Uh...no."

He threw me side-eye.

"Come on, Dal! I woke up late. I didn't have time to grab a bite. I barely had time to jump in the shower and throw on some clothes."

"Okay. I've done enough pruning today. Now I gotta fatten up my skinny boy."

*

BRILLIANTLY WHITE CABINETS with black granite countertops dominated the sprawling kitchen. A butcher block island stood between the 50s-style white stove and white fridge, and over it hung a black metal rack from which an array of copper pots and pans dangled. A huge glass-top table with a white metal base and four old timey–looking black metal chairs sat off to one side before a row of circular windows. The place was retro and modern at the same time.

"Nice," I said, taking it all in. "Stylish and functional. Totally different from my kitchen, but just as homey. I like this."

"Is this what happens when you're hungry? You go all

Martha Stewart?" Dalvin brushed his fingers against mine. "I got sap all over your hands. You can wash up over there at the sink. I'm gonna grab a quick shower, and then I'll get us some lunch."

"Cool—oh, wait, Dalvin. Those props for Film Club, are they by any chance ready to go?"

"Not yet. My pops is really piling on the punishment chores."

"I hate to add to the pressure, but is there any way you can finish them today? I'll be glad to help. If you can't, it's fine—"

"Hold up." He frowned at me. "Z, why are you stressing about those stupid props?"

"Ollie freaked when he couldn't get in touch with you. He wants me to bring the props to him tomorrow morning. He did that manic burn thing with his eyes. You know how that scares me. If I don't bring him those props, I think I might get cut." I didn't mention the part where Dalvin and I could possibly get kicked out of Film Club.

"Oliver Gates can kiss my natural ass. I told him I'd get the props ready for the first run-through, and I will. So don't sweat it. I got this, babe."

Oh my God. Did I really hear that? For a moment, I couldn't breathe. "You...called me babe?"

Dalvin just smiled. "It felt right."

And now, I was smiling through the heat in my face. "Make it a quick shower. Suddenly I'm hungry."

*

HE WAS BACK in fifteen minutes, barefoot, wearing a black Marvel T-shirt and blue jeans. The second he stepped into the kitchen, I did what I most wanted. I grabbed on and kissed him. He locked arms around me, kissing back as if the fate of the world depended on it. We tussled like a couple of grizzlies fighting over territory.

After about a minute, Dalvin pulled away. "Okay, wow. Not that I ain't enjoying this, babe, but didn't we agree you need food?"

Even my eyes felt hot as I gazed him down. "Damn the food. I just want to keep doing what we were doing."

He grabbed my wrists and carefully peeled my arms from around him. "Well, unfortunately, there's not a whole lot of time here. We gotta get you back to school for fifth period, and you need some food in you before you go. So, get your overheated self to the table and have a sit down."

I sat at the table. Dalvin gathered the things he needed to prepare lunch: a canister filled with different types of bread, shaved ham, and a block of cheese.

As he got to work firing up the stove's griddle and slicing and dicing, he said, "You like apples, right?"

"I like apples. Throw some melted caramel on 'em, and I'm in love."

Without missing a beat, Dalvin reached out and snagged an apple from the fruit bowl on the counter.

I got those warm tingles again, so strong I leaned over, squeezing my hands between my knees in a kind of self-hug. The urge to be closer to Dalvin swelled through me, a kind of persistent tugging at my brain and my heart. "So. You've dated guys before?"

"Nope," he replied. "I've never been on a date, period. You'll be my first, and I'm glad."

"Aw. I'm glad too. So you haven't dated; you haven't had sex either, huh?" My hand flew up like a startled bird and slapped over my mouth. "Oh my God," I groaned through my fingers. "Did I just say that? Please forget I said that."

Dalvin looked over his shoulder, grinning at me. "You're so cute when you hyperventilate like that, dude. It's cool, what you said. The answer's no, I haven't had sex. I think I told you when we had that sleepover."

"So...if we ever have sex, I'll be your first."

His expression shifted, becoming completely serious. "I'd be glad for that."

Something hung in the air then, heavy and magnetic. Everything in me was racing, except my lungs. I stopped breathing. My fingers twitched. I felt excited and scared, as if I were watching a collision about to happen.

How could I be sitting there, all happy and excited, when Jemma was going through what could possibly be the worst time of her life? How could I not have her back, especially when I put her in that worst time of her life? The thoughts zoned me out. As I sat at that table, the smile slowly began to freeze on my face.

Dalvin broke the spell. He sort of shrugged and, as he turned back to his lunch making, said, "By the way, I like the stickers on your bike and helmet."

I lowered my head and crossed my arms over my chest.

"Don't worry. Angie and the rest of the cheerleaders are passing them around for Trans Awareness Day. They peel right off, easy."

Whether or not the stickers were hard to remove wasn't even a concern for me.

After another minute of silence, Dalvin said, "Zeno?"

"Yeah?" I didn't raise my head.

"What's wrong?"

"Nothing."

"No, it's something. You shut down on me."

"I'm okay, Dal."

"I know you, man. I know your moods. Two minutes ago, you were happy. Now you look like you've been whipped. Come on, talk to me. Did I do something…or say something you didn't like?"

I shook my head.

"You do this a lot lately. Turn yourself off. I don't want to push when that happens, so usually I just change the subject, and after a while, you come back. I'm not gonna push you now, but I'm here. I'm here if you wanna talk."

I sighed. Dalvin had always been attractive to me, but now, he was beautiful in new and different ways. I so wanted to be closer to this guy. That wouldn't happen if I didn't open up to him.

I raised my head. "A cop stopped me on my way here."

Dalvin dropped the knife he was using. "Jesus. Zeno, are you okay?"

"He didn't hurt me. He just treated me like shit."

"Tell me what happened."

"I was riding down Peabody in the bike lane. This cop pulled me over outta nowhere. He came down on me about the stickers. He thought I was trans and wanted to make me feel bad for it."

Dalvin rolled his eyes. "He was being an asshole when he could've been doing something useful with his time."

"Exactly."

"Shit." He started dicing again. "Lots of people out there like that cop. We go to school with some of them."

"He threw my stuff on the ground. I just stood there and let him do it. He wanted me to feel like dirt, and I didn't fucking do anything—"

"Hey, stop." Dalvin put down the knife and crossed to the table. "The guy was a policeman. What were you supposed to do? Punch him out? That would've given him exactly what he wanted, and your ass would be in jail. But you're here, and you're okay. That's a win."

"It doesn't feel like one."

"Did you get the cop's name?"

"No. I got his badge number."

"You could still file a complaint with the police department."

"Do you really think somebody would actually read my complaint? Do you really think that cop would even get a slap on the wrist? Nobody's gonna give a shit. And I'm not gonna tell my folks. My dad's freaked out enough about the GHB thing."

Dalvin moved behind my chair and looped an arm around my chest, his hand cupping my shoulder. "Then maybe you fight back another day, in some other way. Just tell me one thing. Did the cop make you *feel* like dirt?"

"Hell no. He fucking pissed me off!"

He hugged me tightly from behind. "That's the important thing. You didn't let him break you, so you won. You won, man."

My friend. What would I do without him? Things were better than ever between us, and also very new. What were we becoming? I took his hand and kissed it. The trembles went through me again. I sucked in a breath, squeezed Dalvin's hand, and held on until the shivers stopped.

Ah. Better, for now anyway. "Thanks, Dalvin." Waggling my eyebrows, I smiled at the big-hearted guy who still cuddled me. "Now feed me, boy."

*

WE ATE SANDWICHES: ribbons of sweet Virginia ham piled with spicy mayo beneath thin slices of gouda cheese and thick slices of crunchy Fuji apples on buttery homemade croissants, all grilled to perfection. I never would have thought of putting apple slices on bread, but each bite was like a taste of heaven.

"Dude, this is amazing," I gushed between clenched teeth, trying to keep a half-chewed mouthful hidden. "What in the world made you put apples in a sandwich?"

"You like apples," he said with this glint in his eyes.

We sat side by side at the table so we could watch *Justice League: Crisis on Two Earths* on my cell phone. Neither of us had ever read the comics, but we were heavily into the animated DC superhero movies. By now, Dalvin and I had watched those movies so many times on our phones that we could practically recite the dialogue with the characters.

"Pssh!" I snorted, watching as Batman confronted Superwoman, who casually broke one of his ribs.

"Still not a Bat fan, huh?"

"He's weak compared to everybody else, a frickin' ordinary man in a costume. The only thing he brings to a fight is a bunch of fancy gadgets, and he wouldn't have those if he wasn't rich. I just don't get why he's one of your favorite characters."

"He's badass."

"He's nothing, and this movie proves it. He gets his ass kicked by just about every supervillain who comes at him."

"But in the end, he saves everybody in the multiverse. Not Superman. Not Wonder Woman. Not Flash. *Batman.*"

"Only because..."

Dalvin waited, smiling. "Only because what?"

"Well, because he was able to outthink Owlman, an opponent who was just as smart and many times deadlier than he was, as well as totally insane. And he always knew he could do it. Which, admittedly, is pretty impressive." I mumbled all this to Dalvin.

"See, that's the thing, Z. Batman is badass because he believes he's badass."

"Okay, okay, okay. I'm gonna eat my sandwich now. Is that all right?"

"Yeah. Just make sure you finish *all* that crow, dude."

"I hate you."

We laughed, and just like that, everything was better. It didn't take kissing or touching to get me there. Hanging with Dalvin was enough. I still didn't understand exactly how we'd reached this point.

But it was a damned good place to be.

Chapter Eighteen

THE NEXT FEW days were mostly blurred in my mind. A few incidents stood out involving my steadily collapsing relationship with Jemma. At school, she'd greet me with a generic, no-smile "Hey." Then she'd move on before I could do something radical like start a conversation with her. She ignored my texts, except for the one I sent trying to confirm the date and time for her dance recital. Her response to that was quick and to the point.

You don't have to come. Forget I asked.

Ouch.

I wasn't sure what to do. It didn't feel right to just come out and ask her about the pregnancy thing. I was trying to give her space and let her bring it up when she was ready. Also, I didn't want to go to Mom and Dad until Jemma confirmed it.

Dad broke down and told Mom all about the GHB thing. Because why not? I spent the longest half hour of my life on the phone with her, answering the same questions everybody else had already asked me about that stupid incident. Jeez. The whole world wanted to make a big fat nothing into something.

There was also my encounter with Ollie the morning after my lunch with Dalvin. I spotted Oll in the main hall, huddled in front of his locker as he struggled to pull a book from his backpack. He was muttering to himself as I walked up, so I stood next to the guy and waited for him to finish his conversation, which only seemed polite.

After about thirty seconds, Ollie whipped his head in my direction and snarled, "Anderson, why are you in my face?"

"Hey, top of the morning to you too." Having come to school sans the props Oll so nicely asked me to bring, I didn't want the guy pulling a Ninja on me. I figured I'd better explain myself first. "So. About those props—"

Ollie sighed so hard I half expected blazing sulfur to shoot from his nostrils. "You lit a fire under Drake and got him to have his mom drop off my props for me this morning. Everything's still on schedule. Great. You expect me to thank you for that?" He looked down his nose at me as he shoved a book into his locker. "Stand right there and wait for it."

He slammed his locker shut and almost hit me in the face as he flung his backpack over his shoulder. Then he spun on his heels and marched off down the hall. I smiled.

Dalvin came through. Of course, he did.

I thought about my friend a lot, especially at night, picturing him lying in his bed with nothing on but a pair of shorts. I wanted to see him again or at least talk to him. But Dalvin was on lockdown for the rest of the week.

Not seeing him made Friday night that much worse.

Even though Dalvin wouldn't be on the field or anywhere near the stadium, I went to the playoff game. Kippy, one half of the Film Club's resident acting troupe, got stood up by his girl-friend and didn't want to go alone. I only had one car wash appointment that afternoon and nothing to do afterward, so I volunteered my company. It was all supposed to be no big deal, and it kinda wasn't.

Except MemTech lost 21 to 3.

*

MOM MADE IT home late Friday night after I'd gone to bed. When I strolled into the kitchen Saturday morning in my boxers and T-shirt, she was there, standing at the sink, holding a frying pan in her hand.

"Morning, Mom."

"Hi, Zeno. How are you this morning?"

"Thirsty." I went to the fridge and grabbed a pint-sized carton of OJ. Dad bought the pints for me because I had a tendency to chug directly from the familial gallon-sized jugs, which he considered gross for some reason.

As I swigged my juice, Mom stood there staring at the frying pan in her hand, her thoughts obviously elsewhere. I walked over next to her.

"Are you sure you know what to do with that thing?" I asked, pointing at the pan.

Mom gave me evil eye. "Your dad may do most of the cooking, but he's at the shop right now. If you're expecting someone to make your bacon and egg breakfast, you're looking at your only chance. So, I'd drop the jokes if I were you, smart boy."

"Okay. Point taken. Jokes dropped." I polished off the juice carton. "What's Dad doing at the shop? Today's his day off."

"His foreman called in sick this morning. Your dad has to open up the shop."

"Oh. That sucks. I know how much you guys look forward to your time together."

"He said he'll be back by noon." Mom's evil eye had turned into an inspection as she leaned in on me, squinting. She used to do this when I was little, checking to make sure I wasn't dirty behind the neck and ears or something.

It was freaking me out. "Mom, I just rolled outta bed, okay. I only wanted to grab some juice. I'm gonna jump in the shower before I come to breakfast, I swear."

She ignored every word I said, her squint still trained on my neck. "Is that a bruise under your ear? Dr. Durwin said she didn't find any—"

"Oh my gosh!" I threw up my hands. "Seriously, Mom? You're checking me for *hickeys*?"

"I'm concerned about what happened to you. I'm your mother. Don't I get to be concerned?"

Oh. My. God. I slapped a hand over my eyes. "Okay. Mother dear, the party was over a week ago. Any hickeys I got there would be long gone. If I have hickeys now, I got 'em *after* the party—"

Shit. Did I actually say that part out loud? I looked at Mom just in time to see her eyebrows go up. Way up.

"Zeno. Do you have a girlfriend?"

"Uhmm..."

She put down the frying pan and turned to face me. "Are you having sex?"

"No! Ha ha. Jeez, Mom."

Mom started to speak again and shut her mouth for a second. "Come over here. Let's sit down."

We sat across from each other at the table. I crushed the empty juice carton in my fist, squeezing it over and over as if it were dough. Maybe I could fake a fainting spell.

"Hon," Mom said with her patented little all-knowing smile, which was supposed to relax me. It didn't. "You don't have to feel ashamed or worried. I'm not angry that you're having sex—"

"Except I'm not having sex."

"Sex includes a lot more than intercourse. Oral is still—"

"I know, Mom. Oral is sex. A hand job is sex. I remember everything you and Dad told me about the birds and bees, and I promise you, I haven't had any variety of sex."

Well, except for that weird thing between Jem and me at her party. And that would definitely count, especially if a grandchild pops out of it for Mom and Dad.

"I know you've been over this a dozen times with the police detective, your dad, and me. But think. Do you recall anything, any detail, about what happened to you after you were drugged? Did someone touch you? Was there a condom involved?"

"Everything after the GHB and until I woke up is one big blank, so I don't know. But I do know a condom reduces my risk of disease and daddyhood, and I will use one whenever I decide to have sex. Okay?" I hated lying to her, but I didn't want to say anything about Jem and me yet. I didn't know for sure if my friend was pregnant. I also had no idea if Jemma had talked with her mom and dad about this, and I didn't want Mom to blindside her.

"Good enough." Mom was hunched over the table, propped on her elbows. She sat back suddenly, the lines in her forehead vanishing. "So. Do you have someone special now?"

"Yeah."

She waited a second or two. "You're gonna make me pull teeth, I see. Does the special someone go to your school?"

I nodded. "We met freshman year."

"Ah. Do your dad and I know this girl?"

"Uh...kinda sorta," I said, and when Mom opened her mouth,

I cut her off before she went there. "No, it's not Jemma."

"Well, bring her over sometime, whenever you're ready. We'd certainly like to get to know her."

"Yeah, sure." God. Should I even do this right now? "Uh, Mom?"

"Yes, sweetie?"

"Would it bother you if this special someone...isn't a she?"

The lines came back to Mom's forehead. For a moment, she looked totally confused. Then her eyes flashed. "Are you saying you're gay?"

"Not gay. I'm into girls, and I'm into guys. That's more like, bi. Whatever."

"Ah."

She went quiet on me, snuggled against the backrest of the chair, fingers tapping slowly on the table. I wasn't sure how to take her silence. Was she hurt? Was she pissed at me? Was she already beginning to pass judgment?

"His name is Dalvin Drake," I blurted. "We're both in Film Club. He's great with a camera, good enough to be a pro photographer. And oh my gosh, he makes the most amazing sandwiches and breads. He's on the football team—"

"Yes, I know. I've seen his picture in the Sports section. And your father and I met him earlier, remember? Isn't he also the boy who punched out—"

"Mom. He's a really nice guy. And smart. He's already been accepted into three good universities but he's holding out for his dream school, Howard. He helps his mom with her side job as a baker. That's where he learned how to make these so-freaking-delicious muffins and—"

Mom held up both hands. "Zeno, you're babbling."

"Well, that's because you're not really saying anything. I

want this to be okay. Are you okay? You look spooked."

"I wouldn't say 'spooked.' I am surprised."

"Okay. I get it. You expected straight."

"I assumed it, yes."

Great. I should've kept my big mouth shut.

Mom sighed. "Please don't look so horrified. I know assuming things about you doesn't leave room for who you actually are. Is this something you just figured out about yourself?"

"I noticed the attraction to guys about three, maybe four years ago, but I kinda ignored it and just focused on the feelings I had for girls. For a long time, I didn't really know how to deal with my feelings for boys."

"Why didn't you ask your dad or me?" Her thin, arched eyebrows tightened into a frown again. "We want you to feel that you can talk to us about anything."

I squeezed the smashed-up carton so hard I thought it would ooze out of my fist like pulp. "I didn't know how to even tell you guys. I figured if I told you, you'd just be disappointed. And that's exactly the way you're looking at me now." My heart sank in my chest like a clump of poorly chewed food. "Come on. Please. I'm the same Zeno Anderson I've always been."

"Listen to me," Mom said, leaning forward in her seat. "I'm not disappointed. Okay? But I am worried. That's what you're seeing in my face. You already have one strike against you being Black in this society. Being anything other than straight is another strike. That's not to say you're automatically a victim or you can't be successful and happy in your life, but it's a fact that you're going to face obstacles a heterosexual white man will never see. I want to be sure you're prepared to deal with those obstacles."

"Yeah. I get that." My hands shook.

"I don't mean to scare you, honey. But you're about to

become an adult, and once you step through that door, there's no turning back. You have to be ready to face the real world as it is. Everything you're doing now, from keeping up your grades to your car wash job, is preparing you to make that step. The decisions you make now, about things like college and your career, will set the course for your life. And the kind of person you are also determines what kind of life you have. Being who you are will limit you only if you allow it."

"So...you're not angry or anything that I'm bisexual?"

"How do you feel about being bisexual?"

"Well...I'm okay with it. It's me."

Mom reached over and took my hand. "Then I'm okay with it too."

"You think Dad will be cool with this? And will you tell him?"

"You should tell him yourself, baby boy. You two need to talk this out between you. But your dad and I will always love you. We just don't want your life to be harder than it has to be. We want you to be safe and happy."

"Mom, I *am* happy. Dalvin makes me so damn happy."

She lifted my hand and kissed my wrist. "I'm glad for that."

*

HEADPHONES ON, I sat on the floor, hunched against the sofa, playing a video game via the television in the den. It was maybe a quarter past noon. Despite the shouts and explosions in my ears, I heard the rattle of Dad's key in the lock. I switched off the game, shed the headphones, and made my way to the kitchen. I got there just as Dad tossed his keys on the table and grabbed a can of soda from the fridge.

"Hey, man," he said when he saw me walk in.

"Hey, Dad."

"Where's your mom?"

"She's taking a bath."

Dad popped the tab on his soda. "I'm taking her out for dinner and a movie. You're on your own this afternoon."

"Dad, sit down. We gotta talk."

He'd just lifted the can, ready to take a swig, when he froze. His eyes bugged. "Dang. Am I in trouble?"

That was a perfect impression of the breathless way I always responded when Dad told me it was time for a talk. I had to laugh. "Will you just sit down, please?"

He gulped soda as he pulled out a chair. I took a seat across from him.

"Okay, son. What's on your mind?"

I'd already decided the only way to do this was to simply do it. Without preamble, I said, "Dad, I'm bisexual."

When Marvus was, like, in first grade, he had this major spider phobia. Some idiot classmate pranked him on his birthday with a daddy longlegs wrapped in a little gift box. My ninth-grade biology teacher told me daddy longlegs were more closely related to scorpions than spiders. But again, I digress. When Marvus opened the box and saw the spindly legged thing inside, his eyes popped with such terror you'd have thought he was looking at a maniac clutching a bloody knife.

That was the way Dad looked at me now.

I gave him a minute, my knee bouncing like a jackhammer under the table. "Dad. Say something."

He slammed down the soda can, sending up a volcanic spray of brown foam, got out of his chair, and came around the table in a bearlike charge. In a single breath, I simultaneously grabbed the edge of the table with both hands, braced my feet against the floor, and shut my eyes.

Then Dad was on me.

He wrapped me in the tightest hug.

Slowly, I opened one eye and then the other. *Okay. I'm still alive.* Dad tightened his arms around me even more. I patted his shoulders. My hands were shaking.

"Dad? Are you okay?"

He nodded as he finally let go and stepped back. He looked down at me. "Does your mom know?"

"I told her this morning. Why are you so scared of this?"

"I've heard the stories, Zeno. About transgender people being murdered. About gay men being beaten and all the crazy laws Republicans are passing around the country to make life as hard as they can on the LGBT crowd. When you told me about being bisexual, my mind went straight to the darkest place."

"It's not all dark. I've heard those stories, too, but I'm okay with this. I mean, I have to be. It's my life."

He smiled. "It's good to hear you say that. You know this doesn't change anything between us, right? I'm as proud of you as I ever was."

"Thanks. And Dad?"

"Yeah, son?"

"When I said it's not all dark...there's this guy."

Dad stared blankly at me for a second. "A guy?"

"I *really* like him."

Dad crossed his eyes. "Just when I'm finding my comfort zone, you smack me right out of it. Thanks a lot, son."

*

"MOM, DAD, YOU remember Dalvin."

"Hey, Mr. and Mrs. Anderson. It's a pleasure to see you again."

It was Sunday afternoon. We stood in the kitchen where my parents were tag-teaming on dinner preparations. Dalvin had texted me earlier that his dad had finally ungrounded him.

He stepped forward, extending a hand toward my mom and dad. With a smile full of teeth, Dad reached out to shake with Dalvin. Dad wore an oversized black Batman T-shirt and red baggy cargo shorts. Three inches taller, Dalvin had on starched white jeans and a blue plaid shirt. FYI, it's kinda disturbing when your teenage potential boyfriend looks more mature than your middle-aged father.

"Well, hello there, kid," Dad said, pumping Dalvin's hand like he was hoping for black gold. "I'm glad to see you again too."

Mom took her turn at shaking Dalvin's hand. "So. You're the fella taking my son out on his first date."

"Yes, ma'am." Dalvin's cheeks flashed prominently when he smiled. "I'm gonna show him a good time."

"Well, wherever you're going out there, you two ought to be safe." Dad waved his hands, the wide gesture taking in both Dalvin and me. "This is a helluva lot of testosterone packed into one spot."

"Yes sir," Dalvin said, smiling. "And this is for the two of you." He pulled his other hand from behind his back, offering up a big red tin container.

"Oh my." Mom looked surprised as she took the container. "What's this?"

"I made a batch of butterscotch cookies."

"Well, well. Zeno told us you're a marvelous baker. Thank you. I can't wait to try these."

Dad flashed his eyes at me. "I'd hang on to this one if I were you, son."

Dalvin ducked his head a little, smiling. Blushing was super cute on him.

"Can we get you anything, Dalvin?" Mom asked, placing the cookie tin on the counter. "A snack? Something to drink?"

"Some peach iced tea would be good."

"Young man, this is your lucky day. It just so happens that my baby boy makes the best peach iced tea on this earth. And he stirred up a big pitcher of it just before you got here." Mom turned toward the fridge. "Zeno, get Dalvin a glass."

But Dalvin was already opening the cabinet where we kept the glasses. He grabbed himself a goblet.

Mom and Dad looked at each other. Then they looked at me.

"Sara, honey, get the pitcher and serve Dalvin some tea," Dad said, still locking eyes with me and grinning. "Zeno, let's step out for a minute. I want to talk again about that glow you had on your face last weekend while your mom and I were at the cabin."

I clapped both hands over my face.

Chapter Nineteen

"THAT WAS STUPID of me, Z," Dalvin said as he drove away from my house. "I'm sorry. Did I get you in trouble with your dad?"

"Nah, man. You saw him smiling. He wasn't angry that I had you over. He just wanted to make sure we didn't get into any trouble."

"Trouble as in having sex?"

I pointed at Dalvin. "Exactly. I fessed up, told him we made pizza, drank tea, watched movies, played games, made out, and I had condoms, but we didn't go there."

"And he believed you?"

"It's the truth. I figured out a long time ago, if I tell my parents the truth, I usually stay on their good side."

"You tell your dad I slept over?"

"Do I look suicidal to you?"

We were heading west through Midtown. Dalvin made the turn onto I-240.

"Where are we going?" I asked.

"You'll see. Just sit back and enjoy the ride, babe."

Sunlight glittered like scattered diamonds off the windshields of passing cars. That brilliance came nowhere near the brightness in Dalvin's eyes.

"I hung out with Kippy Friday night," I said in the interest of casual conversation. "We went to the game."

"Yeah?" Dalvin's eyes seemed to cloud over, and the sudden edge to his voice was so cold I was surprised his breath didn't fog the air.

Wow. Definitely not the best topic for the moment. "Hey, I'm sorry the team got knocked outta the playoffs. I know how much the whole thing means to you—"

"It's okay, man. We don't have to talk about that."

"Yeah, no problemo. Say, you check out that crazy new horror movie on Netflix?"

Dalvin broke into a grin. "I watched it this morning as soon as I got ungrounded. That was some seriously freaky shit!"

"Hells yeah!"

For the next half hour, we stayed on the safe ground of maniac slashers and stupid teen victims.

*

FROM I-240, WE took Highway 385 east into Collierville and headed straight for the commercial district. We drove past the usual establishments you'd expect to find in such an area—several restaurants, a Target, a Petco—their parking lots packed with the cars of happy and eager customers lured out by the sunny weather.

I took it all in. "So this is Collierville."

"This your first time here?" Dalvin asked.

"Yeah. I don't have any family or friends out this way, so I guess I never had a reason to come."

"I've been this way a few times. My moms has clients here."

We turned abruptly into a strip mall. At the end of the row of stores, a sprawling brown-brick building loomed. The sign mounted along the wall above the four doors that made up the main entrance read as follows: Collierville Ice Dreams Palace.

"What's this place?" I asked as Dalvin pulled into a parking spot. The name was just a bit ambiguous.

"Come on," Dalvin said teasingly as he climbed out of the car.

We passed through the doors, and I caught a major case of what Jemma called the feels. I laughed and gagged on a sob at the same time, gawking so hard I almost tripped over my own feet. The cavernous space we'd entered was dominated at its center by a huge rink of white ice. Dozens of people flowed around the rink, some of them dancing and bopping to the music—at the moment, Maroon 5's "What Lovers Do"— playing over a kicking sound system.

"Oh my sheez," I practically yelled at Dalvin. "I can't believe you actually remembered that stupid fantasy I told you about."

"Didn't sound stupid to me. Let's get our skates."

At the kiosk next to the entrance, Dalvin told the clerk he'd reserved two pairs of skates. The clerk turned over size thirteen ice blades in exchange for our street kicks. Dalvin and I proceeded to strap on the skates on a bench near the rink. Along the long wall behind the rink, a food court included McDonald's, Pizza Hut, Popeye's, a Thai place, and even a vegan spot. Adults and kids filled the tables there, noshing away and good timing on this wonderful Sunday afternoon.

And then it hit me.

The couples I saw holding hands while skating or having lunch with their kids or just standing around together enjoying the scene...they were mostly male/male or female/female. Frozen, I looked again at a middle-aged white man hooked arm in arm with another middle-aged white man; two twenty-something white girls sneaking quick kisses on the ice; a teen Asian guy hugging another teen Asian guy from behind while placing their orders at the Baskin Robbins; and a thirty-something Latino mom couple ushering a brood of three excited little kids toward the rink.

Amazing.

"Dude," I gasped. "What is this?"

"This place is gay-owned and gay-friendly," Dalvin replied casually. "And every week they do Gay Sunday. That's what you're seeing out there."

Skates secured on his feet, Dalvin stood. He held out a hand to me, smiling that beautiful, chiseled-cheeked smile of his. "Ready to join in?"

There went a fresh round of tingles under my skin. I took his hand. Which turned out to be a *very* good thing. I hadn't been on any kind of skates in years, and it took a minute before I found my balance again. Hand in hand, we set out on the ice.

As far as I could see, we were the only Black couple in the place. Yet, I didn't feel any sense of otherness, didn't feel the need to watch the crowd for hostile faces or to pretend Dalvin was just a friend when he was way more than that. In a sea of racial diversity, I felt embraced and even celebrated. Dalvin and I were among people who were just like us.

And Dalvin? It occurred to me that maybe he wasn't as comfortable with this as I was. When I looked at him, he was gazing at me with eyes full of...adoration? Maybe that was too strong a word, but it was clear how much he liked me. There was no hesitation, no doubt, no unease on his face, just a smile as joyful as any you'd see on a kid come Christmas morning. I wanted so bad to kiss that smile but didn't want to risk taking us both down on the ice. I smiled back at him.

His big hand fit perfectly in mine.

The lights above the rink dimmed suddenly, draping the skaters in a soft blue glow that shimmered like an icy fog. Miguel's "Adorn" poured with ethereal sweetness from the sound system's speakers. We flowed across the ice, holding on to each other, lost together in the music and the glacial light, and for a while, it actually felt like it was just the two of us in that place.

And I kept thinking: *Dalvin made this happen. Dalvin did this for me.*

God. I couldn't help it. Good or bad, I really was falling in love with my friend.

*

BY FOUR O'CLOCK, we were pulling up to the curb in front of my house.

"Come on in," I said. "You're invited to dinner. We usually eat around five. You and I can play video games until then."

"Thanks. That all sounds great, but I gotta get home. I told you how big my family is on church. The only way my dad agreed to let me skip the noon service was if we all went to the evening service. Which starts at five."

"Oh." Picture a puppy locked out in the rain. That was about how I felt then.

Dalvin took my hand. "I had a great time with you today."

"I really liked being with you too. This was so special to me. Thanks."

We leaned in and kissed.

"See you at school tomorrow."

"Yeah."

I didn't want to get out of the car, but I did. I stood on the sidewalk, watching as he drove away. I kept watching even after he turned the corner and vanished.

"Hey."

I turned, still caught up in the haze of tingly feelings my boy had left rushing through me. That haze faded instantly when I saw the person standing behind me.

Marvus.

He wore a gray and yellow tracksuit, the kind of gear he favored in fall and winter. His expression was calm, casual. I automatically stuffed my hands in my pockets, hunching my shoulders like a turtle trying to draw into its shell. I didn't know what to say, couldn't even manage a hey in return.

"Was that your boyfriend?" Marvus asked, and when I scowled at that, he quickly added, "I wasn't spying or anything, man. I was coming to see you and just happened to get here when you guys pulled up."

He paused for a few moments. When I didn't speak, he said, "Can we talk?"

I played in the sandbox with this dude when we were little more than toddlers. We teased girls together at our first middle school dance. He loved astronomy, and we spent endless hours on his roof with him showing me stars and planets through his telescope. He jogged with me when I was prepping for the track and field tryouts. I was with him when he got the news that his sister lost her battle with brain cancer, and I held him while he cried.

Now, I couldn't even look him in the eye. In answer to his question, I nodded toward my house, led him to the porch, and sat on the steps. He sat beside me.

This time, Marvus didn't wait for me. "My ma told me about hiring you the other day. That pissed me off. She really wants to fix you and me, but I told her she's gotta stay out of it. We can fix this on our own. Can't we?"

I stared off at the neighbor's house across the street.

"I think we can," Marvus continued. "There's nothing even broken between us. At least that's the way I see it. Why don't you tell me how you see it?"

It was like a weight dragging on me whenever I hung around Marvus these days. He looked the same, sounded the same, even smelled the same thanks to the coconut-scented body spray he'd been using since puberty hit him. The thing between us was as monstrous as a gargoyle, and I couldn't face it. I didn't know how to explain any of this to him, so I kept silent.

Marvus scratched at his scalp, something he always did when he got frustrated...or pissed. "You know, my ma told me to give you time, give you space, and you'd come around. Well, I gave you time, and I gave you space, and you don't seem any closer to coming around than you ever did. Listen, Zeno, I miss you, man. I miss us hanging the way we used to. I want to fix this, but I can't do it by myself." He stood. "Especially when I wasn't the one who broke us in the first place."

He walked away without a backward glance.

*

AFTER DINNER, MOM and Dad retired to their room to watch a movie, and I set about cleaning the kitchen. I was loading the dishwasher when my phone pinged with a text. From Jemma. I was so shocked to get a message from her that I almost overlooked the actual content.

Have u checked out WarPage? Hope Dalvin is ok.

WarPage was the name of the MemTech football team's Tumblr page. Something about Jem's message caused fear to squeeze like a fist in my stomach. I pulled up the page and read the top two posts:

FUCK DRAKE!

Dalvin sucks shit!

It went straight downhill from there.

*

"THIS IS CRAZY! It's just not right."

"Calm down, Z."

It was after eight, and I'd finally managed to get Dalvin on FaceTime. He sat on his bed in nothing but his boxers, looking pretty cut. I was so upset I almost didn't notice how good he looked.

Almost.

Daaamn!

"I can't calm down, Dal. Seems like everybody at school is blaming you for us getting knocked out of the playoffs. How could it be your fault? You weren't there."

Dalvin sucked at his teeth, a quick click of a sound. "Yeah, that's kinda why they blame me, man."

"What happened to that 'There's no I in team' shit? You're a beast player, but still, you're just one player. You couldn't have lost that game by yourself any more than you could've won the fucking thing by yourself. Win or lose, it's a team thing."

"You know how stuff goes. People gotta have a scapegoat sometimes, and right now, that's me."

"But it's not your fault. If it's anybody's fault, it's mine."

Dalvin lifted his shoulders, extending his hands out to the side in a gesture of confusion. "Okay, babe, how is this your fault?"

"If you hadn't swung on Richie, you wouldn't have gotten suspended from the team. And you wouldn't have swung on Richie if I hadn't gotten my ass drugged at Jemma's party."

"Come on, Z. Are you serious right now? You didn't make me knuck Richie. That's all on me, and I don't want you sweating this."

"Did you read some of the crap they're saying about you?"

"No. And I don't want you reading any more of the crap, either."

"They're saying shit about you knocking Richie out."

"What kinda shit?"

"*Crazy* shit! That you're some asshole jock who punches out guys half your size. That you're trying to make up for having a little brain and a little dick by—"

"Whoa!" Dalvin snapped, waving both hands wildly in front of him. "None of that crap matters. People are only saying that because they don't know what Richie did to make me knuck his ass."

"Somebody has to stand up for you, Dalvin."

"You said it yourself, man. I'm a beast. I can take care of myself. Anyways, Coach already called me. He's having the shit taken down. It'll be gone by tomorrow. I'm good, so stop your stressin'."

He cozied up to his phone, his face filling my screen beautifully. In the process, he developed a serious set of bedroom eyes. "Now let's talk about something else. Like how cute you are."

The charm worked. The tingles started running up and down my spine again, making me wish I could teleport myself straight into Dalvin's room. I grinned, and we went happily into a flirtatious, fun conversation as if nothing serious was going on anywhere in the world. But a nagging sense of dread lingered within me that I couldn't shake. It floated beneath my smile and my sweet talk, like scum on the surface of a pond.

Chapter Twenty

MOM WAS LONG gone Monday morning, off to start her truck route, by the time Dad and I got suited up for the day. In the kitchen, I drained a bottle of water as Dad polished off a glass of cranberry juice. Such was our breakfast.

I grabbed a second bottle of water and lifted my backpack to my shoulder. "I'll catch ya at the shop, Dad."

"Hold up there," Dad said in a rush. "Where's the helmet?"

"I don't need it today. Dalvin's picking me up. He'll drop me off at the shop after school."

"Oh. Okay." Dad crossed the kitchen and put a hand on my shoulder. "I called Detective Hanson yesterday while you and Dalvin were on your date."

Sheez. "Well, that's great. What did she have to say?"

"Your urine test was negative for GHB. She pointed out that's no surprise considering it was done a couple of days after the possible exposure. A girl in the cafeteria says she heard Richard admit he dosed Jemma's cup with GHB and that he knew you accidentally drank it. But Richard denies saying it. The boys who were with him back that up, and the only other person close enough to hear what happened—Dalvin—says he doesn't remember anything about it. The detective has no proof Richard possessed GHB or hurt anybody with it. All she really has is a bunch of he said, she said, and that's not enough to file charges. So, the case is pretty much dead in the water at this point."

Yes! Now I can forget this shit ever happened. My fist was halfway up over my head before I caught the disappointed frown on Dad's face. The fist pump morphed into a woe-is-me smack to the forehead. "Wow. That sucks."

"Don't bullshit me, Zeno. You're glad to let this go. Me, I'm still pissed that this Richard kid drugged you, and the law can't do anything about it."

"I'm sorry. But seriously, it's okay."

His frown melted. The corners of his mouth barely turned up, his eyes a little heavy. He patted my shoulder.

"Go to school, kid," he said quietly as he headed for the garage. "Learn something."

*

DALVIN DROVE UP as I watched from the front steps. Right on time, I might add. He burst into the biggest grin when he saw me walking toward him. For my part, I started smiling the second the car came into view.

So damn happy. I was happier than I'd been in a long time. My big, looming graduation and half-baked career plans couldn't even move the needle on my emotional Richter scale this morning. Dalvin made that happen. He literally turned our first date into a dream come true for me. *He* was a dream come true.

"Hey, Dal." I dropped my butt into the passenger seat.

"Hey, babe." In lieu of a kiss, he took my hand and gave it a squeeze. "Gotcha something. Catch." With his other hand, he made this quick, casual flip.

I brought my free hand up, and the next thing I knew, something bounced off the side of my head and fell into my lap. "Ow!"

"Whoa!" He laughed. "Too slow. Sorry, Z." Dalvin grabbed the object and held it out to me. "I'm pretty sure you didn't have breakfast this morning. Here."

He held a cool, crisp granny smith in his palm.

"Thanks." I took it and started munching.

Dalvin pulled off, driving us toward school. "Talked to Ollie last night. He says the rehearsals have been good and thinks we can start filming next week. We should try and get our next interview out of the way before that."

"I'll see about getting an interviewee lined up. I'll let you know. Hey, Dalvin..."

"Yeah, man?"

"Why didn't you tell that detective you heard Richie admit to having GHB at Jemma's party?"

Dalvin's head tipped to the side as if he'd taken a blow to the face. He grunted. "I dunno. Richie is, or was, sort of a friend. And I don't trust the police to do the right thing. I dunno. I just went with my gut."

He let go of my hand and started rapidly patting his right thigh as he drove.

"You have any classes with Richie?"

"Yeah. Four."

Shit. "Are you okay, Dal?"

He put his right hand on the wheel, holding on tightly. "I'll get there, Z."

*

I WALKED DALVIN to his locker. His friends were happy to see him.

"Whassup, Dal."

"Hey, big guy."

"Glad you're back, man."

They clapped him on the back, high-fived him. He joked with them and laughed as he passed by. Students who weren't his friends just looked away, frowning, like they were refusing to acknowledge his existence. Or they smirked in his wake (never to his face). Whatever. The real trouble came from the jocks.

Three dudes on the basketball team cut eyes at Dalvin as if they'd spotted a child molester walking down the hall. Like they hadn't spent hours after school shooting hoops with the dude. A couple of the football players took it a step further. They casually maneuvered their big asses to block Dalvin's way, standing there like two sides of beef carrying on a conversation. At the same time, they straight stared into Dalvin's eyes, daring him to tell them to move. Dalvin just stepped around them, and we went on our way.

Dang. The basketball players I got; they were Richie's boys. But the football players were supposed to have Dalvin's back. If this was the way they were coming at Dalvin for missing a damn playoff game, what would they do if they found out about him being gay?

"Don't sweat that shit, man," I said as we moved away from the hall blockers.

"Trust, bruh. I'm not."

We made it to his locker, and he started dialing in his combination. His hand was steady, his expression casual. I stepped in close, brushing my shoulder against his, beset by this pressing urge to hold him, to comfort him.

"It's gonna be weird today," I offered.

"It's been weird for days now." He rummaged around in his locker. Lots of banging from there. Like he was excavating or doing demolition.

"Dalvin? You okay?"

"I gotta swing by the office before I go to homeroom."

"Yeah, sure. I should probably start asking around to see if I can line up that interview for us."

"Text me, let me know how you're doing. Maybe we can meet up later, and I'll help."

"Cool."

Our hands were at our sides, between our two bodies. He curled his pinky around mine. I held on for, like, a minute.

"Okay, then," I said as we stepped away from each other. "Catch ya later."

"Yeah, man."

I turned to go and wound up with Richie all in my face.

"Oh," he mumbled, pulling up short in front of me. His eyes went round. "Hey, Zeno. What's up, Dalvin."

Dead silence behind me. My mouth hung open for about fifteen seconds before I managed to say, "Uh, hey."

Richie's hair was slicked back tightly, his hands clenched into fists, his eyes skimming the space between his feet and mine. "I was coming to see Dalvin, but I'm glad you're here too, Zeno. Can I talk to you guys for a second?"

I immediately looked over my shoulder. Dalvin stared blank-eyed at Richie as if he were looking at a shrub or something. He slammed his locker shut and just stood there. So...he wasn't walking away.

I turned back to Richie. "Okay."

Dalvin stepped up beside me. Richie raised his head, looking into our faces, and his Adam's apple bobbed up and down so hard I thought he'd choke on it.

"Uh, guys, I'm sorry about the whole...drug thing." An embarrassed smile broke out on Richie's face for an instant. He looked up at the ceiling and then looked down at the floor again. "I didn't mean for... It wasn't supposed to turn into... I didn't want anybody to get hurt or anything. It was supposed to be fun, you know. But it wasn't. It turned into something stupid and awful. I get that, and I'm really sorry."

Head down, Richie waited. For what, I wasn't sure. Absolution? A smile? A friendly pat on the back? It was still kinda early for that.

There weren't that many students around yet, and the hall was quiet enough that I could hear the click of Richie's throat as he gulped.

Dalvin waited a few more seconds, letting Richie pickle in his own juices, then said, "Is that it? Is that everything you have to say to us?"

"No." Richie looked at Dalvin and then quickly turned away. "I also want to thank you, dude, for not narcing on me. I had a lot to lose if I got hit with charges. Graduation, college, all of that could be gone now. And don't worry. I told my mom I didn't want any charges pressed against you for anything. You had my back with that detective, and I appreciate that you were looking out for me."

Dalvin folded his arms across his chest. "Okay, so now what?"

Richie blinked as if surprised by the question. "I thought we... I miss hanging with you, dude. I thought..."

"What? That we'd just go back to being chill again?" Dalvin clenched his teeth so hard, the joint in his jaw popped like a finger snap. "You thought it was fuckin' *hilarious* that Zeno got blasted on that drug."

"No! I mean...I said that, but it was a joke, like. I didn't understand how bad the whole situation was until that detective came snooping around. I'm telling you, man, I didn't want Zeno to get hurt."

"It wasn't just Zeno who could've gotten seriously hurt behind that shit you pulled at the party. What about Jemma? If she *had* drunk that juice you spiked and faded out the way Zeno did, then what? They don't call that crap the date rape drug for nothing."

"I wasn't gonna rape her!"

"No? Then what was the plan? Were you gonna feel her up? Take off her clothes, snap pics of her, and post 'em all over the internet? What? Explain it to me."

"It was just supposed to be a sweet high, man. Just a little fun, you know."

"Why don't you ask Zeno how fun it was?"

"Dalvin. Come on, dude..." Richie's face sagged as if it were about to drip right off his skull. He held out his hands like a drowning man. "I fucked up, okay? I was stupid."

Dalvin sighed and moaned heavily at the same time. "It wasn't your first fuck up. It wasn't your first stupid. Richie...shit. Listen, I don't want to see you get expelled. I don't want to see you get rejected by your dream college, and I don't want to see you go to jail. But I also don't like the way you treat people. I don't like what you did to Zeno. I don't like what you tried to do with Jemma. And the more I think about it, the more I realize that I don't like *you*. You keep doing you if you want, but please don't do it anywhere around me."

Dalvin turned around and stalked off into the stairwell. That left me and Richie. And yeah, that shit was awkward. Staring after Dalvin, Richie sucked in a breath, a blustery sound as forlorn as anything I'd ever heard. When he turned to me, his eyes were watery and bright.

"Zeno, you gotta believe me. I'm sorry. I'm so sorry."

What could I do? The guy was no friend of mine. I wouldn't even consider him a casual acquaintance. Still, under the circumstances, I didn't want to leave without saying something to him.

"Hey, Richie, I'm over what you did to me. And I believe you're sorry. But I'm not the one you gotta convince."

I gave him a pat on the back before walking away.

*

AFTER HOMEROOM, I passed through the main hall on the way to my first period class. Ahead on my left, standing in front of a big-ass display case with a couple of her friends, was Jemma. She was decked out all in a white—sweater, skirt, leggings, and kicks—her hair tied back in a white scarf. She looked happy, dazzling. Hotter than ever.

The sight of her made me cringe. It had been a minute since we'd seen each other. Time enough, perhaps, for her to get over being pissed at me. Unless she was pregnant. I kept walking, kept looking at her, and as I drew abreast of her chatting little group of friends, I caught the moment Jemma's eyes shifted toward me and widened just a bit. I superprimed my smile, expecting when she fully looked at me, she'd smile back. Hell, she'd probably do that jazz hands thing she did when we hadn't seen each other for a long time, like last year when Mom, Dad, and I spent Christmas with my aunt and uncle in Chicago and were gone for almost two weeks. Yeah, she'd given me jazz hands and a smile.

Only, now she didn't. A moment after her eyes flicked toward me, they flicked away. She turned back to her girls. The smile she gave was solely for them.

I walked on, thinking I had some convincing to do of my own. The problem was Jemma and I seemed to be speaking totally different languages now. I had no idea how to make her understand how much I liked being friends with her. Maybe *that* was the problem. Maybe she wanted us to be more than friends. For a minute there, we were both kinda crushing on each other. I thought we'd gotten over that. Or was it just me who'd gotten over it? You crushed on somebody enough to give yourself to him, you wanted that to mean something to him, right? Dude couldn't even remember the whole precious thing—that's gotta hurt.

And if the dude left you pregnant...

God, Jemma hated me.

But once, not so long ago, things had been really good between us. Until the flirting started back and forth with us. Damn. Why would she ever even like me that way? She was an amazing girl. She could do *way* better than me.

Just like Dalvin was an amazing guy. And he could do a hell of a lot better than me.

I groaned a little, deep in my throat.

Sheez. You're thinking too much, fool. Get your ass into a classroom where you can turn your stupid brain off.

I doubled my pace down the hall.

Chapter Twenty-One

WE'D AGREED TO meet at the student parking lot after the final bell. Having arrived first, I leaned against the side of Dalvin's car to wait. Kids poured out of the building, streaming through the lot. They talked, laughed, and joked within their little cliques as they flowed around me. Kipper exited with his arm draped like a boa around his spunky, redheaded girlfriend's neck. They looked happy together, eyes and smiles bright. Normal kids. Good for them. Kipper didn't notice me as they moved on down to his (or her) car.

God, get me outta here.

Looked like it was gonna be a minute before Dalvin showed. I got out my phone, plugged in my headphones, and started streaming songs from my chill list. Closed my eyes and sorta lay back against the car. Disconnected my brain.

Yeah.

*

THE MUSIC CUT off abruptly for a second to alert me that I'd gotten a text. It was from Dad.

Cust just dropped off car 4 wash Where r u

I checked the time: twenty-six minutes since the final bell.

I turned off the music. Something was up with Dalvin. I stepped away from the car, eyes focused on the school exit before me. Students still filtered out, though the torrent had dwindled to a trickle now. Some small guy, obviously a freshman, eased out of the building, scanning the surrounding area with excess care. When he spotted me, his hands flew up as if I'd pulled a gun on him. Moments later, he apparently realized I wasn't the threat he was on the lookout for. He dropped his hands, scurried across the parking lot, and ran off down the street.

Then Dalvin stepped through the door, backpack on his shoulder. He saw me and smiled as easily as ever. But his shoulders were tense and his stride stiff as he came toward the car. I tensed up myself, unable to smile back at him.

"Sorry I'm late getting out here," he said right off. "Oll held me up. He wants us to scrap the interviews and come up with something else to fill out our screentime."

"Why? What's his problem now?"

"You have any luck today lining up another interview?"

"No. Everybody I asked turned me down." In fact, a couple of guys on the swim team just about cussed me the moment I tried to explain the project.

"That's because somebody put the word out," Dalvin said. "Nobody's gonna help Film Club because that would be helping me."

"This is about that stupid game again?"

"Payback," Dalvin said, nodding.

"We got a lot of footage with Jemma's interview. We really only need one other person. I think maybe I can—"

"Maybe Ollie's right. We should just dump the whole idea." Dalvin moved around to the driver's side.

"I don't want to do that. This isn't right, Dalvin. They shouldn't be doing this to you."

"I can't let this crap fuck up the rest of the club. You guys don't deserve that." He tossed his backpack on the backseat and slid behind the wheel. "Come on. Let's get outta here."

I climbed in and stashed my backpack on the floorboard between my feet.

Dalvin didn't say anything as we rode. He didn't have to, not about his feelings. He kept tightening his jaw, grinding his teeth. He blinked rapidly every few seconds. It had to be hell, having all these people dump on him.

I reached over and gave his knee a squeeze. "This shit about the game, it'll blow over."

"I ain't sweatin' that mess, man. After I graduate, I don't have to see any of those idiots again." He tightened his jaw yet again. "I heard from Howard today."

"Yeah? That's great, man!"

"It was a 'thanks, but no thanks' kinda thing."

I gasped. "They rejected you?"

"Turned me down cold," he confirmed.

This didn't make sense. There had to be some kind of mistake.

"Wait. I've seen the student rankings. There's literally only, like, four kids in this school with better grades than you. Why the hell would Howard turn you down?"

"I figured this was coming," Dalvin said. "The guidance counselor told me last week that Howard had requested my updated files. Somebody tipped them off about the whole knocking-Richie-out thing."

"But who'd do that?"

"My guess is Richie's mom. She's on the school board. Richie must've mentioned that Howard is my dream university. She didn't press charges, but this is almost as bad."

"Damn, man," I said, voice trembling. "Dalvin, I'm so sorry."

He put his hand over mine, and I lowered my head, feeling guiltier than ever.

*

"WHAT'S UP, SON?" Dad asked. "You're never this quiet."

I'd wrapped up my two car wash appointments for the day, and Dad was driving us home. "It's nothing. I've got some things on my mind."

"Is anything wrong?"

"Well...yeah. There's this problem."

He gave me that deep, concerned father look. "You want to talk about it?"

"Not really."

"Okay. Just remember, you can talk to me anytime. And you can tell me anything."

"Thanks. But I already know what I have to do about the problem. I'm gonna make it right."

Dad nodded gravely. "I have taught you well, young Padawan."

"Can we make a stop before we go home?"

"Sure."

I got my phone out and sent Dalvin a text.

*

HE OPENED THE front door as I walked up the steps to the porch. "What up, Z. Come on in."

I stopped on the porch. "Is anybody else home?"

"Just my little brother. He's conked out in his room." His smile was crooked, hesitant. He studied my face. "What?"

I passed him, entering the living room.

He closed the door and slipped his hand in mine. "Come over here." Dalvin took me to the sofa, where we sat down together. "Everything okay with you?"

"I have to say something." Looking into his big brown eyes, I realized this would be a lot harder than I thought. "I'm sorry. I can't keep doing this."

His eyes flickered. "Doing what?"

"This," I replied, lifting our still-clasped hands. "This thing we're doing..."

"Becoming boyfriends."

A tiny pain punched me in the chest. "Yeah, that."

"Zeno, what's wrong? What's happened to you?"

"Nothing."

"Then why are you trying to break up with me before we're even a thing?"

"This isn't fair to you, man. It's costing you too much, turning your whole life upside down."

"What're you talking about?"

"The suspension. Getting kicked off the football team. All that shade you're catching at school. And now you're not getting into Howard—"

"Hold up. Wait a minute. None of that has anything to do with us, Z."

"It has everything to do with us. I can't keep dragging you down like this. You worked too hard to get where you are. I don't want to blow all that up."

"You're trying to take responsibility for shit that's not yours.

I did what I did. That's on me, not you, and I'll deal with the fall-out. The only thing you're blowing up is us. And I really don't want you to do that."

Dang. He was trying to protect me again. He was trying to keep me from feeling guilty, and I wanted to kiss him for that. But there was no way he could change the facts. All the grief he'd been catching since Jemma's party followed from that one punch, a punch thrown because of me. He'd already lost a lot. No way would I stand by and watch him lose anything else.

There was also the fact that I'd made a mess of Jemma's life and had left her to deal with it on her own. If the two of us were on the path to parenthood, I owed her, and I owed our baby. I had to make them my focus, no matter how upside down that turned my world. I didn't want to let go of this wonderful thing Dalvin and I had started any more than he did. But if I really cared about him, if I really cared about Jemma, I had to do what was best for them.

"Sorry," I muttered again as I started getting to my feet.

Dalvin wrapped both hands around mine. "Zeno, this is good, what's happening between us. Don't you see that? And it doesn't happen to everybody. Some people never get this chance. Do you really wanna give this up?"

His voice was shaky. I hated that I was causing him pain. I hated that I was breaking my own heart. But I had to do this.

"I'm still your friend, Dalvin. Okay? I'll always be your friend."

I pulled my hand free.

Chapter Twenty-Two

THE NEXT FEW days sort of blurred together, mostly because I ditched school and doubled back to hang out in my room after Dad went to work. I kept up with my assignments online but otherwise avoided anything having to do with MemTech. Because, you know. Dalvin and Jemma.

I didn't answer Dalvin's texts. I didn't answer his calls. When I thought of him—which was pretty much all the time—my throat seemed to close up. Sometimes I'd swear I was going to choke to death.

I wanted Jemma to be upfront and tell me about the situation I'd put her in. But she didn't answer my texts or my calls, and I sure as hell wasn't about to discuss this stuff with her in the middle of some school corridor. It was necessary that we at least acknowledge her pregnancy before I broke the news to my parents.

Picture my head exploding.

To distract myself, I did lots of workouts (chin-ups, push-ups, sit-ups) and binged on every LGBTQ-themed movie Netflix had to offer. I even watched the foreign language ones, which I usually bypassed. I mean, seriously, *subtitles*? If I wanted to read dialogue, I'd grab a novel. But together, all these things worked, at least for a while, to actually take my mind off the black hole rotating voraciously at the center of my life. Avoidance wasn't a long-term solution, obviously, but for the moment, it was the only way I could think to cope with my feelings.

Each day, I popped over to the auto shop at the appointed time and handled my business. Joked around with Bobbo and the other employees, put on a bright smile for my customers. When Dad and I sat down for dinner, I made it a point to keep the conversation flowing between us as always. And my video chats with Mom were par for the course; she queried me endlessly about college applications, and I threatened to stick my head in a carton of orange juice and drown myself if she didn't stop. All in all, it was a long but uneventful week.

That is, until Friday afternoon rolled around, with three car wash appointments lined up. Helmet on head, I rolled my bike out of the garage, about to take off for the auto shop, when Mom's car turned into the driveway. Ah, she was home early for the weekend. She must be so glad her boss had temporarily switched her to a Monday through Friday shift instead of the usual Wednesday through Sunday.

Hm. I was puzzled, a few moments later, to see Dad's car turn into the driveway behind Mom's. Okay, what was he doing here when he was supposed to be working? Maybe he'd taken off early for some extra time with Mom. Yeah, sure, that was the way they rolled, fun times and all.

Except, their faces were kinda grim as they climbed out of

their cars, looking like a couple of executioners ready to flip some deadly switches.

"Hey, baby," Mom said to me, but there wasn't an ounce of cheer in her eyes. It was so dang chilling when she put on her Batman face. In my opinion, the only thing the Bat had going for him was his mastery of looks-that-kill. You know the look Batman gave a villain while dangling the fool by one foot off the roof's edge of a ten-story building? Yeah, *that* face.

I stood there holding my bike, stuck, rigid as a light pole. I looked from Mom to Dad. "I'm in trouble, right?"

Mom raised a hand, gesturing toward the house. "Let's go inside and talk about it."

"But I've got customers coming to the shop."

"Bobbo's gonna wash any cars that come in for you. And pocket the cash he collects." Dad rapped his knuckles on my helmet. "I'd keep that baby on if I were you. Your mom's ready to go upside that head of yours."

Okay, I'm dead.

*

I COULDN'T WRAP my brain around the concept. "The school emailed you guys?"

Mom, pacing back and forth across the kitchen floor, stopped in front of me with her hands on her hips. "Why is that so hard for you to believe? MemTech has a policy of contacting the parent or guardian when a student has been absent without explanation for three days. It's a reasonable thing to do. I knew about the policy. Why didn't you?"

"I guess because I never ditched school before."

"Which is the only reason you are not at this moment confined to your room with nothing but a mattress on the floor. And really, Zeno, you should read MemTech's student handbook, for God's sake."

Damn. I'd forgotten how scary Mom could be when my antics pissed her off. Dad usually gave me a bit more leeway, maybe because *his* mom had been super strict with him when he was growing up. Dad told me about this time when he was eighteen and got home ten minutes—*ten*, mind you—after his curfew. He let himself in through the front door, and Gramma marched him straight to the back door, where she made him spend the night on the porch. Even now, Gramma can shut Dad down with one narrowed eye. That's some mad mojo to punk a middle-aged man.

Dad was upset with me, obviously, but trying to have my back too. I sat at the kitchen table with him to my right. He reached up and hooked Mom by an elbow, giving her a gentle tug.

"Babe," he said quietly. "Please. Sit down."

Mom clicked her teeth, a sound so full of anger it made me cringe a little. She moved over and took the chair to my left, her eyes cutting my way like a slasher's blade. I didn't get why she was so furious. Skipping school for four days was a bad thing deserving of punishment, sure, but Mom was carrying on as if I'd swung on a preacher. Or carjacked a nun.

Dad took over the interrogation. "We're trying to understand this, son. What happened? Eleven years of school, and you never missed a day except when you were sick—"

"And three months before graduation, you pull a stunt like this," Mom snapped. "The last thing you need this late in the game is a disciplinary mark on your record. You've worked so hard, and all that effort could go right down the drain. It doesn't make sense that you'd do this now."

Dad held up a hand, signaling for Mom to wait. "Zeno, what's going on? You keep telling us you're okay. You smile in our faces as if every day is just another day. But when I got that email from the school, it scared me. Since Jemma's party, I haven't been able to shake the feeling that something is troubling you. Be honest with us. Why did you skip school?"

I could have deflected, obfuscated. (Yes, people, you definitely do use all that school learning in actual life.) That was my immediate inclination. But this had been eating at me for days now. I'd been trying so hard to hold it in, which was a lot like trying to contain an explosion after watching the fuse burn down. Suddenly, I wanted to put it out there.

"Okay. To be honest, I broke up with Dalvin on Monday. I haven't been going to school because everything is so...crazy awkward. I don't know how to be around him, and I don't know what to say to him now. And when I broke things off, I didn't realize how much I was gonna miss him."

Half a truth would have to do for now.

Mom's face softened a bit, and while traces of anger remained, I was glad to see the flash of sympathy in her eyes. "Zeno. Baby. I'm sorry that happened. Skipping school was definitely not the way to deal with your feelings, but we'll get to that in a second. Do you want to talk about why you broke up with Dalvin? He's such a nice guy. Is there any way to fix things with him?"

That was sweet. Mom was so easy on the idea of my having a boyfriend, like it was an ordinary thing for a son to have. Well, actually, it *was* an ordinary thing for a bi son to have.

"I don't know. Maybe after Dalvin has graduated and MemTech is behind us and all." *And I know whether or not I'll be marrying Jemma or something.* "Maybe then we could give it a swing. Maybe I should've told him I wanted to wait, that I'm not ready for us to be boyfriends now."

Mom started to respond, but Dad held up his hand again,

suddenly sporting Batman's face himself.

"What exactly was the plan here? Skip school for the rest of the semester to keep away from Dalvin?"

"Well, no, obviously. I mean, I would've...eventually...come up with—"

"You do this a lot, don't you?" he said. "Anytime there's a problem, you avoid it. Right?"

Okay, that was flat out of nowhere. Caught off guard, I scratched my head, trying to dig up a response. Mom switched her gaze back and forth between Dad and me, totally intrigued.

"I've noticed some things about you," Dad continued. "You and Marvus were thick as thieves from pretty much the time you both learned how to walk. That kid was in this house so much I almost added him as another dependent on my taxes. Then, about seven months ago, boom, no more Marvus. I haven't even heard you mention his name since then. If your mom or I asked about him, you were quick to change the subject."

I turned to Mom, hoping for rescue, hoping she would take us back to the much safer topic of my breakup with Dalvin.

"Your dad's right," she said. "It's obvious something happened between you and Marvus, but we didn't press you. We figured if you wanted to talk about it, you'd come to us."

"It was the same with Jemma," Dad said, piling on. "If you weren't hanging out with her, you were talking or texting with her. For a while there, I was waiting for you to bring her home and tell us she was your girlfriend. But since the party, nothing. It's as if she doesn't exist anymore. I ran into her and her dad at Walmart the other day. I asked her when the two of you would be doing your next movie night. She told me that was up to you, and she was not smiling when she said it. There's something off between the two of you, and yes, sure, you don't have to talk about that either if you don't want to. But is this how you intend to go through your life, Zeno, always avoiding whatever upsets you? Do you ever plan to grow the hell up and face your problems like a man?"

Ouch. That wasn't a rhetorical question. Dad sat there, looking narrow-eyed at me with the full expectation that I would answer him. He was right, even about Jemma. Yeah, I'd texted her and left voicemails, but I was actually relieved she hadn't responded so far. With Dad eyeballing me, my stupid brain went on lockdown. I sat there, blinking at him.

"Fine," he growled. "You don't want to deal with this, we're done talking. If you ever decide you do, you know where to find your mom and me. You're grounded for four days. You will be taking your ass to school come Monday morning, and you will not skip another day. Are we clear?"

I lowered my head like a scolded puppy. "Yeah, Dad."

"You finish your homework and then put your laptop in my room. Give me your phone. Now."

I held out my phone. Dad snatched it from my hand, got up from the table, and left the kitchen. Mom reached over and gave my shoulder a squeeze. Then she followed Dad, leaving me alone with my guilty-ass thoughts.

*

FORBIDDEN TO LEAVE the house, stripped of my phone and laptop, I had lots of time to think Friday night. Yours truly reached many critical conclusions. The first arrived exactly two seconds after Dad snatched the cellie. Pissing my parents off at this juncture was hella stupid. It was way more than the loss of my sole connections to the world's digital network. My parents were my rock. They barely spoke to me the rest of the evening. It was as though we were on different continents, leading different lives. A lot of what it took for me to face the world every day came from knowing they had my back, and now, it felt as if that anchor was slipping away.

Second conclusion. I was tall, strong, handsome (like my dad) and smart, but I really didn't have a lot of swagger. Don't get it wrong; I stepped up when I had to. Like, in sixth grade, I helped Marvus fight off these two big idiots who double-teamed him and tried to take his lunch. And in seventh grade, I refused to accept detention from a teacher who mistakenly accused me of disrupting her class with a thunder fart. (It was the dude sitting behind me.) But the shameful truth was that I hated confrontation, and I needed to get over that, or at least enable myself to work through the confrontation without feeling like I was gonna hurl any second.

Third conclusion. It was time to stop with the avoidance. If I could hide from an ugly or disturbing situation, I did so without hesitation because it was the easiest option. But I knew from experience that hiding wouldn't fix things. Hiding also had some pretty severe costs, and your boy here had paid through the fucking nose.

Fourth conclusion. Most people finish high school at eighteen, but I was doing it at sixteen, and I had to be ready for what was coming next in my life. I might not have settled on a career yet, but I knew I wanted to step out in the world on my own terms and call my own shots. I'd still be sixteen when I started college in the fall. If I expected my parents to let me begin my next stage of life in an out-of-town university—which I really, truly wanted—I had to convince them I was capable of functioning as an adult. So far, admittedly, I'd been doing a poor-ass job of that. Also, daddy-hood would bring a big change to all of my plans.

Final conclusion. I had a lot of shit to straighten out.

Time for me to take a page out of Batman's book. I had to believe I was badass.

I thought some more and came up with a plan. How good or successful it might be, I had no clue... Wait. Be Batman, remember? The plan was gonna work. I was gonna *make* it work.

I woke early Saturday morning, determined and eager to get started. I took a shower, pulled on black sweatpants and a black Wolverine T-shirt (what better way to boost your confidence than wearing a badass, adamantium-clawed killer mutant on your chest), and went to the kitchen to start breakfast. I made a pot of strong coffee, set the table, stuck English muffins—Mom's favorite—in the toaster oven, sizzled six slices of bacon, and scrambled a big batch of eggs.

Cooking provided the desired result.

"Man. Something smells damn good in here," Dad said behind me. I turned as he entered the kitchen with Mom close behind him. Mom sported a severe case of bed head, but she'd at least taken the time to put on her slippers and robe. Dad wore only a pair of pajama shorts.

"Good morning," I said with my biggest smile. "You guys sit down. I got ya this morning."

They sat. I poured their coffee, their orange juice, and filled their plates with food. I even provided butter and jam for the muffins. Mom loved it.

"Mm," she cooed. "The sight of my baby boy serving breakfast really warms my little heart. Great job!"

"Thanks, Mom." I took my seat across from them. After I swilled down half a glass of juice to fortify myself, I cleared my throat. "Guys, I've got some things I wanna say. Is it okay if we talk?"

"Of course, son." Dad looked relaxed as he spread jam on his muffin. Maybe there was actually some hope for my longshot plan.

"What's on your mind this morning?"

"Well, first up, I gotta apologize for the whole ditching school drama. It was a dumb thing to do, and I'm sorry for getting you guys all upset. But I also gotta ask you something about, you know, the reason I did it. Dalvin called and texted me a lot while I was out of school. I never answered. I know the guy, though, and I'm pretty sure that if I don't talk to him soon, he's gonna show up here, probably today. I'm grounded and—"

"If he shows up," Dad said around a mouthful of English muffin, "we'll let you hang out with the kid." Seated next to him, Mom nodded.

Ooh. I blinked. That was not what I was going for at the moment. When my parents laid down a punishment, they usually stuck with it until the very end. Being grounded meant I couldn't have any visitors. So, this unexpected give on their part was definitely good and more reason for me to be hopeful.

"Okay, so how do I talk to him? He's gonna be all about the breakup."

"The best way to talk to anyone about anything is to be honest with them and yourself," Mom said. "Whatever Dalvin asks you, tell him the truth, honey."

Didn't I do that already? Well...not exactly. I didn't tell him everything.

Dad must have seen the uncertainty in my eyes. "Do you want to tell us why you broke things off with the guy?"

I was about to get ahead of myself. Until I talked to Jemma, I had to keep certain details to myself. "Okay, this is gonna sound so cliche but...it was for his own good. Dalvin got suspended from school and kicked off the football team because of me. He didn't get accepted to his dream university because of me. And I'm not worth it—"

"Whoa!" Dad's eyes flashed, and it was a good bet every hair on his body stood on end in his sudden outrage. "What's that supposed to mean?"

"I don't know. I mean...it's me, just me. Dalvin's not supposed to sacrifice everything important to him for that."

Dad put down the muffin and rubbed his eyes as if he'd been through the toughest day ever. "For God's sake, Zeno. I can't stand to hear you talk that way about yourself. You always sell yourself short. And I get it. You live in a world that's constantly telling you lives like yours don't matter. Your history doesn't matter, your pain doesn't matter, your rights don't matter, *you* don't matter. But you can't buy into that crap, or you'll lose who you are. I know because I spent too many years myself thinking I wasn't worth anything, and I'll be damned if I let you make that mistake. You're an intelligent kid with a kind heart, and you have so much going for you. You have to believe that you matter, because you do. To me, to your mom, to your friends, to yourself."

"And to Dalvin," Mom chimed in, smiling. "That's so obvious. Why else would he be going to all this trouble to reach out to you after you drop-kicked him?"

"But I shouldn't hurt somebody I like. Right?" I looked from Mom to Dad. "I mean, I shouldn't hurt anybody, period. But I especially don't want to hurt Dalvin. And that's what I've been doing—"

"How?" Mom asked. "Let's take the suspension. Dalvin was suspended for hitting another student. How was that your fault?"

"Come on, Mom. We all know why Dalvin hit Richie."

"The key words there are *Dalvin hit Richie*. The why doesn't matter. Dalvin hit that boy, not you, and he has to face the consequences for that."

"Dalvin said the same thing, but—"

"No, there is no 'but' here," Mom said. "You have to let Dalvin take responsibility for what he did. And instead of cutting yourself off, you should stand by him through this. If you care about him as much as you say you do, walking away is the worst thing you could do right now."

"Here's another thing," Dad said. "Your feelings, what you want—that matters too. You deserve to be happy as much as anyone else. You like this boy, you want to be with him, go for it. Leave it to him to decide whether having you in his life is a good thing."

Huh. It made sense, what they were saying. I wanted Dalvin in my life. Not just as a friend. More. I wanted to be closer to him. I wanted my first time to be with him.

Ah. Right. My virginity was long gone. Dead and buried.

Best that I stick with my plan and see how things work out.

"Okay, guys. About Jemma and Marvus. I kinda wrecked things with both of them. But...I don't wanna tell you the details. Okay?"

"That's fine, honey," said Mom. "Is there anything we can do for you?"

"Yeah, actually. I wanna fix things with them. I wanna do it today. And I'm grounded."

Dad, munching on bacon, looked up at me sharply. "Damn right you're grounded."

"And I so deserve it. Which means I don't ask what I'm about to ask lightly. Three hours. Just let me leave the house for three hours today. I promise I won't go anywhere except to Jemma's and Marvus's houses to see if I can get back in their friend columns. You can add another day to my sentence to make up for the three hours."

There. I'd made my case, hopefully like a man. My parents watched me as if they were either very impressed or highly offended. I wasn't sure which way they were gonna go on my request, but I was proud of myself.

I waited with a smile.

Chapter Twenty-Three

THE DOOR OPENED with a familiar squeak. *All this time, and they still haven't squeezed some oil on that damn hinge.* I laughed in my head. Outwardly, my hands were shaking a little, and my face was so frozen with apprehension I was afraid it would crack if I tried to smile.

Holding the edge of the door in one hand, she looked out at me, squinting something fierce. The late morning sun flared behind me, undoubtedly surrounding my body in a corona of white. She raised a hand, shielding her eyes and getting a good view of the person who'd arrived rudely unannounced at her home. The laugh that burst out of her was like the caw of a big startled bird.

"Ha! Well look at this," she bellowed, an impressive feat for such a small woman. "As I live and breathe. At long last. Here's Zeno Anderson back at my door like always."

"Hi, Mrs. Ahern," I said, finally able to crank out a smile. "Is Marvus home?"

"It's not yet noon on a Saturday. You know where to find him. Come on in."

She waved me in. I locked my bike to the porch's metal rail and stepped through the door.

Too bad I didn't think to ask for my phone back when I requested the reprieve. I could have called ahead and arranged meetings. Without the phone, I'd have to trust blind luck that my friends would be home when I got there. In the case of Marvus, that was a pretty safe bet. Dude loved sleeping in on Saturday. Unless his mom or dad insisted he join one of their excursions (or his dearly departed kid sister had dragged him to her soccer games), he wouldn't come up for air until lunchtime.

I walked down the hall. Nothing had changed. The walls were still the same cool light gray, the carpet black. Or charcoal, as Mrs. Ahern preferred. Pictures of Marvus and his sister hung on the walls, a timeline from toddler to teenhood. It felt like I'd been here only yesterday. I rapped loudly on Marvus's door.

"Leave me alone, Ma!" he shouted from within.

I resisted the urge to adopt a falsetto and drop a roundly insulting motherly reply. "Marvus, it's Zeno."

There was a moment of total silence, then a thump, followed by a rush of footsteps. The door ripped open, and Marvus, in a white T-shirt and purple polka-dot briefs, stared me down. He wore his hair in a close fade now, so he had no bed head to worry about. However, one corner of his mouth had produced a thin line of dried drool down to his ear, and there was enough crust at the edges of his eyes to make a sweet potato pie.

I covered my mouth to hide my chuckle. Sheezus, I couldn't believe I'd actually kissed this dude. And God, I couldn't believe I was mildly amused by the whole thing now. That kiss had been an epic cosmic disaster.

"It is you," Marvus huffed. "I didn't think I'd heard right. What...what're you doing here?"

"Your moms let me in."

"Yeah, of course she did. And I look like shit." He wiped a hand quickly over his face.

"Nah, you look cute." *Fuck! What the hell's wrong with me?* I wasn't flirting when I complimented his looks. I was trying to give him a boost to kinda smooth things over for our talk. Now wasn't the time, however, for putting anything out there that could be misinterpreted. "Sorry, man, I shouldn't have said that."

He seemed willing to let it slide. "Come on in."

His bed was a mess, the covers mostly on the floor, along with one of his pillows. The rest of the room was typically neat (we had that in common). School books stacked on his desk. Clothes folded nicely over the back of the chair. Shoes lined up along the wall by the closet like a row of mini-tanks. Posters of NBA players adorned the walls, and a collection of model US fighter jets covered his dresser, arranged by the year introduced into service. Yep, Marvus's little cave was still the same.

In an awkward rush, he scooped up the pillow and covers from the floor, returning them to the bed. Then, he grabbed some clothes from a chair.

"Have a sit-down. I'll be back in a sec." He slipped out of the room like a ghost, and a few seconds later, I heard the bathroom door close.

I snagged a controller, flipped on his TV and PlayStation, and settled in for some gaming while I waited. About three minutes into the session, it hit me. Did I still have such privileges in this house after ghosting Marvus for months? I was lucky the dude was willing to even talk to me. I shut off the game console and the TV, put the controller back where I found it, and sat my ass down like a good little boy.

My timing was excellent. Marvus walked back into the room mere moments later. He'd washed his face and pulled on the jeans and gray sweatshirt he'd taken with him. Halfway into the room, he stopped, shoved his hands in his pockets, and looked right at me.

"Okay, man. You wanna tell me why you're here? Is this a good thing?"

He wriggled his fingers in his pockets. The dude seemed a little nervous. Our situation had been brutal for way too long, so I got right to the point. "Marvus, I'm really sorry about the kiss."

Marvus frowned, his eyes crinkling. "Yeah, you said that right after you kissed me." He sat down heavily on the bed. "What I want to know is why you stopped hanging out with me. You cut me out like...like I stole from your grandma or something. You'd see me coming and turn the other way. That shit hurt, man. Why'd you do that?"

"Because I was ashamed." I narrowed my eyes, driven by a sudden hot rush of anger. "I wasn't sure of myself then, the feelings I was having...the way I was starting to feel about you. I was trying to figure out if I was gay or whatever. I was scared."

"How was I supposed to know any of that? You didn't tell me."

"I thought you felt the way I was feeling. We were watching that Ohio State game, ragging on their players. We were laughing, and you kept putting your arm around my neck, and it was, like, we were so close. You looked good. Your arm felt good around my neck. It felt so right that we were friends, and I kept thinking how much I liked your cocky ass. And then I kissed you..."

I watched for the expression on his face now to mirror the expression on his face then. Marvus's lips were pulled in, his mouth a grim line. I recognized the look. It was his I'm-trying-not-to-cuss face.

I was close to cussing myself. "You pushed me back so hard I hit my head against the damn wall. And the way you looked at me, you weren't just freaked. You were disgusted. I disgusted you. How am I supposed to hang around somebody who feels that way?"

"I noticed you checked out guys sometimes. I figured you were gay—"

"I'm bi, actually. I figured it out."

"Okay. Bi. My point is that I don't have a problem with any of it."

"I saw your face, man! You looked like you'd just eaten raw brains. You sayin' I imagined that?"

"Zeno, be real. I'm not gay or bi. I'm only into girls. What you did felt wrong."

"Yeah. 'Hate the sin, not the sinner.' Uh-huh."

"I don't mean, like, universally wrong. I mean wrong for me. The kiss was wrong for me. If I looked 'disgusted' or anything, it was because of that, not because I thought there was any problem with you being you. I love you like family, but hell, I don't want your tongue in my mouth."

Oh. Okay. That made sense.

"You know what really bothered me about this?" Marvus said, leaning toward me. "You didn't even ask if it was okay with me before you did it. You just glued your mouth to mine all out of the blue. I'd only met Katina a couple of days before—"

"Katina?"

"My girlfriend. I was already starting to get into her, she's that kind of special, and I wanted her to be my first kiss. But your tree ass got in there first." He reached over to deliver a soft jab to my shoulder, his mouth a crooked, joking grin. From the distant look in his eyes, however, I could tell his thoughts were shifting to his girl.

I could see how much she meant to him.

Damn.

"I'm sorry, Marvus."

"You don't have to keep apologizing. I already accepted the first one. I'm sorry I made you feel disgusting when you're not. Now, can we drown this shit and be boys again?" He stood and held out his arms.

I got up. We hugged. Marvus was, like, six inches shorter than me, which put his head against my shoulder. We must've looked mighty awkward standing there together.

But things between us were better than ever.

We let go, stepped back, and cheesed at each other.

"Okay, are we good now?" I asked.

"Hey, I was always good with us."

That was all I needed to hear. He held up a fist, and we dapped.

"So," I said. "Katina, huh?"

"Yeah. She's something, man. She does the gymnast thing. Says she's gonna be the next Simone Biles. You gotta meet her."

"I want to."

"And tall boy I saw you with the other day. I thought there was a spark between you and dude."

"Most definitely." I couldn't help it. Thinking of Dalvin made me grin like a fool.

"He your boyfriend?"

I laughed, shaking my head in wonder. "I, uhh, gotta work on that."

"I bet you will. When do I get to meet him?"

"I'll let you know. His name is Dalvin, by the way. He's on MemTech's football team. You probably would've heard about him by now if you were into any sport other than basketball."

"I'm hungry. I'm gonna get Ma to fire up the griddle. You want some breakfast?"

"I already had breakfast. It's almost lunchtime, and I can't stay long."

"Aw." Marvus poked out his lower lip. "You can't hang long enough for me to spank that ass at Monster Hunter World?"

"Oh. You're like MLK. I see you have a dream too."

He punched me on the shoulder again. "Come back later. I got this new model kit, an F-22A Raptor. We can work on it together. Then I got a date with Katina tonight. You can meet her before we go out."

"I can't. I'm actually grounded right now. The only reason I'm here is because my folks let me off punishment for a couple hours so I could fix something I broke."

He nodded. "Ya know, I always liked your moms and pops."

*

JEMMA WAS WASHING her Bug in the driveway, barefooted and her hair loose. She wore a pink bikini beneath an oversized T-shirt. Even wet, the shirt was far from diaphanous. The only way I knew she had on the bikini was because one of the bra straps showed within the loose, floppy neckline. Her back was to me as I rode down the street. To avoid startling her, I climbed off, removed my helmet, and walked the bike the rest of the way.

I leaned my bike against the trunk of the oak tree in the Haynes' front yard. "Hey, Jem."

She looked over her shoulder. Straight deadpan. "Hi." And she turned back to her work.

I grabbed a sponge from the bucket she was using, went around to the other side of the car, and started sloshing sudsy water over the roof.

"There are such things as automatic car washes, you know."

Jemma didn't take the let's-start-with-light-and-friendly-banter bait. "Why are you here, Zeno?"

Okay. Straight to the point. I can deal with that. "I wanna talk about what happened at your party after I passed out in your room. I want you to know that I'm here now, and I'm not going anywhere. I'll be with you every step of the way, no matter what you decide to do."

Jemma frowned hard at me. "No matter what I decide to do about what?"

"I wish you'd just told me."

"Zeno, what the hell are you talking about?"

I sighed. "I figured it out. Why can't you say it? Why can't you say I got you pregnant?"

She tilted her head to one side, looking at me like a confused puppy.

"God, Jem, I'm trying to step up here. Say *something*."

"You're an idiot."

"Look, I'm sorry, okay? But I'm not a deadbeat. I'll take responsibility for—"

"Oh stop it! I'm not pregnant. What in the world are you thinking? We'd have to have sex for that to happen."

"Uh, didn't we?"

"Of course not." She covered her mouth with her hand, gasping out a breath. "Oh my God. You think I had sex with you after Richie hit you with that GHB? Zeno! What kind of person do you think I am?"

"But you said we made love."

"I said we made *out*. We kissed and stuff until you completely blanked, and I feel guilty for even doing that. I couldn't live with myself if I'd had sex with you while you were blitzed out of your brain."

Thank you, God! Thank you, Jesus! "Okay, but remember when you drove me home, and we were talking about all this? You said you had a decision to make. And then you said you had to get rid of it."

"Get rid of it?" She frowned, obviously confused again. Then she threw up both hands, flinging streamers of soapy water into the air from her sponge as she chuckled. "You thought I was talking about an abortion? Seriously? I was half in love with you. I thought I had to decide if I could still be friends with you while I felt that way. I hoped I could kill those feelings if I stayed away from you."

"Ahh. Shit. I really got that twisted, huh?"

"You think?"

"So how's that whole kill-your-feelings thing going for ya?"

"They're not on life support yet, but they're getting there."

Her eyes grew shiny again. Dang. It was more comfortable for me to check out the surroundings. Some of her neighbors were having a busy Saturday. A man three doors down was washing his pickup. At a house across the street, a woman trimmed hedges with a pair of old-fashioned manual hedge clippers, while another woman at another house dug up her flowerbed, preparing it for planting. Gus, the thirteen-year-old kid who lived next door, snuck looks out his upstairs window at the car wash operation. Little pervert. He'd had the biggest crush on Jemma since he hit puberty a year ago.

"I'm glad we're still friends," I said. "And with all due respect to your God-given hotness, I'm glad we didn't have sex."

She sniffed softly as she half-heartedly swirled her sponge around in a little circle on the Bug's hood.

"Not that I wasn't into you at one time," I continued. "I really wanted us to be more than friends, but that was before Dalvin and I started feeling...stuff for each other. My first time having sex means something to me because I want it to be with him."

"I'm sorry for ghosting you. I should have made it clear I needed space to deal with my feelings. But I was also angry at you for not taking any of this seriously. Hell, Richie drugged you! You thought I took advantage of you a lot worse than I actually did. I wanted to slap myself, and I wanted to totally destroy Richie, but you were like a person having a day at the beach. What happened to you is not okay. I want you to understand that. I tried to explain this, and you completely blew it off!"

"I know, I know. You're right, and I get it now. I love that you stood up for me when I was too stupid to do it. Really, thank you for being there."

Jemma rubbed the back of her hand over her eyes. "God. I don't know why I'm crying."

"Aw, Jem. Please don't—"

She dropped the sponge and stormed around the car like, well, a storm, hair flying back, eyes fierce and streaming tears. I threw down my sponge before she reached me. She grabbed me by the shoulders, looking me in the eyes. "Zeno, I'm sorry things got so horrible with us."

And the dam broke. Jemma wrapped her arms around my shoulders, her face pressing against my neck. Within seconds, my skin was wet with her tears. I slid my arms around her waist and held her. Every few seconds, I swiped a finger at my own eyes, trying not to cry myself. God, if her dad looked out here right now and saw her sobbing all over me, he'd probably think I did something to hurt her and come out here and kill me.

"Hey, hey. Come on now." I tried patting her back gently. "It's over and done. And we are okay."

"I can't tell you how much I hate hurting you..." she mumbled, and she started crying even harder.

Oh my gosh! "I know, you're sorry. Okay, and I love you, and I forgive you, I really do. We gotta let this go, both of us, and move on. Come on, please. You're getting snot all down my neck."

She swatted my chest, shaking suddenly with a combo of sobs and laughter. "Oh shut up!" Wiping her eyes with her knuckles, she pulled away from me, backing up a couple of steps. Her eyes, when she met mine, were big and damp and shiny with regret. "Zeno..."

"Nah!" I made a quick cutting motion across my neck. "We're done with this thing. Fini. It's on a one-way rocket to the freakin' dark side of the moon!"

She laughed out loud in a blubbery sort of way. "Oh my God. You're an idiot. Thanks."

"For being an idiot?"

"Yes. And for being a friend."

I slapped both hands over my eyes and exhaled loudly. It felt as if I'd gone all bubbly inside with emotion. Another second, and brother was gonna be spinning around, arms out, head thrown back like a drag queen in full-on Diana Ross mode. Before I went there, I gulped a breath and said, "Come on. I gotta get back home in a bit. Let me help you finish washing your car. I'm a professional, you know."

"Is that your subtle way of letting me know you expect to get paid?"

"No. That's my subtle way of saying you suck at car washing. Look at all that grime you left on the side of this fine vehicle!"

"You distracted me!"

"And you can't even take responsibility for your suckage. What kind of person are you?"

"You know, I think I liked it better when we weren't talking."

We picked up our sponges and went back to work. And just like that, things were sweet between Jemma and me again.

For about five whole minutes.

Jemma had picked up the hose, ready to start rinsing the Bug, when her face went slack. "Wait a second. Did I hear that right?"

"Hear what right?"

"You have a thing for *Dalvin*?"

"Oh. Uhm, yeah. And I just legit outed him, didn't I? Dammit, I'm a big dummy. Please don't say anything about that to anybody."

"Of course, I won't."

"Thanks."

"So you're gay?" Her voice went totally flat.

I folded my arms across my chest. "Why is gay the default when a guy likes a guy? There's a spectrum, ya know. I'm bi."

"You're bi."

"Yeah."

"And you didn't tell me, your *bestie*?"

Uh-oh.

She aimed the hose nozzle at me.

I put a ton of bass in my voice. "Don't you dare!"

*

I COASTED OVER the little crest of my street. The shuddery feeling started rolling from my chest down into my stomach, a clash of joy and fear. My house had come into view ahead of me. Dalvin's car—actually, his dad's car—was parked in front.

I knew he'd come. I'd been banking on it. But after breaking up with the dude and then ghosting him for almost a week, I wasn't expecting him to be in the best of moods. He was probably here to cuss me out.

I swung into the driveway, dismounting as I did so. As I walked my bike toward the garage, Dalvin stood up on the porch.

"About time for you to show up."

I left the bike in the driveway and took off my helmet as I crossed to the porch.

Dalvin frowned. "Man! What happened to you?"

Though no longer dripping, I was still drenched from my hair to my kicks. Jemma and I had fought quite the water battle.

"Nothing. I helped this friend of mine wash a car."

"You must've used your whole body to scrub that car down."

I shrugged and climbed the steps. "You been waiting long?"

"I got here maybe ten minutes ago. Your dad told me you're on lockdown but said it'd be cool if I hung around."

"Why were you sitting out here? You insulted my dad or something and he wouldn't let you in?"

"I thought we'd have more privacy if we talked out here."

"I'm glad you came."

"You are?"

"Sure. I want to talk to you."

"Then why didn't you answer my calls or my texts? I tried a hundred times to reach you."

"I know. And I'm sorry. Sometimes I run away from things I don't wanna face. But I won't ever do that to you again."

Dalvin took my hand. "Zeno, if you want to break up with me because you don't want to be with me, I have to accept that. But don't break up with me because you think you're some kind of bad influence or whatever. You don't have to feel responsible for—"

"Dalvin, I take all of that back."

"What?"

"I was stupid. That girl I was with—I was worried I'd gotten her pregnant, and I figured I'd have to be with her. Only I was totally wrong. We didn't have sex, and I'm cool with her now. Also, I got scared there for a minute, at what you and I were doing and what it would mean for you, for us. But I'm over it." I squeezed his hand.

"You sure?"

I took his other hand and squeezed it too. "Damn sure."

Dalvin gasped out a breath, a half-smile on his uncertain face. "So...you're still my babe?"

I nodded, smiling full on. "And you're mine."

He threw his head back, eyes squeezed closed, and mouthed a very enthusiastic *Yes!* Then, looking at me, he said, "I'd kiss you right now if that wouldn't out you and me to your neighbors."

"Actually, I don't give a shit about the neighbors seeing us."

"Well, hell..." He leaned in.

Sweetest smooch ever.

We let each other go and stood there, face to face.

I started squirming. "Oh...uh...I should tell you. Today my friend Marvus said he saw you and me together and figured out what's going on between us. And I accidentally, not too long ago, outed you and me to Jemma." I immediately squinched my eyes shut, waiting for the explosion.

It never came. Instead, I got a gentle tug on my right hand.

"Hey," Dalvin said softly. I cautiously opened one eye. Seeing his crooked little smile, I opened the other eye. "I guess we started a trend." He tipped his head at something over my shoulder.

I turned. Across the street, my middle-aged, matronly

neighbor stood frozen in her yard, midway between her parked car and front porch, frozen with several bags of groceries dangled from her hands as she stared at us, slack-jawed.

I waved. "Hi, Mrs. Kaybak."

She closed her mouth, returned the wave, and hurried into her house.

"Too bad you're grounded," Dalvin said. "I'd take you out to celebrate all this."

"I won't be grounded next weekend. I'll take *you* out."

"Cool. Oh, and you don't have to worry about finding another person to interview for our film project. Richie called me last night and said he wants to do it."

"Richie?"

"Yep. Says he'll do it as long as he can talk about bringing GHB to Jemma's party."

"But that's, like, a confession."

"I told him that. He said it's what he wants to do. What about you, Z? Are you okay with Richie talking about this?"

"If that's what he wants, I say let him go for it."

"Okay. I think you need to stay out of this one. I'll talk to Ollie, get him to come up with the questions, and do the actual interview."

"Cool."

"Your dad said I shouldn't stay long after you got back, so I'm gonna go. But before I do, Zeno..."

"Yeah, Dal?"

Face seriously grim, he grabbed my wet shirt with both fists, right beneath my chin. He said through his teeth, "Never. Break up. With me. Again." He pulled me in for emphasis, bringing us nose to nose. And broke into a goofy smile. And pecked me on the lips.

I smiled back. Best demand ever. We were definitely on the same page. So, I grabbed his collar, giving him a good dose of grim-eye. "And don't you even *think* about breaking up with me."

Yeah, I'd say our relationship was off to a healthy start.

Dalvin laughed and nodded. "Wanna hear something good?"

"Hit me."

"I told my dad I'm not going to church anymore."

"Okay. But why is that good?"

"I haven't liked going to church since I was thirteen, when I first heard our pastor preach that gay people are abominations who'll go to hell if they don't stop being who they are. I don't believe God hates me, but I don't feel like I belong in that church anymore either."

"Why didn't you tell your parents when you were thirteen?"

"I thought my dad would kill me."

"Damn. That was your big fear, huh?"

"Yeah. I finally faced it. And you wanna know what made me do it?" He nudged my shoulder. "You."

"Me? How?"

"You didn't let that transphobic cop kill your self-respect. I realized every time I walked into that church, I lost another slice of dignity. I decided I had to do something about that."

"So what did your dad say when you told him?"

"He was pretty cool about it actually, which surprised the shit out of me. He said I was old enough to make my own decisions when it came to religion and left it at that."

"Wow, Dal, that's great."

"Yeah." He hitched up his pants, a smug grin on his face. "I feel like a man. Now I just have to work my way up to telling him I'm gay."

*

IN BED, STRIPPED down to boxers and a T-shirt, I was finishing a homework assignment on my laptop. The knock at my door surprised me. My parents and I had said our goodnights, it was closing in on midnight, and the Andersons were snug under their covers. Or so I thought. "Come in."

Mom and Dad were still in their clothes. Odd. Something had to be wrong. Was someone in the family sick? They walked in and stood next to my bed, looking down at me.

"Hey, Z-bo," Dad said. "We saw the light under your door. Since you're still up, we thought we'd have a little talk with you."

Oh crap. "Am I—"

"No, baby boy, you're not in trouble." Mom laughed. "We wanted to say that we're proud of how you handled things with your friends."

"Yeah," Dad said. "You told us you faced your problems instead of dodging them, made some clearheaded decisions, had some tough conversations. And you worked things out with Dalvin, Jemma, and Marvus."

"That was very mature of you," Mom continued, "and it's helped us make a decision about where you're going to college in the fall."

Okay, *that's* what this is about. I had to brace myself. I closed my laptop, put it aside, and took a breath.

"All right. Let's hear it," I said. "Are you letting me go out of state, or is it U of M, here I come?" I couldn't read either of their faces. Good thing I submitted an application to U of M this evening. And thank God U of M is accepting applications until June third.

"We've decided," said Dad, "to let *you* make the decision whether to do college here in town or out of state."

What? WHAT? Did I hear that right? "Really?"

"Yes, really." Mom's face was practically beaming. "It's your life, Zeno. You're growing into quite the man. We trust you to know yourself and to make the choice that's right for you."

"Exactly," Dad said, and suddenly, his face went dead serious. "Don't muck this up!"

"I won't, Dad. I promise." I grinned like crazy. "Thanks, you guys, for believing in me. This means a lot."

"Shaddup," Dad said, waving me off with a smile. "It's late. Get some sleep."

He took Mom's hand, and they left my room, closing the door after them. I plugged in my laptop to charge, lay down, and pulled the covers over me. Wow. So many amazing things happening in one day!

Who the hell could sleep?

Chapter Twenty-Four

THE FOLLOWING SATURDAY afternoon, I took Dalvin on a date. As the host this time around, it didn't feel right for me to have Dalvin drive, and it would have been way weird to get Mom or Dad to chauffeur. So, I called up an Uber and decided it was time for me to start driving lessons.

Dalvin answered the door with his frohawk stylishly frizzed, wearing faded jeans and a loose pink pullover sweater. "Hey, bae."

I was all smiles. "You look good. Shall we?"

We nudged shoulders as we walked toward the hired car.

"So where are we going?" he asked.

"You'll see," I said confidently, even as I crossed my fingers behind my back. *Please let him like this.*

Around fifteen minutes later, our Uber driver turned into the parking lot of the Memphis Museum of Science and History Central, better known as the Pink Palace because of its salmon-colored walls of Etowah marble.

"Huh. I haven't been here since seventh grade," Dalvin noted.

"I've been here lots of times with my friend Marvus. He loves the Planetarium. But this trip's about you, and there's something else I wanna show you right now. Come on."

I led the way through the main hall into the Arts and Sciences gallery. Dalvin's eyes sparked when he saw the title of the new exhibit, just installed there.

"The History and Future of Computer-Generated Imagery." He was jazzed to where he threw his arm around my neck and tugged me into a bro hug. "Dude!"

I was so happy *he* was happy; it made me blush. He slid away from me and plunged right in, bypassing the introductory video for a display highlighting a breakdown of the opening credits of *Vertigo*, an Alfred Hitchcock movie. In the sequence, the camera dove into a human eye, which led to a series of spiraling shapes.

"Those look like spinning galaxies," I ventured.

"Says here these are staircase motifs meant to simulate vertigo," Dalvin said, reading the copy. "This is one of the earliest uses of a computer in producing a movie image."

I took a glance at the copy. "It says this movie was released in 1958. Wow. I thought CGI was a fairly new thing."

Dalvin gave my shoulder a quick squeeze. "So did I. Now we know."

Visiting museums was always a group thing, in my experience. We'd arrived together, but I inevitably drifted away from my little group, taking in the exhibits at my own pace. Not this time. For the entire two hours of our Pink Palace visit, Dalvin and I stayed side by side. We explored the abbreviated history of CGI and speculative future applications, sighing and laughing, intrigued, enlightened, and thoroughly entertained. While Dalvin hung on every word, dazzled by every image, I leaned into him, or brushed my fingers over the back of his hand, or sneaked a look at the joy in his eyes. With every touch and every glance, something in me opened like a gush of water, filling me from the inside until I couldn't get a breath. It might have been an attack—asthma or panic, though I'd never experienced either before. But I knew what it was. And it prompted me to wonder: Why is falling in love like choking?

I didn't want the date to end.

Upon finishing a tour of the exhibit, patrons had the option of creating their own CGI souvenir using one of several prepro-grammed scenes. Dalvin and I walked away with a picture of us that featured a giant, ferocious Dalvin clinging to the top of the Empire State Building with one hand and clutching a tiny, comically shriek-ing me in the other, all while being buzzed by two Curtiss F8C Hell-diver biplanes. We stopped outside the exit of the Arts and Sciences gallery, taking in the picture together as I held it in front of us.

"This looks so real it's scary," I said. "And all we did was pose in front of a green screen."

"Magic," Dalvin sighed. He reached over, taking the edge of the picture in his hand, his thumb settling over mine. For a long moment, neither of us moved.

"Sooo..." I relinquished the photo to him and slipped my hands into the pockets of my hoodie. "You ready for some eats? There's a pizza place not too far from here."

"Actually, Z, I'm not hungry. And my folks are on their way to the zoo with little bro, so no one's at my house right now." He carefully rolled the pic into a narrow tube and tucked it into my back pocket. A smile twitched at one corner of his mouth. He wouldn't look at me.

His sudden sweet shyness melted me inside because it was a

facet of him only I ever saw. I'd planned more for our date. A late lunch. Followed by a movie. And then a stroll in Overton Park, where evening shadows would provide cover for Dalvin and me to explore our feelings for each other.

But that was before Dalvin announced his house was vacant.

I leaned in close, planted a little kiss on his right ear, and whispered, "Let's go."

*

WE LAY ON Dalvin's bed, my head on his shoulder, my hand on his chest. He traced his fingers back and forth across my cheek. His phone was on the dresser, and he had a playlist of chill songs going in the background as a soundtrack for this moment between us. I could feel his heartbeat beneath my palm. *Boomp. Boomp. Boomp.* Urgent, ready. The music was great. He and I were into a lot of the same artists, the same genres. Everything was perfect.

"I really like this," I murmured into his chest.

"Mm. Me too."

"Your body…I love the way it feels. So different from a girl's."

"Yeah? You think?"

"Shut up!" I gave his pec a little swat and then slid my hand over it. "I guess what I'm trying to say is that I'm used to touching girls. Everything feels soft and silky, which is great. But I like the difference when I touch you. The way your muscles are so thick and your chest is hairy. I like the 'guy' in you."

Gently, he shifted our bodies around until I lay on my back as he propped on his elbow, looking down at me. "Do you like the guy stuff more than the girl stuff? Is it, like, one turns you on more than the other?"

"No, I don't think so. To me, girls are hot and guys are hot, just for different reasons."

"Well, total homo here. Nothing about the female form appeals to me. I've had girls flirt hard, rubbing their boobs against my arm and stuff. It freaks me out, man, doesn't feel right. I'm just not wired that way."

"I get it. And that's okay. I like girls who are really feminine and guys who are really masculine. If I have a 'type,' that would be it. What's your type?"

"You."

"Aw. Good answer."

He leaned down. I closed my eyes. We kissed, my hand around the back of his neck, his hand cupping my face. The kissing, though soft at first, a gently coming together of lips, quickly grew more passionate. Dalvin climbed on top, weighing me down with his body. I gasped and turned my face away.

"Zeno?"

"I'm cool, Dal. It's fine." I turned back, joining his lips to mine once more. He squeezed my shoulder, my arm, his hands finally settling as he gripped me by the waist. The choking sensation started again, but not in a good way like before. I anxiously sucked in a breath. This was definitely a panic attack. I realized now the same thing happened when Dal had started making out with me during our sleepover, only it was much worse now. What the hell? I liked this guy a lot. And a dude couldn't get any more masculine than Dalvin. This should have been my own personal heaven.

I pushed the squirming discomfort down and tried to will it away. Wrapping my arms around Dal's shoulders, I pulled him closer, kissed him back like I had a point to make. Next thing I knew, Dalvin was tugging at my hoodie. I sat up, raised my arms; he pulled the thing over my head in one swoop and tossed it aside. I yanked my dislodged T-shirt down as Dalvin began pushing me back to the bed once more. My stomach cramped, making me gasp.

He froze, his hands on my belly. "Z, what's wrong? You're acting the way I do when a girl smashes up on me with her chest."

"I'm sorry." Feeling like crap, I rolled away from him and shook my head helplessly. "I don't know what's happening here."

"Maybe...maybe you're just not into me."

"Dalvin, you're cute, and you're hot. Believe me, I'm into you. It's me who's the problem."

"Oh shit." The thought that hit him was so terrible it made his eyebrows arch. "This is about that date rape situation, isn't it? You got some kinda PTSD behind that shit."

"Nah—"

"I googled it, man. People get doped with GHB, it can mess them up. Maybe you need to talk with somebody, ya know?"

"That's not it. I already dealt with that. That stupid YouTube video is gonna haunt me forever, and I may never do karaoke again, but I'm not stressing with anybody, not even Richie."

"Then what...?"

In the silence that followed, everything became clear to me. I was afraid, not of sex but of being with Dalvin. Afraid of the homophobia we would inevitably stir up together. Afraid we wouldn't know what the hell we were doing. Afraid that if this romantic relationship didn't work, I'd lose him completely, even as a friend. Basic fucking fear. I'd allowed it to dictate the terms of my life. I'd seen where that would take me, running, ducking and dodging all over like a fool, and I was done shoving my head in the sand. This wasn't some random hookup. Our entire friendship had been building to this moment. Dalvin and I wanted to be closer to each other, to deepen the bond between us in one of the most intimate ways possible. It could be a very beautiful thing for us. All I had to do was man the hell up.

I rolled over to face Dalvin again, gazing into his eyes. His kind, loving, wonderful eyes. I shrugged out of my T-shirt, took his hand, and placed it on my chest, making it clear that I wanted his touch. My breathing became heavy. I felt my own heart thudding beneath Dalvin's palm. And I saw the uncertainty that shimmered into Dalvin's face.

"Z, are you sure you're cool with this? I don't want to hurt you."

"You won't, Dal. I trust you."

"Good. Okay. Don't be afraid." His voice shook a little.

I smiled. "Are you talking to me or to you?"

"Both."

*

WE LAY TOGETHER naked on Dalvin's bed, cuddling. I was tired and breathless and sweaty, but also happy. Very, very happy. So happy I couldn't stop smiling. I'd never been high before, but it must feel like this. Some transformation had taken place, one so profound it had me wondering if I were now a whole new person. I felt I'd taken another huge step on the road to manhood. And Dalvin was right there with me.

"What's so funny?" Dalvin asked.

"Huh?"

"You keep giggling back there."

"I'm just feeling good." I had my arm wrapped around him from behind. I kissed the nape of his neck. His soft, frizzy hair smelled like cocoa. "You okay, Dal? Was it... Did I hurt you?"

"Nah, I'm good. You were amazing, Z."

"So were you. I mean, I don't have anything to compare it to, but I was not disappointed."

"Dude!"

"I guess this means we have officially gone from friends to boyfriends."

"Yeah, definitely. And I'm not ashamed of it. I like what we have, man. I don't want to hide it or anything."

I squeezed my arms around him. "I think that's the sex talking, babe."

"You're probably right." Dalvin took a quick breath and turned his face toward me. "Wanna go again?"

*

AFTERWARD, THE SEQUEL.

Dalvin lay over my back like a weighted blanket, his hairy chest tickling delightfully at my spine. His hands covered mine, our fingers interlaced. It was fantastic, being so close to another person. Not somebody random out to use you for fun, but a person who really cares, who holds you tenderly, who makes you feel precious. Our bodies buzzed like my dad's electric shaver.

"Whew," Dalvin sighed.

A snarky grin spread across my face. "Took your breath away, huh? I knew I rocked that world."

"You're so modest." He nuzzled the top of my head with his nose. "I love your hair. It always smells amazing."

Sweet. That made me smile again.

"Hey, what I said earlier about not wanting to hide us...I was thinking. This is kinda last minute, but will you go to senior prom with me? As my date?"

"Babe, I'd love it."

"We can do tuxes in yellow and black."

"And we'll get corsages for each other."

"Wait, I'm not *that* gay," Dalvin said. "How about boutonnieres?

"That's my dude. We'll do a limo. And dinner."

"Dinner, yes. But not at a restaurant. I wanna cook for you."

"Aw."

"And we gotta do ice skating again. That was fun."

"Yeah, you're awesome on the blades."

"You too. We should go bike riding. I haven't been on my bike since I was fourteen, but watching you, I kinda miss it. My old bike's still in the garage, probably just needs some air in the tires."

"Better let me inspect it. Make sure it's safe. I gotta protect my investment, ya know."

Dalvin suddenly shuddered, sliding his arms under my chest and hugging me hard. "Damn, Z. I'm loving this."

"Me too. Can we be here like this forever?"

"Oh yeah, babe. We can have forever."

There was a click, followed by the loud thrum of the garage door opener kicking into operation.

Dalvin jumped off the bed as if there were no such thing as gravity. "Or we can have until my folks come home!" He snatched my boxers off the floor and flung them at me. "Quick! Put your clothes on!"

The good times were just beginning.

Chapter Twenty-Five

"WELL, THIS SUCKS."

Marvus sat on the floor, slumped against the side of my bed. I lay on my back on the floor, my feet propped on the mattress. We were googling colleges on our phones.

I peered over at him. "What sucks?"

"This thing with you graduating and going off to college a whole year early. We were supposed to graduate together."

"Well. Sorry about that. But it's not like you didn't know this was coming."

"Truth. It still sucks. I'm kind of jealous too. Why'd you have to be so smart?"

"Seriously, Marvus? You're whining?"

"Just kidding. I'm happy for you, bro. I'm glad to do senior year and graduate with Katina. We're talking about applying to the same colleges."

"So those colleges you're looking at now are ones Katina wants to attend?"

"Yeah. She sent me a list."

Almost a month had passed since Marvus and I reconnected. Among the many dates Dalvin and I had been on over that time, one was a double with Marv and his girl, Katina. Lithely muscled, tall, pretty, and brown-haired, she was a few shades lighter than Marvus's medium brown tone. She also had a potty mouth and snappy wit that would put a stand-up comedian to shame. Dalvin and I liked her right off, and she seemed to reciprocate on the good vibes.

"It's good you two are starting your search now," I said. "Some idiot, who shall not be named, waited until he was almost midway through his senior year to start. You got a major in mind?"

"I'm thinking early childhood education."

"Yeah, right. Do you even like little kids?"

"Of course I do. Especially the little badass kids. They're the ones who need me the most. They need somebody who understands them. I was a little badass boy in elementary, remember? Most of my teachers wrote me off instead of trying to help me."

He cast a look at my phone and frowned. "You're checking out Howard University?"

"Yeah. Just going over what kind of degree programs they offer."

"Is that a good idea? Dalvin might have a problem with you going to his dream school after it rejected him."

"We talked about it. He's cool. Anyway, I sat down with my dad yesterday, and we did a video conference with Mom. The decision's been made. I'll be going to the University of Memphis in the fall."

"Aw, that's tough, man. So, your moms and pops decided you're too young to go off on your own, huh?"

"It wasn't like that. I made the decision. I think it's the right one for now."

And no, I didn't take that option because I thought it was what my parents secretly wanted. It dawned on me that, for the past few months, I'd been carrying on like a scared, oversized tween. I figured I needed a little more time to grow the hell up.

"U of M offered me a scholarship," I continued. "With the John Lewis Memorial and the Excellence in Academics scholarships, I'm set financially for the freshman ride. I can keep my car wash thing going, save some more money, and then transfer out of state for my sophomore year. I'll be on better financial footing than if I went out of state this year."

Marvus nodded. "Sounds like a good plan. Two scholarships! Man, all those stellar grades paid off. You got a major yet?"

"I've narrowed it down to criminal justice or communications. After I finish undergrad, I'm going to law school."

"Wait. I thought you said the legal system in this country is corrupt and racist and all. I don't get why you want to be part of that."

"For the same reason you want to work with disadvantaged little kids," I said. "Yeah, the government in this country is broken and big money calls most of the shots. Yeah, our justice system is driven more by bigotry than justice. I'm not fool enough to think one Black man with a new law degree is gonna fix any of it. But if I work with the Innocence Project or the ACLU or start my own advocacy group, I can help make a real difference."

"What about Dalvin? Is he heading for the U of M too?"

"Nope. MemTech's coach and a couple of teachers pulled some strings. Dalvin is committed to playing football for the University of Southern California. He's going into their animation and digital arts program."

"So, you guys are gonna do the long-distance thing?"

"Sophomore year, we plan to be at the same university. Unless Dalvin really likes the USC program, we're gonna transfer to Howard. He seems pretty jazzed about the program already, so I think I'll be heading to southern Cali. But freshman year, yeah, we're gonna be long distance."

Teeth clenched, Marvus hissed out a breath. "Shit. I don't think I could do that with Katina. I'd miss her too much."

"Dalvin will be coming home for fall, winter, and spring breaks. We'll video chat while he's in California. We even plan to video date every weekend. This is gonna work for us."

"But what if you get to college and start meeting a lot of hot dudes. Or hot ladies."

"What if you get to college and start meeting lots of hot ladies?"

Marvus shook his head hard enough that it seemed his ears would fly off. "Uh-uh. Doesn't matter, man. I'm all about Katina."

"Then you know how it is for me. I see lots of hot people now. At school. In the store. My dad's repair shop. Everywhere. But the only person I want is Dalvin."

"Well shut my mouth."

"Wait! I haven't even told you the best part about going to the U of M. Guess who else is going?"

Marvus narrowed his eyes. He was totally puzzled. "Who?"

"My *mom*."

"What the fu—?"

"She got accepted into grad school. She's gonna cut her work schedule to two days a week, and in a year or so, she plans on having her master's in biology."

Marvus still stared at me as if a connection had snapped in his brain. "Dude. You're going to college...with your *momma*?"

"It's not like that, Marv."

"It's exactly like that, Zeen. You and your moms are about to be students on the same campus. At the same damn time."

"And?"

"Come on, dude. You'll be in college. How's anybody supposed to take you seriously when you got your mommy right there holding your hand?"

"I told you, it won't be that way. Most, if not all, of Mom's classes are gonna be in some science building. My classes are gonna be in buildings scattered all across the campus. We won't hardly see each other, except if we meet for lunch or something."

"Yeah, well, I can see things getting awkward. You know your moms is hot, like for real."

I gave Marv serious crazy eye.

"Don't scowl at me like that. Your mom looks way younger than she is. I can see some college dude make a move on her right in front of your clueless ass. Shit, I used to have a crush on her myself when I was eleven—"

"No! Stop!" I frantically formed a cross with my forearms, warding Marvus off as if he'd turned vampire. "I don't even want to hear that mess. Ugh!"

"Dude. You can't relate because she's your moms. But I'm telling you, the lady is gonna turn heads on that campus. You need to recognize, Zeen."

"Marvus, you are a freaking disturbed individual. This is the most disturbing conversation I've ever had, and it's got me feeling very disturbed. I feel so disturbed my skin is starting to itch. Thank you."

He puffed up his chest. "Hey. Just doing the best friend thing."

*

"ZENO," DAD CALLED from the kitchen. "Dal's here."

Still slumped on the floor, Marvus and I were dueling via our cell phones in an online game with a couple of guys in Japan. Things were pretty even, neither side able to command much of a lead. At Dad's announcement, I tossed my phone aside and jumped to my feet.

"Hey," Marvus growled, sounding offended. "You can't walk your happy ass out in the middle of this game."

"Watch me." I headed for the door.

"Bet you don't get this excited when I drop in."

"You think?"

It took major effort not to fly up the hall.

In the kitchen, Dad washed turnip greens at the sink. The man cooked a mean pot of greens. We're talking slap-yo-mama eating. Speaking of mamas, mine was due home any minute now on this fine Friday afternoon. Dad would welcome her with a good ole Southern dinner.

My eyes went immediately to the tall, beautiful bumblebee in a yellow-striped hoodie and black jeans. Yeah, dude was rocking my fave colors. He graced me with a happy smile. "Hey, Z."

"Hey, Dal. So you've been sprung from babysitter prison, huh."

"Yeah, my dad just got home. I came right over. Oh, hey, Marvus."

Marvus moved past me into the kitchen. "Whassup, man." He and Dalvin clasped shoulders and went for dap.

"I'm making fried pork chops, turnip greens, candied yams, and hot water cornbread," Dad announced. "You friends of Zeno's staying for dinner?"

"My mouth is doing a happy dance right now, Mr. Anderson," Marvus said. "Hate to pass up a mighty meal like that, but

Katina's gonna be finishing her shift at Mickey D's in about fifteen minutes. I'm gonna swing by and pick her up. We got a study group this evening."

"More for me, then," said Dalvin. "Count me in, Mr. A."

"See ya, Marv," I called to my departing friend.

Marvus rolled his eyes toward Dal. "Yeah, like you're gonna miss me." He smiled as he let himself out the back door.

"You can head on back to my room, Dal. I'm gonna have some juice. You want anything?"

"Nah, I'm cool." He sauntered off down the hall, leaving a breeze in his wake.

Ahh. The heavenly, citrusy scent of my boy's soap.

I grabbed the bottle of apple juice I'd left chilling in the freezer. I'd caught it right at the point where it was pure icy slush. Excellent. As I turned to go, Dad held up a hand to stop me.

"What?"

Dad leaned toward me. "Keep that door of yours open," he said quietly.

"Okay." I ducked around his hand.

"I mean it, Z-bo."

"*Okay*. Sheezus."

Dalvin pounced the moment I walked into my room. He wrapped me in his arms, kicked the door shut, leaned me back and planted a kiss on my lips, all in the space of about two seconds.

"Hey, babe," he crooned when he finally gave me space to breathe again.

Finally, a proper greeting.

"Whew." I almost dropped my bottle of juice. As soon as I steadied myself, I reluctantly reached back and opened the door.

Eyeing the open door, Dalvin said, "Your dad?"

I nodded. We'd had more than a few seriously hot and

substantial make-out sessions behind that closed door, always when both of my parents were MIA. But that was all we'd done so far at my house. One afternoon, not so long ago, Dad had come home early. Even with our mouths suctioned together and our hands under each other's shirts, we heard the back door click open. By the time Dad let himself into the kitchen and called out for me, Dalvin and I had straightened our clothes and were sitting side by side on the floor, controllers in our hands, playing a video game. We didn't think about the closed door. When Dad opened the door and looked in, he saw our wooden postures and expressions and heard our heavy breathing. He'd added it all up in half a minute.

So here we were now, Dalvin and I, with the door open. He took my hand, pulling me to the bed. We sat, and he threw his arm around my neck. I put the juice on the nightstand.

"Did you see the post from the Faculty Advisors Committee?" he asked.

"No. Marvus and I have been checking colleges and playing games since I got home from school."

"Film Club took Best Achievement for our little movie slash documentary project."

"Wow. For reals?"

"Kid ya not."

I shouldn't have been surprised that Film Club had won the biggest award among all the senior extracurricular projects. The acting was great, the camera work was excellent, the writing was awesome (I'm brazen enough to say so myself), and the directing was impeccably anal. The mini documentary had been the most impactful, however. Jemma's interview was relatable and passionate. Richie's interview was absolutely riveting. Gone were the snarky, bad humor and the greasy attitude. He looked right into the camera when he answered the questions Ollie pitched at him, a sad, sincere kid connecting with every viewer. He explained that he'd done something he regretted so much it kept him awake at night. Amazing because it was so totally unlike him.

And yeah, it was a confession.

Our film had been screened at the assembly on Monday afternoon. Before the auditorium even cleared out, Principal Ghoudry stopped Ollie and asked for a copy of the film. The next morning, Detective Hanson had shown up bright and early, put handcuffs on Richie, and read him his rights as she marched him out of homeroom.

"I feel sorry for him."

"Who?" Dalvin asked.

"Richie."

"Hey, he knew what he was doing."

"But *why* did he do it? He was in the clear. All he had to do was keep his mouth shut."

Dalvin shrugged. "Part of it was guilty conscience, I think. The other part has to do with fear. Remember in the interview, he said his big fear is not having friends. Well, he doesn't have a lot of those. Most of the players on the basketball team think he's a joke, so he puts on this asshole act to fit in with them. He needs a real friend. That's why I started hanging out with him. The only other real friend he had was this girl in the band named Zoey. When she heard what he'd done at Jemma's party, she stopped having anything to do with him. Just like I did."

"So, he got himself arrested, and that's supposed to get you and this Zoey girl back in his corner?"

Dalvin shrugged again. "It was the right thing, owning what he did. I have to give him that."

"He's gotta be in so much trouble. I hope he's okay."

"I called him last night. He was glad to hear from me. He said in addition to being suspended this week, he's not gonna be allowed to walk the stage at graduation. The police released him to his parents the same day he was arrested. He says their lawyer told them it's a good chance she can get the possession charge dropped, or she can get Richie off with community service and no criminal record to chase him. He's not us, Z, so he'll be okay."

Yeah, the criminal justice system would surely be easy on Richie. I turned my thoughts to Jemma. She'd blown away the audience (Dalvin and me included) at her dance recital. In June, she would take off for New York City, where she had a summer job lined up teaching dance to little kids at some kind of dance camp. And in the fall, she'd begin the next stage of her life at Juilliard. She was pretty excited about it all, of course. We were back to hanging out like always. Things were good between us.

"Babe?" Dalvin touched a finger to my chin. I looked at him. "Where'd you go just now?"

"Thinking about Jem. I'm gonna miss her when she's off on her own." I took his hand, interlacing our fingers. "I'm gonna miss you too."

"Hey, this isn't the end of anything. Our lives are getting bigger and better." He lifted my hand and kissed the back of it. "I told my parents about me. About us."

Wow. Dalvin and I had agreed we would officially come out as boyfriends at the senior prom, which was next week. I'd suggested he come out to his parents beforehand. A high-profile student athlete debuting as half of a same sex couple was sure to make waves in local sports news and social media. I didn't think it would help Dalvin's teetering relationship with his dad for the man to learn anything so major about his son secondhand.

"I didn't tell them your name or anything," Dalvin added.

"Just that I had a boyfriend—"

"Baby, it's okay if you tell them I'm the boyfriend. They're gonna find that out anyway, like, next Saturday. When did you do this?"

"Today. Right before I left to come here."

"Oh shit. Are you okay? How'd they take it?"

"Mom was surprised as hell, but she was quick to let me know I was still her son. Dad was the one who took it hard. He didn't yell, kick me out, disown me, or anything. He didn't say a word, just stared at me for what felt like a hundred years and then got up, walked out, and shut himself away in his room."

"That part sounds bad, Dal."

"Mom said I should give him time. His religious beliefs are telling him I'm damned, but he loves me. He's gotta figure all that out. Mom says he will. I hope he will. But whether he does or doesn't..." Dalvin kissed my hand again. "*This* is here to stay."

I could have floated off the bed and taken Dalvin with me.

"Babe?" Dalvin gently nudged his body against mine. "You went away again."

"No, I'm here. I was...feeling stuff."

"Is something wrong?"

"No. Everything's good. Just...I love you, Dalvin."

His smile was slow and sweet. "I love you, Zeno."

Best moment ever.

Epilogue

I STOOD IN the door of my room, giving the place another once-over. I'd changed the bed, dressing it in clean covers even though Mom told me I didn't have to. My movie and game posters were gone, tossed out with the other unwanted items I'd cleared from the room. The game system, television, and laptop had been packed away with the rest of the stuff going with me.

Stripped down to the basic furnishings, the room seemed blank, sterile, sort of like a hotel room. Then again, that bed...aside from sleepovers at Marvus's house, that bed was the only one I'd slept in for as far back as I could remember. And the big drawer at the bottom of the dresser was where Dad said two-year-old me hid when we played hide-and-seek. God. Even sterile and bland, this room was a part of my life.

No, not part of my life, not anymore. Now it was part of my history.

"Zeno?" Jemma appeared at my side, sounding impatient.

"What're you doing back here? Dalvin's ready to go."

"I'm double-checking, making sure I'm not leaving anything behind," I offered lamely. "Come on." I took her hand, and we walked up the hall together.

Everybody was in the driveway.

The electric-blue SUV parked there had been packed with Dalvin's duffel bag and just about everything I owned. In front of the vehicle, Mom scatted a jazzy ditty while Katina showed her some new dance step. No, wait. I got that backward. Mom was showing Katina the dance moves. Katina hummed along, smiling like a little kid at a birthday party as she tried to match Mom's moves. They were having a good time.

At the back of the vehicle, with the rear door raised, Marvus searched dutifully for spaces to shove various objects—shoes, candles, a dirty pair of socks found under my bed—within the overstuffed trunk. And on the passenger side, Dad stood with Dalvin, who showed him footage from a twenty-minute digital animated film he'd made with a couple of other USC students during his freshman year. The movie was about a little boy who wished himself into a dinosaur to get his too-busy parents' attention. Cute film. Dad went "Aww!" a lot.

It was August twenty-fifth. The dog days showed no signs of waning. The merciless sun blazed from a cloudless sky, with very little in the way of a breeze, the temp already in the mideighties, and it wasn't even nine a.m. yet.

"There he is," Marvus said as he continued arranging things in the trunk. "Dang, dude. You were in there so long I was starting to think you changed your mind."

"Nah, Marv," I said, "I'm ready to leave Tennessee behind."

It had been a good year. Marvus and Katina had graduated from high school in June. They'd settled on and accepted offers from Georgia Tech, where Marvus would double-major in psychology and education and Katina in aerospace engineering (on an athletic scholarship for gymnastics). Mom had earned her master's degree a couple of weeks ago and was about to plunge right into the U of M's doctoral program in biological sciences. The simple thought of all those science courses gave me a headache.

I'd selected political science as my major at U of M and had completed my freshman year with a 4.25 GPA. In his freshman year, Dalvin fell head over heels for the animation and digital arts program. He wanted to work in movies. USC offered a degree program in communication (I decided to switch majors) and had a highly regarded law school. It was the west coast for us.

I lingered on the steps with Jemma, still holding her hand. "I'm glad you stopped by."

"I'm only in town for a couple of days," she said, "but you know I wouldn't miss seeing you off." Her body was more toned than when she left for Juilliard last summer, and she seemed happy, content. "I've been meaning to tell you...I met this guy."

"Oh, really?" Despite the exaggerated arch of my eyebrows, I was actually surprised. "Well, tell me about 'this guy,' huh? Name, rank, and serial number, and let's see a photo. I have to figure out if he passes muster."

"His name is Chuck, he's from Philly, and his major is drama." She produced her phone. "And this is him."

The guy pictured had clean-cut, country-boy looks: large, expressive brown eyes, big pink ears, and longish, silky black hair. He had an easy, innocent smile, and a lean but firm-looking body that appeared to have spent years pitching hay, chopping wood, and doing other country-boy type chores. If he made it to Hollywood, he'd probably end up like Nick Robinson, playing teen boys until he was well on his way to thirty.

"Okay, he's nice looking," I said. "But is he nice?"

"He's sweet. A little shy. He kinda reminds me of you."

"How? He's white. And half my size. No, dang it, he's a midget."

She reached up and swatted the back of my head.

"Ow. Okay, I deserved that."

"Yes, you did. Chuck and I have been dating since May. I like him. And he's crazy about me."

"Hey, that's great, Jemma. I'm happy for ya."

"Thanks. If I haven't said it before, I'm happy for you and Dalvin."

"You have. But it's nice to hear it again." I looked at Dalvin. He was acting out a scene from his new digital project. (I knew because he'd acted out the same scene for me last night.) His cartoon expressions and exaggerated movements had Dad throwing his head back in laughter. Ah, my big goofer.

Marvus slammed down the rear door. He picked up the one remaining item: my bike. "Hey! Somebody wanna give me a hand mounting this thing in the rack?" Dalvin and Dad went to his aid.

Mom and Katina came over to the steps.

"Can we have a hug too?" Katina said.

"Come here, you." I opened my arms, stepped down, and consumed sassy Katina in a hearty bear hug. We did the rocking from side to side thing. Over the past year, she'd become a good friend. She made Marvus happy, and that made me happy.

I let go of Katina and went to Mom. She held out her arms to me, her expression as proud as anything. We hugged, and I held on for a minute.

"Well, well," Mom said, patting my back, a smile in her voice. "My baby boy is finally checking out of the Hotel Anderson." For the first time today, I felt my eyes sting. I rubbed a hand over my face.

Mom let go and took a step back. She reached up and patted my cheek, her way of saying, *You got this.*

Jemma. Katina. Mom. My ladies, standing together, letting me go, pushing me onward with their smiles.

"Come on, Z-bo," Dad called. "You're losing daylight."

I turned. My bike was secured to the back of the SUV, and Dad, Dalvin, and Marvus stood together by the driver's door.

Ah, well...

I walked over to them and hugged Marvus first. "I'm gonna miss you."

"I think you mean you're gonna miss hanging with me," he said, hugging me back. "I'm gonna miss hanging with you. We'll be on opposite sides of the country, but we're only a text or FaceTime away. You'll still see me just about every day."

As I backed away from Marvus, Dad grabbed me by the arm and pulled me in.

"Be safe, son."

"I will, Dad."

He kissed me on the forehead before letting go. Dalvin slid an arm around my waist.

Dad looked us both in the eye. "You boys take care of each other."

Dalvin nodded, giving me a quick squeeze. He opened the driver's door, holding it while I climbed behind the wheel. I'd bought the SUV last week with part of my savings, all of the financial gifts from my high school graduation, and a generous donation from Mom and Dad that was sort of a going away present. Dalvin and I would be living together in a dorm room. I planned to get around on my bike, mostly, and Dalvin had bought a new bike of his own so we could do recreational riding together. But there would be times when we'd need reliable transportation for the both of us.

Dalvin climbed into the passenger seat. For our high school graduation, he'd traded in the frohawk for a nice conservative buzz cut fade. It was a peace offering for his dad, who (no surprise) hated the frohawk, especially after Dalvin came out to him. During his freshman year, Dalvin had begun growing out his hair into locs. Mr. Drake wasn't happy with that. Of course, he wasn't gonna be happy with much of anything Dalvin did, short of bringing home a girlfriend. He loved Dalvin enough that he maintained a relationship with him. He even seemed to take it pretty well when Dalvin finally brought me home at Christmas and introduced me as his boyfriend. Mr. Drake asked me to help him make his eggnog pudding—trust, it tastes a hella lot better than it sounds—and he and Dalvin put up the Christmas tree as per their annual tradition.

But Mr. Drake was always a little distant with us, a tad off, as if he was just going through the motions. I didn't think the man would ever be fully comfortable with the fact of his gay firstborn.

What mattered, however, was that Dalvin and I were comfortable. With each other, and the path we were taking together.

The world was big and beautiful and full of wonders. We would stop and explore one of them, the Grand Canyon, on our way to California. The world was also fucking scary as hell. College had focused my mind on a lot of things. Climate change. Pandemics. Cyber security threats. Weapons of mass destruction. Human overpopulation. Terrorist groups, foreign and domestic. Any of these could lead to the collapse of our civilization. Scarier still was that many of the government leaders expected to deal with these issues rejected science and rationality in favor of conspiracy theories and one-upmanship.

The Supreme Court of our country was doing everything possible to undermine or invalidate policies and laws designed to protect against discrimination on the basis of race, sex, and sexual orientation. A clear majority of Republican legislators no longer even pretended there was such a thing as democracy in the USA, stacking the deck in their favor so those who disagreed with them had no vote and no voice. The Supreme Court said it was okay for Republicans to do that. The Democrats, due to ridiculous Senate rules, were essentially sitting on their hands and letting this happen. It was still legal in most of the country for LGBT people to be fired from their jobs and kicked out of their homes for being who they were. Congress wouldn't eliminate qualified immunity, the doctrine that allowed police to harass and kill Black and Brown people with impunity. Nothing was being fixed.

Such was the world Dalvin and I were walking into. Driving across the country instead of flying or taking the train increased our risk of a problematic police encounter. But we couldn't—and *we weren't going to*—let fear dictate our lives. We were jumping into that crazy world with both feet. We were gonna change the things we could, vote for candidates who best represented our interests, and try not to worry too much about the rest. We mattered; our feelings mattered. We were gonna make the most of every day that came to us.

I looked again at the people I was leaving. God, I loved them all. My eyes started to sting again. I blinked.

"Shit-a-goddamn, Zeno," Marvus barked, swiping a quick hand at his own eyes. "Start the damn car!"

Everybody laughed. I fired up the engine, smiling at my family and friends.

"I'll be in touch," I said to them.

Dalvin waved goodbye to everyone, and then I shifted the SUV into drive and pulled out of the driveway. Minutes later, I turned on Madison Avenue, heading for the interstate.

Dalvin rested a hand on my knee, his grip strong. With my

eyes on the road ahead, I could feel his smile, his warm, loving gaze. "You okay, babe?" he asked.

I took Dal's hand in mine. "Yeah. Always."

About the Author

A former corporate writer of business correspondence, policy, and training manuals, Gene Gant lives with his family in a quiet little neighborhood outside Memphis, Tennessee.

Email
writegenegant@gmail.com

Facebook
www.facebook.com/gene.gant.7

CONNECT WITH NINESTAR PRESS

WEBSITE: NINESTARPRESS.COM

FACEBOOK: NINESTARPRESS

X: @NINESTARPRESS

INSTAGRAM: NINESTARPRESS

BLUESKY: NINESTARPRESS

THREADS: @NINESTARPRESS